MOTTKE
The Thief

MOTTKE
The Thief

BY SHOLEM ASCH

Translated by
WILLA *and* EDWIN MUIR

C.1

GREENWOOD PRESS, PUBLISHERS
WESTPORT, CONNECTICUT

CONTENTS

*

BOOK I

BOOK II

BOOK I

CHAPTER I

*

How His Father Came to Marry His Mother

THIS is how it happened that Mottke's father, "Blind" Leib, came to marry Mottke's mother, "Red" Slatke.

As a young man Leib had a fine reputation in the little town. He worked for Selig the cobbler (the same Selig whose wife had a child every year), and he was a worker, too; you wouldn't find another like him in the whole world. He had golden hands. He was so skillful that he could make double-handsewn shoes—that was to say, he could lay one sole on top of another so that they looked like steps, and then he would sew one step with yellow thread and the second with black. This was a fashion he had invented himself, and when he went out into the streets at the beginning of the Easter holidays in his double-sewn shoes the whole town came running to gaze at the marvel. All the other young men were simply green with envy and there wasn't one of them who didn't want shoes exactly the same, double-sewn, with one row of yellow and one row of black stitching. But no one was skillful enough to copy Leib's invention, and he himself obstinately refused to sew a pair for any one else, not even for mountains of gold: "I made these for myself, and nobody but me is to wear shoes like that."

Yet what good was all his skill when he was so taken up

1

with pigeons that he didn't want to work? In the very busiest times, before Easter, for instance, or in autumn when the work simply burned under one's fingers, it was enough for Leib to hear a whistle beneath the window and in a trice his head was out and he was gaping into the street. And if he saw the baker, that Goy, letting out his pigeons, there was an end to Leib's work; he would be up on the roof in half a second letting his own pigeons out of their cote—and then away he would scramble, across all the roofs of the town, driving his pigeons with a stick and watching them fly up into the sky that arched so quietly over the houses. And if his master dared to say a word to him about it, Leib would throw the shoes he was working at right into the man's face and fling off his apron and march out of the shop. He had never stuck to one job for so long as six months, and once he even took his fists to his employer. After that the Cobblers' Guild decided that he was to have no more work. Yet before a week was out there was Leib cobbling away again, this time for "Yellow" Selig.

"What's a man to do?" said Yellow Selig, defending himself before the Guild. "After all, he's the best hand-worker in the whole town. And if there's a high-class job to be done there's nobody can do it so well as Leib. When he likes, he can turn out a pair of ladies' shoes that could be set straight away in the finest shop-window in Warsaw. A pair of ladies' shoes that could dance all by themselves!" he added, licking his lips with pleasure, which he always did whenever he was talking about Leib's work, for Selig was an artist at his trade.

It was just about this time that Leib got engaged to Red Slatke. He had been walking her out for a long time, and you could meet the pair of them any Friday evening in the gardens outside the town, until well on in the night. Red

Slatke couldn't keep a job either, all because of Leib; for whenever it came into his head he used to fetch her away at any time, by broad daylight, and simply vanish with her in the gardens until the evening. And meanwhile in the kitchen the milk would be boiling over and the plates lying unwashed and the meals uncooked. The housewife would be nearly out of her skin with rage: "Such impudence as servants have!" And when Red Slatke came back she would find her trunk standing in the lobby and herself out of a job.

Besides, people said in the town that Red Slatke stole the best tit-bits from the kitchen to give to her sweetheart. It was a fact that you could often find hidden under her pillow a freshly roasted chicken wrapped up in paper, or a bit of fish or some of the best pastry. Yet nobody believed that Leib would ever really marry Slatke. More than one of her mistresses had prophesied to her that he would get her into trouble and leave her in the lurch, and all the respectable people said that Leib was the very man to ruin an orphan (Red Slatke was an orphan, without father or mother). But no one knew how to prevent him, for who wanted to risk his neck by reading the fellow a lecture? Leib himself, however, decided privately: "If all the people in the town have such a bad opinion of me and think I'm the kind of man to ruin a girl, then I'll just show them what I am!" And so one evening after the Sabbath he went to the Rabbi and said:

"Rabbi! I want to swear before you and pledge my hand on it that I'll marry Slatke as soon as I've served my time in the army."

The Rabbi replied:

"Much good it is pledging your hand on it. Do you know what it means when a Jew pledges his hand on anything? And what if you break your pledge, which God forbid?"

Then Leib swore it to him by the grave of his father and

by his sick mother, and that made the Rabbi believe him. So the Rabbi sent for Berisch the butcher, who was the orphan Slatke's uncle, and that very evening in Berisch's house the betrothal contract was drawn up in the presence of the Rabbi himself.

When Leib took his betrothed out walking on the next Friday evening—this time he had made new shoes for himself and for Slatke too, and they were triple-sewn shoes, one row of red stitching, one of black, and one of yellow—no one had a word to say against him. Quite the other way about: the citizens of the little town greeted the couple with great friendliness and called "Good Sabbath" to Leib just as if he were the respected head of a family, and said to each other: "Look at that, now. Let him be what he likes, he's a decent fellow after all; he's going to marry the orphan."

Yet hardly four weeks had passed before Leib was breaking the vow he had sworn to the Rabbi by the grave of his father and by his sick mother; he had begun to run after Basche the dressmaker. People said afterwards that it wasn't really his fault, but that deaf Jeche, the dressmaker's mother, had set herself to catch him, being vexed to think that her daughter, who was no common servant-girl but a dressmaker, should be left stranded, while an orphan, "a girl that was nothing and had nothing," walked off with such a good bridegroom as Leib—for since his betrothal he had given up his pigeons and settled down to work in earnest.

Anyhow, there he sat at the dressmaker's Friday evening after Friday evening and right through every Sabbath day. In the dressmaker's there were books and novels to read, and on Friday evenings a band of young men and girls used to go there for a sing-song, and sometimes there was even dancing. No wonder Leib liked to go there. He was a little ashamed, all the same, to show himself with Basche in the street, and so they always sat indoors. Meanwhile, Red Slatke sat at home in her mistress's house every Sabbath day, dressed up in her best and waiting for Leib. The poor girl nearly cried her eyes out, but little good that did her. The whole town was talking about it, and Slatke's mistress said that she had told her so, and that she had warned her not to have anything to do with the fellow, since it was bound to end badly. Red Slatke had nothing to say in answer.

It came to the first day of Tabernacles. Slatke stood in the dark passage beside Basche's flat waiting for Leib. When he came in at the front door she saw by the crack of light that he was wearing the triple-sewn shoes he had made in honor of their betrothal. That gave her such a sickening stab in the heart that she flung into his face the whole contents of the bottle of vitriol she had been hiding under her apron.

The agonized man shrieked and fell down on the floor, but Slatke did not run away. Instead, she rushed out into the courtyard shouting for help. When the people came running they found Leib writhing beside Basche's door, blinded and seared in the face, his clothes burned, and his fine triple-sewn shoes on his feet. And beside him Red Slatke was kneeling, tearing her hair and beating her breast, screaming: "Help him, oh help him! Look what I've done to him, look! . . ."

A doctor arrived, and Leib was taken to the hospital. The red-haired girl carried his hat and collar behind him, still tearing her hair and screaming: "Help him, everybody! Look what I've done, look!"

She was taken to the police court, but in a day or two she was set free again. At once she rushed off to the hospital where Leib was lying. But they would not let her in to see him, and so she wandered round and round the building for a while like a lost dog. Then she went into service again and roasted chickens for Leib and carried them to the hospital. The attendants took the victuals but would not let her in. "He doesn't want to see you," was what they told her. That did not stop her from bringing strong soup and roast chicken every day to the hospital.

At last one day she slipped a rouble into the attendant's hand and managed to get in. When she saw the invalid she felt sick. He did not look human, he was like some monstrous abortion with his eyes plastered over. She flung herself on her knees before the bed, clasped his legs, pressed her face into them and kissed them, weeping loudly.

At first Leib said not a word and did not even move. But then he stammered out a few words, and she understood she was to come nearer. She moved nearer to him, crawling before him like a dog. And with all the strength he had Leib brought his fist down on Slatke's head. She came nearer still to make it easier for him, and after every blow the tears started from her eyes and her face shone with joy. But an attendant happened to come up, and when he saw what was happening he drove her out.

After that Red Slatke let no evening pass without coming to the hospital with broth for Leib. Whenever she had any free time she stood under his windows, pestered the attendant with questions and ran after the doctor to kiss his hands. The blows she had got made her less timid about pushing her way into the sick-room, and every time she did the scene of her first visit was repeated.

Some weeks later Leib was let out of hospital. His face was still plastered up and his eyes were bandaged. Red Slatke, meanwhile, had sold all her trousseau, a whole trunk-ful of garments that she had sewn herself, and the bed-linen she had inherited from her mother. She had a few roubles besides, which she had saved out of her wages during Leib's stay in hospital. And so she rented a room in a tailor's house and took Leib there and made strengthening broth for him and went begging for him in the kitchens where she had once been a serving-maid. In the evenings she could be seen setting the blind man before the door and propping him up with pillows to make him sit more comfortably. And when he was able to walk again, Slatke led him by the hand through the streets.

Every now and then, when the familiar whistle sounded with which the Christian baker cajoled his pigeons from their cote to send them circling over the market-place, Leib threw up his head, listening to the rustling of the wings above him, and then his hands would grope around uncertainly as if they were seeking something. Slatke knew at once what Leib wanted; she would push her face close up to him and he would begin to beat her with his fists on the head or wherever came handiest.

Some months later the plaster and bandages were taken off. His face was quite covered with scars which were not yet healed, so that there was raw red flesh everywhere. One of his eyes was destroyed, but the other had been saved, although he could see very little with it. That was when people began to call him "Blind" Leib.

Not long after that he was quietly married to Slatke. Not a soul was invited to the wedding, which was conducted by the "Dajan," the Rabbi's deputy. Uncle Berisch brought some ribs of beef from his shop, so that they had a fine dinner. Then the young couple rented a small house for a year, and Uncle Berisch set them up with some pieces of furniture.

Leib did no more work—he swore that he had quite forgotten how to cobble. So he loafed about the streets while

Slatke went out to service. She used to bring him his meals from her employer's kitchen, and the little money she saved he spent on drink. Only when Slatke became incapable of working during the last months of her pregnancy did Leib make up his mind to earn an honest penny himself, and so he became a porter.

CHAPTER II

*

How Mottke the Thief Came into the World

THE news of Mottke's coming was not exactly received with delight. This is how it happened.

Blind Leib (everybody called him that now) was living with Slatke in a cellar. It was a place where people lived who paid no rent but had established a kind of settled right to house-room there. It was a vaulted cellar under the ruins of a long-deserted building, and in the old days it had contained a bakery. One half of it was reserved for Feigele the fruit hawker and all her baskets, old sacks and filthy bast matting. She really had a right to her share of the cellar, for she had lived there while it was still a bakery. Another part of it was occupied by the long-legged weaver whom the school-children used to gobble at in the streets because of the huge Adam's apple he had. In the summer-time he used to twist, every morning, long white strands of yarn that stretched across half the street, and the children could never understand how he could accommodate all his own length and all the length of his yarn in such a small cellar. The third tenant was Meier, the teacher, from whom the girls learned a little reading and writing. He had a natural claim to a share of the cellar, since he was Feigele's son-in-law. He owned the corner by the window. He was called "the girls' teacher," but in reality he had long ceased to have

9

any right to the name, although a few little girls still arrived after breakfast to learn by the window the rudiments of reading, guided by Meier with the help of a slate-pencil and a prayer-book. What he really did, however, was to act as letter-writer, and many women brought him letters to read for them or got him to write their letters. Then Meier would mount an enormous pair of spectacles on his nose, hold the letter up to one of the small window-lights, and read it over aloud, while the owner of the letter was lost in wonder at his cleverness in finding so many things to read out of such a small piece of paper.

The fourth and most important tenant of the cellar was Blind Leib. He had not the shadow of a right to live there, but who could stand up against him? One winter he had simply walked in with Slatke and taken up a whole wall with his bedding—for even then he had a large family. Slatke had a child nearly every year, for that was how she earned the most of her living. She was well spoken of as a wet-nurse, and people said that children grew fat on her milk. So she brought her own infants up on the bottle and hired herself out as a wet-nurse. And since her husband needed an income every year, Slatke had to go on having children; any extra expenses were paid for out of Blind Leib's work as a casual porter.

One evening not long before the Jewish New Year, that is to say in the autumn when the days were beginning to shorten, Blind Leib came home. The whole cellar was full of smoke and steam. There was a smell of frying and something was sizzling and sputtering at the fire. It smelt as if Slatke might have been cooking goodness knew what, and yet it was only onions that were frying in the pan and sending such clouds of smoke all through the room. Blind Leib's mouth watered, and he ran out into the street to gather in his offspring. From all sides small children of various ages came flocking, some of them still on all fours, popping like mice out of their holes. With this assembly Blind Leib marched into the cellar again and clapped his hands to hurry Slatke up. At that she lost her temper:

"Would you harry the very soul out of my body? And me hardly able to stand on my feet!"

These words made Leib rather uneasy. He knew that she never said anything without meaning it, and that she wasn't the woman to be afraid of work. He peered at the huge basket of onions which she hawked from house to house, and convinced himself that it had not been moved since morning. That was really upsetting, and he asked:

"Slatke, haven't you been on your rounds today?"

"I only hope you'll be as sick as I've been the whole of this day. I've been turned inside out!"

"Why, what's the matter, Slatke?" he asked, picking up one of the children, while another clung to his boots.

"What's the matter? Just look at the creature," she shouted from the fire, turning an evil eye upon him, "he doesn't know, not he, what's the matter! Ask the policeman, if you don't know yourself maybe he'll be able to tell you."

"What, Slatke, is there another bastard on the way?" cried Leib, half anxious and half surprised.

"Another . . . What kind of father is it that calls his own children bastards? . . . The devil take you!" returned Slatke, spitting at him in her anger.

Blind Leib's heart grew warm, and he said with a smile that looked like the grinning of a death's head, thanks to his sightless eye:

"Slatke, is there really another kid coming? Eh, you're a grand wife!"

"Much it matters to you! What have you got to give it? All its grandmother's legacy, I suppose?"

"Legacy or no legacy—give us something to eat, Slatke!"

Slatke produced a large dish of fried potatoes and set it on a box. The children at once began to rummage among them with their fingers. Blind Leib plied his spoon lustily, with his free hand drawing in an upturned box as a seat for his wife. Slatke took it, sat down and picked up a piece of potato in her right hand, but made no attempt to eat; she only groaned and rested her head on her other hand.

"What are you groaning for, Slatke?" asked Blind Leib, preoccupied by a bit of potato which was so hot that he had to shift it to and fro from his tongue to his teeth and back again. "If we get another kid that means good money again."

"Money!" groaned Slatke, glaring at him angrily.

Blind Leib knew his Slatke well and realized that it would be unwise to quarrel with her at the moment. "The good money will come in, anyhow," he thought, applying himself once more to the appetizing potatoes and nursing another hot piece in his mouth.

Some time later, just as Red Slatke was bargaining with a peasant over some potatoes, she was hailed by Jente the dealer, who always wore such wide skirts that people swore she kept hundredweights of stuff under them for smuggling across the border. Slatke's condition was now clear and after one sharp glance at her Jente passed her tongue over her thin lips like a cat and said:

"In the family way again, Slatke? Well, good luck to you!"

"It's as God wills." Slatke gave an embarrassed smile.

"Soon?" Jente ran the eye of a connoisseur over Slatke's body.

"Likely in my seventh month. . . ."

"Likely enough," confirmed Jente with a nod of the head, scrutinizing Slatke once more. "Then you'll be confined just about the same time as the Shochliners' daughter-in-law."

"Why do you say that?" asked Slatke inquisitively, although she had already guessed what was in Jente's mind and felt a little on edge about it.

"I was only thinking that that would be a good job for you. The Shochliners would pay you well and treat you like a queen."

"Won't the young wife be able to nurse her baby, then? Is she too delicate?"

"Delicate!—what has that to do with it? Don't you know that a rich woman can afford to hire a nurse? She has everything she can want. God grant that you and I may be as well off as old Shochliner's daughter-in-law."

"What's she willing to pay, then?"

"Oh, there won't be any trouble about that. They've been at me for a month already to find them a good wet-nurse. And is there any better nurse than you? It won't take long to get the wages settled, believe me."

"Maybe ..." replied Slatke, whom Jente's compliments had again embarrassed. "Well, they can ask in the town about me and my milk. I nursed Moische Pinschewer's grandson, and two of Silberberg's I brought on wonderfully, and I've been wet-nurse in the richest families in the town. They can soon find out if my milk's good or not."

"But we all know that, Slatke. There's no need to argue about that. Well, it's settled, then. I'll go straight to the Shochliners now and take you with me. Only you'd better put on a clean apron. You'll get an advance straight off the reel."

"A clean apron wouldn't make me any different."

"No, Slatke, this is serious. The Shochliners won't want

to have any Christian nurse in the house. The son's very pious and insists on a Jewish nurse for his child. He says that children who suck in Christian milk grow up stupid and learn nothing. Weeks ago they asked me to find them a Jewish nurse. You can earn your pile in that house."

And so, on that very same day, Slatke accepted an advance of money on account of the milk which nature was bestowing on her in trust for her own child. And that evening Blind Leib, who had been given a meat supper, clapped her on the shoulder and said:

"Well, Slatke, wasn't I right? Another kid on the way, that means good money!"

Slatke had been in a bad temper all evening, without knowing why, and she interrupted him brusquely:

"God, if only a bone would stick in your throat and choke you, you glutton, and then there would be less of your lip!"

Meanwhile, Mottke lay serenely in the body of his mother, accompanied her to all the markets, scrambled with her over all the vegetable carts, dragged with her the heavy sacks and baskets, and cared less than nothing for the fact that she had sold her milk, since for the present he had all the nourishment he needed. And what did the affairs of the outside matter to him? He wasn't out in it yet. . . .

When the time came for Mottke's appearance in the world, old Frau Shochliner took it on herself to look after Slatke, whose milk had been sold in advance to her daughter-in-law. The women of the Mothers' Union spread fresh sheets over the bed in the cellar. The midwife arrived in plenty of time. Boiling water was kept steaming at the fire —in short, every one took the greatest trouble about Mottke the Thief. Slatke herself did not make much fuss—she was well accustomed to the business—and even before Blind

Leib came back from the synagogue with the written prayers that were to keep off all evil spirits, and to that end were to be pasted on the walls, even before then a terrible outcry had set the whole cellar a-bustling. Mottke the Thief was announcing his arrival.

For the first eight days of his life, until he was circumcised, he enjoyed himself very well. He was carefully bedded on a pillow, with nothing much showing but glittering black little eyes that were as quick as mice in his small dark face. Old Frau Shochliner saw to it that Slatke gave him the breast often enough, for she wanted Mottke the Thief to suck strongly and much, so that Slatke might have enough milk for her grandchild. For the same reason she brought Slatke all kinds of fine things to eat, sometimes broth, sometimes stew, and now and then even a bottle of wine. That was a good deed, for she was being charitable to a poor mother, and at the same time it was useful, for the milk of her grandchild's wet-nurse would be rich. Mottke did not stand on ceremony, either: he nuzzled and sucked strongly at his mother's breasts and sweated in his pillow as if he were in a Turkish bath. Thick beads of sweat stood on his small dark forehead, on which a damp lock of hair curled exactly as on the forehead of Blind Leib.

Four written prayers stuck up on the walls protected him from evil spirits. Every evening the boys came from the school to greet the new sojourner on earth and to say in his stead the prayer for the night.

On a Friday evening the porters of the town, Leib's colleagues, appeared to give the little man the "Sholem aleichem" that was his due. Old Frau Shochliner, who had obtained for her son the right of holding the child at the approaching circumcision ceremonial (which counts as a meritorious deed before God), had provided the regulation

beer and dishes of peas for the guests, and the porters
sweated in the cellar, drank the beer, ate the peas and congratulated Blind Leib. He loved these ceremonials in which
he could play the leading rôle.

Every time his wife bore him a son he felt as if he had
been raised to a more exalted position. People all came to
see him then, the Rabbi, the circumciser and other respected
Jews. They all crowded into his cellar, addressed him as
"Reb Leib," and showered marks of honor upon him. Every
one wanted to shake him by the hand, and there was roast
goose to eat and beer to drink, and, most important of all,
nothing whatever to pay.

So this time Blind Leib gathered honor from the produc-
tion of Mottke the Thief, who was presented on a clean pillow to the Porters' Guild.

Old Frau Shochliner's son was holding him, the same
young man whose child was to be nursed by Slatke. He
brought Mottke into the room and handed him to his father,
who was robed in a long, broad prayer-mantle. In his turn
he handed the child to the Rabbi, who sat in a chair. And
as Blind Leib looked round the cellar and observed that he
had the Rabbi on his right hand and the rich young man on
his left, he was filled with pride.

Immediately after that Mottke let out a yell that made
the walls tremble: the first injustice of his life was being
wreaked upon him and he did not know what he had done
to deserve it. . . .

Slatke stood there, pale and weeping, in her new white
hood and white cape which the old Shochliner had given
her in honor of the day. The solemn faces round her and all
this deference to her did not go with her weathered sun-
burnt face, which was as dark and tough as a piece of
leather.

She stood there, overcome with confusion, and she could make neither head nor tail of what was happening round her. Who was she after all, God help her? Slatke, the beast of burden. How did she come to be the mother of a new-born Jew? And while she was thinking this the Rabbi said to her: "My congratulations, mother!" Then the old Shochliner herself came forward, along with her young son. . . . They were all attentive to her, begged her to take a chair; they put her child in her arms and congratulated her. . . . And who was she, after all, God help her?

But Blind Leib sat in the place of honor beside the Rabbi. Honey cakes and brandy were handed round, everybody drank his health and congratulated him, and he thought to himself: "A fine business, a circumcision! You get honey cakes and brandy and money into the bargain, everybody pays you honor and you feel you're a human being. A pity that a man can't have a circumcision every day."

*

Mottke Refuses His Rag Dummy

ONE fine sunny afternoon a few weeks later Mottke was lying in an old basket in which Feigele the hawker stored rotten apples during the winter. Round his little body was wrapped his mother's scarf, which she wore in all sorts of weather but was already past using. His mouth was stopped with a dummy made of a wet linen rag wrapped round a piece of sugar, and Mottke kept sucking at it without stopping. The vigorous muscles round his little lips were drawn tight in his effort to draw living nourishment out of the rag dummy. His black eyes were half shut and his little face seemed drowned in sleep. All the top part of it, the eyes, the compact forehead with the damp black lock sticking to it, reminded one of Blind Leib his father; but the lower half with the energetic mouth, the short chin and the soft smile resembled the mother. The child's face was so peaceful that he looked as if he were asleep. But he was not asleep, for every now and then he gave a doleful cry and went on yelling until his little sister, who spent her time between sitting beside him and playing with the other children in the street, hurried to the cradle and stopped his mouth once more with the rag dummy. Old Reb Meier, too, rose from his place at the window and stuck Mottke's own hand into his screaming mouth. Mottke began at once to suck and suck, both at the dummy and his own hand, as if a fountain of milk had been set to his lips.

18

I can't say whether at any later time in his stormy life Mottke ever had leisure to reflect on himself and his fate. But I fancy that as he lay in the old basket, warmed by the sunbeams which first had to pass through a grating and then the cellar window, stuffed with rags, before they at last reached his basket—that as he lay there comfortably enjoying the warmth, sunk in a philosophical semi-dreamlike peace, he reflected on very important things indeed. He wondered why at one time, whenever he moved his lips, something liquid had gushed out, stilling his hunger and blissfully warming all his limbs, while now, in spite of all his pulling and sucking, no liquid came at all, none whatever, so that his little stomach remained empty and his belly quite cold, and he felt as forsaken as an orphan. Once when he pressed his mouth to his mother's breast it had been so warm and comforting and he had felt so near to her and so at one with her. Where had it vanished to, that warmth which had enveloped him so pleasantly? What had happened during these last days to make that warmth disappear all at once?

This is what Mottke must have been thinking while he sucked at his fingers. But soon his philosophical calm deserted him and he began to cry and wail until the whole cellar and the whole neighborhood rang. Something had gone wrong, and so he yelled for all he was worth. At first nobody paid any attention either in the cellar or in the little street, for people were accustomed to children crying and screaming, and so Mottke's complaints made no particular impression on them. But Mottke wasn't like other children. He was resolved to let the whole world know of the injustice that he had done to him. He yelled and yelled and would not stop.

Old Reb Meier, who was sitting in his window with his

glasses on his nose writing a letter to America for some woman, was the first to remark Mottke's bawling. He thought at first he had to do with an ordinary fit of crying such as he often heard in the cellar or in the street: that is, with the crying of a hungry child. So he got up calmly, stepped over to the basket, and as before stuck Mottke's hand into Mottke's bawling mouth. But Mottke refused to be fobbed off any longer; he knew by now that the hand was no use. Thereupon Reb Meier stopped his mouth with the rag dummy; but after a few pulls Mottke saw that it was no use either, dropped the dummy and began to bawl afresh. Old Reb Meier gazed at him in astonishment and marveled at such obstinacy. It was the first time that such a yelling had been heard in the cellar. Up till now the usual procedure had been something like this: when Slatke went off to do her wet-nursing and left one of her children with a rag dummy in its mouth, it cried and screamed until it was tired and then began to suck at the rag. In the end the child either died or sucked its way through the bad days and survived until its teeth began to come and it could eat anything at all. But this child simply refused to stop crying. Old Meier went back to his interrupted letter, foolishly expecting that Mottke would quieten down by and by. But Mottke had no intention of doing anything of the kind. He refused either to let old Reb Meier write his letter to America or give the little girl her reading lesson out of the women's prayer-book. So old Meier stepped out into the street to call Mottke's eldest sister Hindele, who had been entrusted by her mother with the task of looking after the child.

Hindele was eight or nine at most. Ever since she had been four she had looked after her younger brothers and sisters. When her mother went off to do her wet-nursing, she left the last baby to Hindele's keeping, and it was Hindele's job to feed it with the bottle and the rag dummy. Hindele had already "brought up" four children in this way; two of them had died, certainly, but the other two had scraped through with the help of the rag dummy and the lump of sugar. Yet Hindele herself was only a child still. And apart from the fact that she naturally liked to play with the other children in the street, she had to fend for her own food, for Blind Leib treated his children as if they were wild birds instead of human beings. He packed them out into the street, where they had to snatch what food they could find. That consisted, as far as Hindele was concerned, sometimes of a crust of bread and occasionally of remnants of meat which people in rich houses gave her for running errands or washing dishes or suchlike services.

When Mottke began to scream so alarmingly, Hindele happened to be with Blümele the dressmaker, where she had been given a piece of bread and a plate of vegetable soup in return for washing the dishes. Old Meier had to search for a long time before he found her. At the news that Mottke was crying and screaming so terribly that old Reb Meier himself had had to go and look for her, Hindele left the dishes standing and rushed home. She was just as astonished at the child's obstinacy as the old teacher had been, and set about trying to quieten it first with the usual well-tried methods that she had always found to work until now. She stuck Mottke's hand into his mouth first, then the rag dummy with the sugar lump, and finally snatched up her trump card—a bottle filled with water, a little milk and some dregs of soup which she had gathered from various pots and pans.

But even the bottle failed. Mottke would not take it between his lips, kicked his legs until he was out of his scarf and screamed until the ceiling rang.

At that Hindele got scared. It was the first time in her experience that any child in the cellar, any child of Red Slatke, had refused the bottle. She did not know what to do. The child kept up a continuous howl. She took him in her arms, she dandled him, she sang to him, but it was no use: Mottke would not stop his screaming. In her despair Hindele, too, burst into tears. She forgot her duties for the moment and evidently seemed to think that she was a child too, with as much right as Mottke to cry to her heart's content.

But old Reb Meier soon woke her out of her childish delusion and recalled her to her duty.

"What are you standing there for, like a Golem? What are you howling about? What are you thinking of, Hindele? A great big girl like you! When your mother hears about this she'll give you a fine hiding. . . . Standing there howling! You should be ashamed of yourself!"

"I don't know what to do. . . . The baby won't take the bottle . . ." replied Hindele, still sobbing.

"Go and fetch your mother. The child is ill," said old Reb Meier.

Hindele was surprised that she had not thought of that herself. But at the bottom of her heart she was afraid to go for her mother, for she knew that her mother had been sold to another child. Nevertheless, she followed the old teacher's advice, snatched up her coat and ran to the Shochliners' to tell her mother.

But she wasn't admitted to her mother as quickly as she had expected. When Slatke served as nurse in a big house she was always well treated, and at the Shochliners' they were as reverential to her as if she were a queen. She slept with the baby in the biggest room in the house, and the mistress saw to it that she was always neat and clean and wore white blouses and newly washed aprons. The old Shochliner was always bringing her something to eat. Whenever there was good strong soup they remembered the nurse. "It'll strengthen the baby," they told one another. And actually when she was on duty Slatke had a very good time; while she was nursing other people's children she had a rest from the burden of pregnancy, from her trotting round the markets with her heavy baskets and her haggling with the peasants. She ate well and slept as long and as often as she liked. Yet the thought of her own child that she had to leave to itself every day kept coming back like a pain. And every time she bared her breast for the stranger's child she sighed heavily. In her simplicity she often thought that it would be lovely if she could give suck to her own child and be as well treated for it. The stranger's child could not suck all the milk in her breasts, and sometimes when she had to press out the remainder with her own hands she thought of her Mottke lying in the cellar; and then she hated the stranger's child.

Hindele was kept standing a long time in the kitchen waiting for her mother. They would not let her any farther, for at the moment Slatke was sucking the child, a little girl of the same age as Mottke. When at last Slatke came out of the warm nursery to speak to Hindele her heavy breasts were showing through her open blouse and milk was still dropping from the nipples. For the moment Hindele did not recognize her mother; she had never seen her looking so rested and so well before. Slatke's cheeks were red and full, she had a white cap on her head and over her white dress she wore a clean white apron. Hindele started back, almost trembled with reverence as if she were facing a strange fine lady, and felt ashamed to state the reason why she had come.

"What has happened?" asked Slatke in alarm.

For a moment Hindele could say nothing. Then she burst into tears, as if by doing that she justified herself before her mother and showed that she was not to blame. At last she said:

"Baby's crying. . . . He won't take the bottle. . . . He's ill, mother!"

As soon as Slatke heard that her child was ill she forgot that she had sold herself, threw her scarf over her head and ran as fast as she could, her blouse still open, across the market square towards the cellar.

A moment later Mottke was pressing his hot, tired face against his mother's breast and sucking at it with his strong little mouth without stopping or taking a breath. It was as if he wanted to drink into him all the fountains of life at one draught. And his little body was soon filled again with that blissful warmth which he had enjoyed so often and so gladly in the first days after his appearance in the world.

But Mottke was to enjoy his happiness for only a short time. Presently appeared the old Shochliner, on her head a hood richly adorned with ribbons, round her sagging neck a gold chain that fell half-way down her bosom. She put on a hypocritical expression, turned up her little short-sighted eyes, and with a hateful smile on her thick lips inquired:

"What's wrong with the child? Is he ill?"

She stepped nearer, prodded Mottke's little paunch with her short, thick fingers and repeated with a self-satisfied smile:

"What ails the child? Is he ill?"

Slatke felt ashamed before the rich old woman. She vio-

lently tore her breast from Mottke's mouth and replied
awkwardly, as if in apology:

"He's only a baby. . . . He can't get used to the bottle."

Her heart was filled with bitterness, and to lighten it she
screamed at Hindele:

"Why did you fetch me here? Why don't you look after
the child? What do you do with yourself all day?" With
that she began to beat the girl.

The old Shochliner pacified her, pulled some small coins
out of her purse and divided them among the children, who
had come rushing to the house from every corner of the
street as soon as they heard that their mother was home.
But the old lady gave Hindele more than the others. She
handed her a whole five-kopek piece and said:

"Come and see your mother sometimes and bring the
baby along, too. There's no reason why you shouldn't do
that. You can go to the kitchen; the maid will give you
something to eat. Why have you never come before?"

Then she smiled at Mottke and tickled his little paunch
with her thick fingers again.

"You little Turk, you! . . . What a strong little rascal
he's grown into already! Why, he's twice the size of our
tiny tot!" she cried, patting Mottke on the thigh. Then she
smiled ingratiatingly at Slatke and led her away.

Hindele was left alone with Mottke. He began to cry
again. And again she did not know what to do, for the child
would neither look at the bottle nor suck the rag dummy
or his own hand. He went on bawling until Blind Leib came
home. Leib treated him without ceremony. He shouted at
him, and when that did not work turned him over and gave
him a sound walloping. But even after that Mottke went
on howling until sleep dried his tears and stopped his mouth.
And while he slept they pushed the rag dummy with the

lump of sugar between his lips. After that he learned to suck it.

From time to time Hindele took him to see his mother. Slatke was greatly pleased by these visits, and if nobody was looking she would take her own child in her arms and give him the breast. But Mottke would have nothing to do with his mother's milk now—he had got used to the rag dummy.

CHAPTER IV

*

Mottke Gets His Teeth

MOTTKE hadn't a very bright time lying in his basket and waiting for his sister or Reb Meier to remember him and give him his bottle. Every time he had to yell as hard as he could before he could make them realize that he was still alive and in need of food. But as soon as he outgrew the basket and found that he could move about, though only on all fours, he began to look out for himself. He ate everything he could get his hands on, from crusts of bread to old boot-soles and loose withies from his basket and coarse strands from the sacks; everything he found he stuffed into his mouth. But his chief source of nourishment was Feigele's fruit baskets with the rotting winter apples.

Year in, year out, they stood in the corner of the cellar, these baskets with last year's apples, rotten pears and frost-bitten plums. In the long winter nights the fruit in the baskets froze together and became one putrid mass. You couldn't recognize the different fruits any longer; they were all covered with a layer of mold and sent out a powerful smell that spread through the whole cellar, producing warmth. This corner of Feigele's became Mottke's food depot. It was as if Feigele had gathered together all this unusable fruit, these last year's apples and decayed pears, simply and solely that Mottke mightn't starve. In the long winter nights, when the wind battered at the ice-bound window, Mottke nourished himself on them.

27

The first time that he found this store of food and glutted himself upon it he fell so ill that everybody thought he was going to die. They sent for his mother. She took him in her arms, but he would neither look at her breast nor at the bottle. She sat beside his bed and cried. It was late in the night. Everybody in the cellar was asleep. From one corner came the whistling snore of Blind Leib. And Slatke sat by her child, crying. He lay in the basket with his eyes shut; he was fevered and breathed heavily. When he came to himself and saw that his mother was crying, he raised his heavy lids and stared at her with his black little eyes. It was as if he understood her and was having a good look at her to fix her firmly in his memory, so that later, when he grew big, he might remember that once she had cried over him.

Towards morning he began to recover, and he started once more upon Feigele's baskets. But from then on they did him no harm. He could eat anything now. He seemed to have a stomach of iron and bowels of steel.

All this happened in winter, when Mottke was still confined to the cellar. But soon the spring came. The sun entered the cellar. It lay on the steps of the stair and its rays came into the room. And in the cellar everybody began to prepare for Easter. Slatke, pregnant again, carried her furniture out into the street to wash and scrub it. Mottke arrived there too along with all the old furniture. He made a supreme effort, crawled out of the place on all fours, clambered up the steps, threw a glance at the street and decided that the world was far bigger than the cellar.

For a few minutes he stayed where he was. The sun warmed him and gave him a comfortable feeling. Mistrustfully he peeped out into the street, afraid to go any further. Between the entrance to the cellar and the street there was a wide gutter which had to be jumped if he was to reach the pavement. He made several attempts to get over this gap on all fours, but it was no use. He looked round him and waited to see if anybody would help him. And his sister and guardian Hindele helped him to overcome the gutter that lay at the threshold of his life. She took him by the hand and jumped him into the street.

There children were playing about and women washing and scrubbing their chairs and benches and tables and tubs in preparation for the coming festival, scrubbing everything indeed that was made of wood and they could lay their hands on. In many houses the walls were being freshly painted and all the furniture and the children along with it turned out. Mottke crawled about among the furniture and the grown-ups and the children. His feet were often stepped on, and once a chest almost fell on him. But he was everywhere, crawling about tirelessly and disturbing everybody and sticking his nose into everything.

Then he caught sight of a little girl sitting in the doorway of a house; she held a spoon in one hand and was greedily supping up curds and whey. The sight of the food was too much for Mottke. He crawled as fast as he could to the doorway, stopped when he got there and reflected for a while, gazing enviously at the little girl. Then he came to a decision, stuck his nose straight into the plate and began to lap it up just like a dog.

The little girl looked at him first in surprise, without understanding what he was at. Then she raised a great howl. Her mother ran out, and this is the sight that met her eyes. Mottke was calmly licking up the curds, while her daughter sat beside him crying, with her spoon in her hand. The mother began to scream:

"Who is this? Whose child is this? Get away from here!"

But Mottke refused to be scared off and did not let the plate go until it was torn out of his hands.

"May the devil fly away with you! Who does this child belong to?" the woman asked.

"Why, that's Slatke's youngest," she was told by another woman, who had stepped out of her house on hearing the noise.

"Oho, so this is the latest brat that Blind Leib has flung into the street. Soon it'll be unsafe to let your own children over the doorstep. Get out of this double quick!" shouted the girl's mother, pushing Mottke away.

He crawled away. The sun was shining on the street; it was warm and lovely. So, staggering along on all fours, he went his way.

On the doorstep of another house he caught sight of some small children of about his own age, who were sitting on a mattress spread out among the tables and chairs and eating buttered rolls. One of the children dropped his roll and began to howl. Nobody paid any attention to him. For a moment Mottke gaped at the boy in astonishment; then he calmly lifted the roll from the ground and began to bolt it.

When the boy saw that Mottke had got hold of his roll he raised such a caterwauling that you might have thought he was being murdered.

His mother appeared in the doorway. But this time Mottke found himself face to face with Sprinzele, the dress-maker. This woman had a sharp tongue and whenever any one injured her the whole street soon came to know about it. Everybody was terrified of her, for if she was given the slightest handle her words grew into a devouring flame that spread and licked up everything.

When she saw Frau Slatke's "new brat" come out into the street to "murder people," she raised such an outcry that everything with legs rushed up to hear.

"Look at him! Just look at him! Help! The boy's eating me out of house and home! That woman Slatke has sent her brat out into the street to destroy our children in broad daylight!"

With that she took Mottke by the hand, dragged him back to the cellar and screamed:

"Keep this brat inside! Why do you send the hooligan out into the street to fall upon our children in broad daylight?"

Slatke was washing one of Blind Leib's shirts. On hearing some one shouting into the cellar she climbed the steps just as she was, with her sleeves rolled up and her hood on her head. As soon as she caught sight of Mottke in Sprinzele's hands and faced the deluge of pitch and brimstone that poured from the dressmaker's mouth, her first thought was for Mottke. The boy looked quite wretched in Sprinzele's hands. He quivered with terror and couldn't make out why he was being screamed at so terribly. But at the sight of his mother he began to howl, and that sent a pang to Slatke's heart. She rushed out, tore the child away from Sprinzele and cried:

"Why are you screaming at the child like that? He's trembling from head to foot! What has the child done to you? My baby, my darling!" and she clasped Mottke to her breast and kissed him tenderly, probably for the first time in his life.

"Look, people, look! She's kissing him for his fine doings! Of course she put him up to it herself. He'll grow up to be a regular thief yet, you mark my words!"

"May your tongue rot! . . . You'll never live to see that day!" shouted Slatke. "He'll be a Rabbi yet!" she added, kissing Mottke tenderly on the head.

The boy buried his head in his mother's arms and, feeling safe now, peeped round with his sparkling little black eyes.

He listened to the argument that was being carried on about him, but showed no interest in it; it didn't concern him in the least. He felt happy and comfortable in his mother's arms, and gave himself up completely to his pleasant sensations.

"You'll grow tall and strong!" Slatke said to him as she led him down to the cellar, and she kissed his face over and over again. Then she set him down and commanded: "There! Stay now with mama. That woman, the things she says! But she'll never see them come true!"

But as soon as Slatke was deep in her work Mottke crawled again up to the street. For he had found a new fount of nourishment.

After that the street was Mottke's pantry. There was enough there to quench his hunger and he took whatever he found. He crawled through open doors into houses, and if he saw anything eatable on a table he gobbled it up without further ado. If he caught sight of another child with a roll—whoosh, it was away and in his mouth. If he saw a woman standing about with a basket of apples he would creep up and quietly have a good go at the fruit. Slatke was often enough put to shame by him. And a little too often some woman would appear at the cellar dragging him by the ear and prophesying an evil future for him. He became the terror of the street. When he was seen crawling out of the cellar the mothers called their children into the house and hid them; and as he drew near doors were shut and one neighbor would warn another, as if a storm were coming:

"The thief! The thief!"

And that title, along with his first name, stuck to him all his life.

CHAPTER V

*

Mottke Goes to School

IT was a cold gray winter morning. The frost, which had whitened the little cellar window all winter, had now spread from the window and the door to the walls and was beginning to decorate them too with its chill rime flowers. Everything in the cellar was frozen. The fruit in the baskets shrank and gradually turned into a single block of ice. Old Reb Meier crouched in his corner beside the window murmuring psalms. Feigele the hawker, literally muffled in jackets and skirts, sat walled in among her baskets of fruit and vegetables, silently peeling a heap of potatoes in her lap and dropping them into a pot. Blind Leib, who had just got up, his wild hair still covered with feathers, was looking in every corner for old baskets, barrels and hoops to use as kindling wood for the little stove. He always cursed when he got up with an empty stomach, and he was cursing and swearing now. But Slatke, surrounded by all her children, still lay in bed, covered up with all the old rags, rugs, coats and clothes that could be found in the cellar. Slatke's corner was the only warm corner in the room. Her baby was lying beside her, warming her with its little body. Mottke peeped out from under her other arm. His black eyes sparkled in his dark, round little face, which still had traces of the potatoes he had eaten the evening before. He felt warm and comfortable in his mother's bed.

33

On one of these mornings his fate was decided. For when Blind Leib caught sight of him happily peeping out from under his mother's arm, he suddenly remembered that he was a father and that it was time to think of the youngster's future. So he began:

"Just look at him! Lying there beside his mother, the brat! Out of that bed! Get up and bring me some wood to light the stove!"

Mottke shrank back and tried to hide himself behind his mother. Slatke took pity on him:

"What do you want him for? He's only a baby. And it's so cold in the room. Let him lie for a little while longer."

"Oh, indeed! Just look at the 'baby.' The little rascal is five past. When it comes to eating he can put away a whole plateful of spuds like any soldier. But when it's a matter of getting a bit of wood to light the fire, does he stir himself? Get out of that bed, I tell you, or else I'll fetch the strap."

"It's high time the boy was out of this," old Feigele said from her corner, moving her toothless gums like a great bird. "It isn't safe to leave anything in the cellar. Yesterday I made a plate of cabbage soup to eat in the evening and left it standing on the shelf with a slice of bread. I came back—and where was the soup? Where was the bread? Of course, Mottke had smelt them out and gobbled them up. One can't leave anything that can be eaten in this place now...."

"He's capable of eating me up, skin and bone!" cried Blind Leib. "And am I to work for a rascal like that? The brat should have been earning his keep long before this. Out of that bed! And make it quick!"

"The way you all go on at him! Is he such an eyesore? The child will get his death of cold, the room's freezing...."

I won't let him out of bed. Lie still, Mottke, stay beside your mother," said Slatke, pressing him still closer to her. And Mottke stuck his head under his mother's arm so that nobody could see him.

"He should be sent to school, to the Talmud-Torah, so that he might learn to pray at least and recite a blessing. Otherwise he'll grow up a regular heathen," said Reb Meier from his corner.

"If you had been a good father you would have seen to that long ago," said Slatke, turning to Blind Leib.

"All right. You chuck him out of bed and I'll take him to the Talmud-Torah."

"God knows it's what I would like to see! If you would only start and be a good father to my poor childhen. It's certainly high time!" sighed Slatke. "Come, Mottke, get out of bed, my darling, father will take you to school," she went on, stroking Mottke's head.

But it wasn't so easy to get Mottke out of bed. He pretended not to hear his father's shouts and his mother's pleadings, and remained curled under Slatke's arm as if they were speaking of somebody else. He didn't budge until his mother got out of bed herself and his father forced him to follow with the strap.

Then Slatke fished out an old vest of Blind Leib's and buttoned it on Mottke. She put her own best shoes on his feet, the shoes she wore only on feast days and had bought only a few weeks before. In such ways she tried to work upon Mottke and awaken his desire to attend school. Feigele presented him with the two best apples out of her basket. Hindele ran to the grocer and got two poppy cakes for him. And old Reb Meier gave him his new prayer-book with the big letters, which he used as a reading book when he gave the little girls their lessons.

Mottke took the apples, the poppy cakes and the prayer-book, but all the same he wouldn't go to school. He clung to his mother's apron, while his father belabored him with the strap. Tears poured out of his eyes, wetting his face, he kept nibbling at one of the apples, but he wouldn't budge from the spot.

Then Blind Leib lost his patience. He simply set Mottke on his shoulders and rushed with him out of the cellar. Mottke bellowed so loudly that everybody rushed up, and kicked so wildly that his mother's new shoes flew into the street; after that he dropped his cap, later his poppy cakes, and finally his prayer-book. Slatke, who had run out of the cellar after him, picked them all up, carried them behind him and kept saying:

"Mottke, be a good boy, go to school!" And she wiped the tears from his face with her scarf.

But Mottke went on screaming and howling and bellow-ing. All at once he slithered from his father's shoulders and fell on the pavement. There he bellowed still louder, while Blind Leib stood over him with the strap, struck him over the head, and shouted without stopping:

"You'll go to school, I tell you, you'll go to school!"

The mother stood before Mottke, so that the blows rained down on her. But she paid no attention to them and kept on pleading with Mottke:

"Mottke, be a good boy, Mottke! Go to school!"

The Jews going about their business stopped for a mo-ment at the noise and asked what was the cause of it. When they heard that the boy refused to go to school they yelled at him angrily:

"Go to school, you silly brat! To school with you!"

Then they went about their business again.

With God's help Blind Leib managed at last to drag

Mottke to the Talmud-Torah, though more dead than alive. Blind Leib was hot with belaboring his son and the sweat ran in streams from his face. And Mottke, properly tanned, stood at last before his teacher, the half-eaten apples and the poppy cakes in his hands, and gaped at this man walking up and down the room with a thin strap in his hand, and at the children sitting on low benches against the walls.

"Dear, kind Herr Teacher, please teach my boy to pray!" said Slatke imploringly.

The teacher's long thin neck shot out like a snake between his sloping shoulders. Then he bent his whole body down towards Mottke and with his green eyes, which glittered strangely in a white bloodless face, began to scrutinize him.

"So this is the lad who won't go to school? You come here, my lad," he said at last, pinching Mottke's cheek so hard with two lean fingers that tears started to the boy's eyes. "Do you know what they do with a boy who won't go to school? He gets a good licking with this," and he showed Mottke the thin strap.

Mottke had been terrified of the teacher from the first minute, and so he held his tongue.

"I'm a poor woman," Slatke began again. "I can't pay much. Two roubles a month at most, with God's help. I'll spare the last bit out of my mouth if you'll only teach him to read, so that he can read the prayers out of the book. God help me, I'm sometimes afraid the child might become a—no, I won't take such a word in my mouth. The boy refuses to go to school!" Slatke ended, bursting into tears.

"Just you leave him to me! I'll soon teach him what's what," retorted the teacher, and he took Mottke by the hand, pushed him on a bench, sat down beside him and opened a book whose pages were soiled and moist with the tears of many children.

"Now, my lad, you look here. What is this thing? Say 'A,' my lad; say 'A.' "

But Mottke didn't even look at the book. He was gazing at his mother. And when he saw that she was preparing to go away he slipped one foot to the floor.

And no sooner had the teacher sat down beside another boy than Mottke was at the door. One tug and he was running as fast as he could pelt across the market square.

When Slatke saw him standing before her in the cellar she thought the ground would open under her feet. At first she felt like flinging herself on the boy and beating him soundly. But then she saw his eyes gazing at her so innocently and imploringly and that stabbed her to the heart. She swallowed down her tears. She clasped him to her breast, kissed him and beat him by turns, and said:

"My boy, my bad boy, what is to become of you? O Father in heaven!"

And when Blind Leib unbuckled his belt in the evening to give the boy another drubbing, Slatke stood in front of him and took the thrashing herself and cried:

"Leib, he's only a child, and it's so cold outside. . . . Let him stay at home until summer, do. . . ."

But Mottke was never sent to school again.

CHAPTER VI

*

Mottke Makes a Friend

IN the last few years Mottke had grown a great deal and now earned his keep. He began by helping his mother to carry her baskets from house to house. He went with her to the market too, climbed over the peasants' wagons, helped her to bargain with her customers, took a hand in counting the eggs that she bought, and often made a few extra ones disappear into his pockets. Later he handed them over to her and she took them and said nothing, quite satisfied. So he was always to be seen with her at the market. If he caught sight of a chicken in a peasant's wagon he would give her a wink. The peasant woman would scream at him not to touch the chicken, but too late—it would be lying in Slatke's lap, where he had flung it. And Slatke would stick some money into the woman's hand and bargain with her for the chicken.

Once he was actually admitted to the old Shochliner's kitchen along with his mother. Since Slatke had nursed the grandchild of the house she had become almost indispensable there; for she brought the family butter and eggs from the market. So she was kindly received in the Shochliners' kitchen and the servants made much of Mottke.

"So this is the noisy ruffian," said the old Shochliner, looking at Mottke, who awkwardly crept behind his mother's skirts.

39

"Yes, he's grown a big boy, thanks to God," replied Slatke, feeling embarrassed.

"And is he going to school?" asked the old Shochliner.

Slatke grew still more embarrassed.

"He's only a baby still . . . a mother's son. . . ."

"Ah, that isn't good. . . . A boy should go to school and learn his lessons," replied the old Shochliner, shaking her head, and she looked at Mottke as if she thought he was as good as ruined already.

Then Chanele came running into the kitchen: she was the little girl that Slatke had nursed. She was fresh and rosy and had cheeks as smooth and bright as apples. Her hair had just been washed and she was wearing a clean dress and a new apron.

Slatke always had a strange feeling for the children she had nursed; she felt close to them and yet alien to them. She loved and hated these children that had sucked her milk. But she could never feel indifferent towards them. So when Chanele entered her heart sincerely warmed to her and she took her in her arms and kissed her.

"My Chanele, my little Chanele!" she cried. "How are you? Have you forgotten your Nannie? And yet I nursed you, Chanele."

Mottke watched his mother taking the strange child in her arms with curious feelings. He hated this girl that his mother was clasping as if she were her own child, and yet he loved her at the same time. He was ashamed to look at the two of them and turned away. Then the old Shochliner spread a slice of bread with goose fat and put it into his hand.

He began to eat and forgot his mother and the girl. But he soon stopped eating and kept staring, now at Slatke, now at Chanele.

The old Shochliner took Chanele from Slatke's arms, wiped away the traces of the former nurse's kisses from her cheeks and led Slatke with her basket of butter and eggs into the next room. For a moment the two children stood eyeing each other. Mottke felt awkward, and held the slice of bread in his hand as if he did not know what to do with it. The girl was less tongue-tied; she stared at him and showed him her new apron, then her ear-rings and finally her coral necklace. Mottke gaped at them and said nothing. Then the girl took him by the hand and led him into the nursery.

Mottke looked round him in amazement; everything was so clean and so dazzlingly white, and everywhere he looked there were toys. Here a great horse with a real wagon, there two birds and a damaged soldier carrying a drum. The girl showed him her playthings and asked him if he had toys, too. Mottke shook his head and still said nothing.

Then he began to play with the lovely things, laughing. He pulled the horse by the tail, so as to make it go. For in the market square he had often seen the peasants driving the cattle in that way when they refused to move. The girl laughed.

"You see, you've got to pull a horse's tail if you want him to go," said Mottke at last, showing the girl how it was done.

The girl laughed again. She pointed at the cat, which was sitting near by, and asked:

"Must you pull the cat's tail, too, if you want it to go?"

Mottke looked at her sarcastically, shook his head and explained:

"You don't play with a cat. You aren't supposed to pull a cat's tail."

That sounded so superior that the girl grew quite red and felt ashamed of her silly ideas.

But then Mottke stopped playing with the toys and began
to look at the girl. He stroked her cheeks with his dirty
warm hand. The girl made no objection. Then he had a
sudden idea. He came close to her and began, just like a
puppy, to lick her cheeks and neck with his tongue.

The girl did not object to that either; she simply laughed
uproariously and said:

"What a silly boy you are!"

Mottke did not make a single friend among the boys of
his own age. Whenever he met any of them there was a
fight straight away. The result was that all the boys in the
street avoided him and gave him a wide berth. The only
place where he found a friend was in the market place, but
it was a friend of a different kind. It was the organ-grinder's
dog.

On every market day Note, the organ-grinder, appeared
among the crowd of buyers and sellers with his barrel-
organ. Usually he took up his stance in the center of the
market square, where he was a great draw with the peasants.
He had a blue bird in a cage which for five kopeks would
pick out of a little box your "fortune," on which in black
and white was written all that was to happen to you in your
lifetime. And Note had a girl too in a tricot who turned
somersaults. Mottke was so fascinated by all this that whenever he saw Note with his barrel-organ, his blue bird and
his girl, he left his mother to herself and rushed away after
the organ-grinder. But he was most taken of all by the dog
that always followed Note and answered to the name of
Burek. It was a poodle with curly hair like sheep's wool.
Note had shorn him in the French style, so that from the
middle he was quite bare except for a little tuft at the end
of his tail. On market days the poodle was no longer a dog

but a curious creature in a little suit, with a cap on his head. Whenever Note played a tune Burek would go round the peasants carrying their "fortunes" in his mouth and collecting coins in a plate. Mottke couldn't bear to look at him while he was going through this performance. He felt sorry for him and hated the organ-grinder for forcing a dog to be something that wasn't a dog.

But Mottke loved Burek when Burek lay, a real dog, in his kennel in the courtyard, barking like all dutiful dogs at every passer-by and tearing at his chain.

Mottke first came to know Burek in the market square. Burek was going round on his hindlegs in his filthy suit, looking very hungry, with a little plate in his mouth, begging for coins from the peasants. Mottke was filled with pity at seeing him do something so far beneath his dignity as a dog. He followed the organ-grinder home and saw him chaining the dog up. He tried to get near the dog, but Burek barked at him furiously. That pleased Mottke too and he began to sue for Burek's friendship, offering him all sorts of scraps of food that he had picked up, mostly rolls and pieces of bread. And once when he had stolen a whole half-pound of butter out of a peasant's basket—he had intended to keep it for himself—he remembered his dog and actually brought the butter to Burek. In time he managed to win Burek's friendship and the dog let him come near him. After that Mottke was continually visiting the kennel. He would sit down beside Burek, take him in his arms and talk to him. He opened his heart to him and confided all his sorrows to him. And once, after his father had beaten his mother and he had been so terrified that he did not know what to do, he ran to Burek, crept into the kennel, pressed the dog's warm muzzle to his lips and whispered in his ear:

"Burek, father has beaten mother. She cried. When I'm a big man I'll pay him back. I'll give him a black eye!"

The dog listened to his story, became grave and reflective, lowered his eyes, stared fixedly before him and began to growl.

"And they dress you up like a girl! They put a coat on you and a round hat on your head. Don't you stand it, Burek!" said Mottke a little more loudly.

Burek became still graver, rolled his eyes and sniffed through his nose.

"They've turned you into a girl, a girl with a round hat! And I *won't* go to school! I won't and I won't! He can thrash me as much as he likes!" cried Mottke still more loudly.

The dog stretched out his front paws, lifted his muzzle, shut his eyes, pricked his ears and began to howl in a low hoarse voice that sounded almost human. It was as if he were trying to say something.

Mottke understood him.

CHAPTER VII

*

Mottke Learns a Handicraft

AFTER a while Blind Leib remembered again that he must look after his son's future. It must be admitted that he did not hit on this idea himself; it was the oldest cobbler in the place, Berisch Chwat, who brought home his paternal duties to him. This was the same Berisch that had once taught Blind Leib his trade. They happened to meet one Friday evening in the house of another cobbler, where the members of the craft assembled to hold their prayers. Although Blind Leib had not cobbled now for a long time, he nevertheless often attended the cobblers' prayer house, and the others still counted him as one of themselves. Old Berisch Chwat gave him a good talking to:

"What sort of end do you think that boy of yours will come to? You let him idle about as he likes and the young ruffian does nothing from morning to night, not a thing! What do you think will become of him? A thief?"

"Well, what can I do if he won't go to school?"

"Apprentice him to a trade as your father did with you. I can remember as if it was yesterday the day when your father, Selig the carrier, brought you to me; it was a Sunday morning. Oh, you were a young limb, too! You wouldn't even wax the threads for me at first."

"Oh, yes! And then you gave me such a tanning with your strap that I can remember it to this day," said Blind Leib, smiling with both his living and his dead eye.

"Bring him to me. I made a man out of the father, and with God's help I'll make something worth while out of the son, too."

"How long?" asked Leib.

"As long as you were with me, so long he'll have to stick it out. How old is the boy now? Seven? Well, then he'll have to stay with me till he's eleven or twelve, that is until he's honestly learned his job. I'll give him his board and lodgings, and I'll provide him with a suit every Easter as well. Later on, when he's learnt something, I'll let him have five roubles for the first year and a whole ten roubles for the second. You know yourself that a strange child is always well looked after in our house. You know my old woman; she has no children of her own, but she's just like a mother to other people's brats."

"Oh, I can remember your Dobsche all right. And her tongue, too! And I can remember her simply tearing a chunk of flesh out of my arm once and flinging me out of doors in the middle of winter and giving me watery soup to eat. Reb Berisch, you've got a handful of a wife!"

"Well, I don't propose to divorce her on account of any apprentice," replied old Reb Berisch, laughing. "She may have given you the edge of her tongue, but it doesn't seem to have done you much good, for you can't say that you're exactly perfect even now. Come along to Chane-Surele's; we can talk things over there and arrange everything."

And in Chane-Surele's "pub," where you could have an illicit glass of brandy with pastry or pickled herring to make it go down, the father sold Mottke for six whole years to Dobsche, Reb Berisch's wife, just as his mother had sold him before. He pocketed a rouble for himself, too, as an advance on the pay that his son would be earning in five years' time. And over the brandy old Berisch declared:

"But he isn't to run away, mind you; he's to obey me and my wife. And he's to run the errands. Tell him that, and tell him he must obey. Is that understood?"

"Don't you worry, Reb Berisch, he won't run away. If he does I'll drag him back by the ears."

Next morning promised to be the beginning of a lovely autumn day, one of those days before the Jewish New Year when the pears and apples hang ripe from the trees almost begging to be plucked and eaten. Leib took Mottke by the hand and went with him to Berisch the cobbler to begin his apprenticeship. The little market square was full of ripe fruit which the peasants and dealers had brought into the town. Everywhere was the smell of apples, vegetables and fish.

And on this glorious morning Mottke arrived at the little stuffy house where Berisch the cobbler lived. All the windows were fast shut, for Dobsche suffered from ear-ache, was terrified of draughts, and even in summer would never allow the windows to be opened. The room was filled with a strong stench of rotting leather, which for many years (perhaps as long as Berisch had been a cobbler) had moldered in the corners of the place. When Mottke arrived Dobsche wasn't to be seen. Berisch sat with his journeyman and his two apprentices, who were all bent over their work at a round table, hammering away.

"Here is my lad," said Leib.

Old Berisch raised his thick eyebrows, pushed his broken glasses from his nose on to his forehead, gave Mottke a fleeting glance and cried:

"Dobsche! Dobsche! Come here a minute! We've got a new apprentice."

Then there crept out of a nook behind a bed a black and meager shape as closely muffled up as if it were the middle of winter. Round its face was bound a head cloth whose ends stuck out in two sharp points. This strange figure had the look of a witch. The impression was strengthened by the fact that all she wore was dark gray and that her face, too, was the same color. It was Dobsche, the cobbler's wife. She said nothing, looked at Mottke with her dead gray eyes, which reminded one of the eyes of a dead horse, and ran her pointed tongue over her dry lips, which seemed to be covered with dust like everything else in the place. Some time passed before she spoke and when she did it was not like a woman speaking, but like a hollow sound coming out of an empty barrel.

"Whose boy is this?" she asked, coughing.

"Leib's," replied the cobbler, jerking his thumb in Leib's direction.

The woman turned her face towards Blind Leib, stared at him for a while and then pronounced:

"He'll grow up into as big a rascal as his father."

Then she nodded her head like a goat, made a hopeless gesture with one hand, and returned to her corner.

"I'll leave him with you, Reb Berisch. Be a father to him," said Blind Leib. "You can do what you like with him. Give him a good hiding if he doesn't obey you! Seeing you're feeding him you can wallop him, too. Do you hear?" he shouted, turning to Mottke. "You're to do what Reb Berisch and Frau Berisch tell you, or else I'll half-kill you, do you hear?"

Mottke made no reply, and his father left.

Berisch told the boy to sit down and gave him a thread and a lump of wax, instructing him what he had to do with them. But Mottke did not know how to set about waxing the thread, and so he stared round the room with wide eyes. He gazed at the two tall beds which took up the greater part of the room—the huge piles of pillows and quilts on them reached almost to the ceiling—scrutinized the dusty photographs ranged on the walls, representing relatives who had gone to America, the shelves stuffed full of old boots and shoes of all kinds, boot-uppers and pieces of leather. He stared his fill at this new home where he was to pass six whole years, and examined his colleagues—the two apprentices and the journeyman, an old fellow—as they sat cutting out soles. Then he sniffed in the peculiar smell of the leather steeping in tubs beside the benches. Finally he turned to the window ledge covered with threads and paper patterns and the window panes darkened with cobwebs. He watched the sunshine creeping nearer outside and trying to pierce through the window and come into the room; but it was hindered by the cobwebs.

Then some one dug him in the ribs. He turned round; beside him, as if she had risen from the ground, stood Dobsche, and from under her skirt peeped a black cat with glittering eyes, which started to wash itself at once with its red tongue.

"Go and fetch me some water," Dobsche commanded, putting a pail in his hand.

Mottke obeyed gladly. Everything here was so new that it delighted him. He took the pail, went to the well and brought the water. The mistress showed him where the water barrel stood, and he poured in the water and ran off to the well again. In less than two minutes he appeared again with a full pail.

Then he sat down again to his thread and his wax, but could not master them, for the wax was too hard. So he began to look round the room. Now his attention was caught by the black tom-cat, which was tied by a long cord to the end of one of the beds and was perpetually peeping from under the mistress's skirts and following her about wherever she went. It seemed to Mottke that the woman and the cat were related, so that neither could get on without the other.

Then some one gave him another dig in the ribs.

"Here, chop up some wood for me," said the mistress, holding out an ax to him.

Mottke took the ax and set about this job with real pleasure, for he had got used to it at home. When his eyes fell on the cat he felt a strong temptation to chop off its tail.

After he had finished chopping the wood he sat down at his bench and again began to draw the thread through the wax, staring round him at everything. The mistress lighted the fire, then sat down in a dark corner and fell asleep. The tom-cat sprang on her lap and did likewise. The room rang with the sound of hammers beating on leather soles. The master was working at a top-boot, the journeyman and the apprentices sat over their work, and the clock on the wall went tick-tock. All at once the whole room, including the master and the mistress and the tom-cat, seemed so tiresome and disgusting that he wanted to run away. He longed to be out in the street, and stared at the sunshine which was climbing the wall opposite and could not get into the room. His heart sank. He wanted to get up and slip out through the door, but a vague fear hindered him. Yet he could not sit in peace any longer, kept wriggling about on his seat, and no longer made any attempt to wax the thread he was holding. He hated everything here. But he hated the cat particularly and thought to himself: "This would be the real time to chop off its tail, now that it's sleeping."

He looked round him for the ax and caught sight of it in the corner where he had chopped the wood. He stood up and took it in his hand. The master looked up from his work and asked him:

"What's that you're doing?"

Mottke held the ax in his hand and said nothing.

The master's question wakened the mistress, and with that the cat woke, too. The two of them looked round in a dazed way. Suddenly Frau Dobsche seemed to remember something, got up hastily, went over to the dresser, took out a few coins and gave them to Mottke, telling him to go for a loaf and two herrings.

Mottke pocketed the money and ran to the door. He knew that he would not come back again, and the only thing he was sorry for was that he hadn't chopped off the cat's tail; but he consoled himself with the thought that he might manage it yet, some other time.

So he slipped out into the street. The sun took him in its arms as if it were glad to have him back again. The money burned his fingers. He started to run as fast as he could for pure joy. He was soon in the market place, breathing in the smell of the apples and the pears, and his heart became light and happy. As he ran past a baker's shop the smell of newly baked rolls met him. He stopped, went into the shop, bought as many rolls as he could stuff into his pockets, and began to eat.

In the distance he caught sight of Feigele sitting walled in among her sacks, baskets and barrels and shouting her fruit and vegetables. He crept near and grabbed a few pears.

Feigele saw him and began to shout:

"What are you doing here in the middle of the day? Have you run away from your master? Your father will kill you!"

Mottke began to think over what he had done. Half the rolls were gone already. He couldn't go back to the master. But he felt no remorse and all that he was afraid of was the

thrashing he would get. He felt that soon everybody would
be hunting for him.

He saw that he must hide somewhere. So he began to run
again, left the market place and came to a little narrow
street. Then he had an idea, climbed over a wooden fence,
found himself in Note's courtyard and crept into Burek's
kennel. There he curled himself up and lay low.

The dog smelt him and began to lick his face and his
hands, filled with joy at seeing him again. Mottke pulled
the remaining rolls out of his pocket and shared them with
Burek.

He knew that the master, the mistress and his father
would be in the market place now looking for him with
sticks. But in spite of that he still felt no remorse, nor even
any fear of the thrashing he would get. But his heart beat
loudly and his eyes gleamed. He lay half under the dog and
peered out of the kennel into the courtyard; but nobody
came.

He lay there all day and all evening. When night came he
felt cold. He pressed closer to the dog, and Burek, who understood, lay on top of him and licked him.

Late in the night Slatke heard a scratching at the cellar
door. She had not been able to sleep for anxiety, for she
had been waiting for some sign of Mottke. When she heard
the scratching her heart stopped for a moment. She stole
softly out of bed and listened to make sure that Blind Leib
was asleep. He was snoring loudly, so she went over to
the stove, took out a bowl that was standing ready in the
oven, and set it without a word outside the door. Then she
snatched up an old rug that was lying in a corner and carried it outside, too. Mottke was crouching there among the
baskets, shivering from head to foot with cold. She handed
him the bowl and the rug and whispered:

"Make yourself scarce in the morning first thing, for if your father finds you here he'll kill you."

Then she returned to the cellar and slipped quietly under the bedclothes. Blind Leib must not know what she had done.

CHAPTER VIII

*

The First Punishment

EARLY in the morning, just when Mottke was enjoying his sweetest sleep, he felt fiery blows raining down on his face, his eyes, ears and hands. He raised his head and dimly saw that his father was standing over him and belaboring him with a whip. He did not cry out or make a sound. He merely tried to hide his head under the rug. But he didn't manage that either, for his hands were tied with a rope behind his back. His father had bound him while he was asleep.

Mottke looked Blind Leib straight in the eyes, although every stroke of the whip almost blinded him; it was a dog whip furnished at the tip with a piece of lead. Nevertheless he lay still and merely tried to hide his face as well as he could. His mother was standing beside his father now. She pulled Blind Leib by the coat-tails and then flung herself between him and his son. But the whip did not stop, so she got the blows that were intended for Mottke.

Then Leib violently flung her back. She gave a loud cry of pain. Mottke gathered up all his strength and tried to stand up and rush at his father; but he could not move, for his feet were tied as well as his hands. So he gave up all resistance, remained lying like a beast to be slaughtered and let his father do what he liked with him. And Leib thrashed him until the whip fell from his hand.

Then he seized his son by the ears and dragged him out into the street. There he began to belabor him with his fists, shouting:

"Go back to your master! Go back at once to your master!"

This time Slatke did not come out to follow him with rolls and poppy cakes, as she had done the day when he was taken to school; she felt ashamed of having given birth to such a son, stayed inside and wept over her bitter lot.

The passers-by stopped and looked on while Leib dragged the boy through the streets by a rope, and praised the father:

"Quite right! You're his father. . . . Be a proper father and show him the road he should go."

And Aaron-Meier the water-carrier, passing with his wooden buckets, prophesied:

"Leib, you'll have lots of trouble with that sprig of yours yet. Don't give him any rope. If you do he'll turn out a monster that the world has never seen the like of before."

"Don't worry, I'll thrash the thief out of him yet! I'll make him into a decent human being," retorted Blind Leib, letting fly at Mottke again:

"Come on, you bastard, come on!"

Mottke made no resistance. Blood was flowing down his face and the rope cut into his bound wrists.

Berisch Chwat the master, Dobsche the mistress, Henoch Picknick, the journeyman, and the two apprentices were waiting to give Mottke a good reception when Blind Leib dragged him into the work-room and flung him on the floor like a sack of potatoes.

"Reb Berisch, do with this boy what you like! You feed him and you have the right to thrash him. You're just as much his father as I am. He's eaten your bread, stolen your money—so wallop him."

"I'll see to that all right. I'll teach him to run away from his master and steal his master's money!" retorted old

Berisch, who had grown as red as a beet-root with fury at the sight of Mottke. Then he bit his lip, climbed up on a chair and began to look for something on a dusty old shelf.

"Where did you find him?" he asked, fetching down the pigskin strap that he whipped his apprentices with. "Dobsche, bring me some vinegar. I want to moisten the strap, it's got dry and might break," he added in an indifferent tone, feeling the strap with his fingers.

"He had the nerve to come home and sleep all night in the cellar!" replied Leib. "And my wife smuggled a pot of potatoes out to him, too. The two of them thought I was sleeping, but I heard them all right and I just waited till the rascal was asleep. Then I bound him hand and foot and gave him what for. My old woman tried to stop me and she got her whack, too."

"His mother is to blame for everything! She's the one that's spoiled him. She always sticks up for him. Did you hear that? She let him in and gave him food into the bargain! How can he help turning into a thief?" Dobsche's hollow voice boomed out of the clouts covering her face. And she wet her hands with vinegar so as to moisten the strap.

All this time Mottke lay bound on the middle of the floor listening to what they were saying about him. The apprentices stood by with white faces and glittering eyes lit up with enthralled expectation of what was to come, and gazed at him with mingled pity and curiosity. The cat slinked up to him, stared at him with interest, licked him with its little rosy tongue and went away again. Mottke could do nothing against the hated animal, for he was bound.

Then he felt that a knife was cutting through his skin and flesh. It was the pigskin strap hurtling down on him. But this time he didn't hold his tongue. When he saw the strange old man standing over him, purple in the face, and the mistress licking her dry lips with her tongue just like the tom-cat squatting beside her, and the apprentices looking at him with terrified faces and sparkling eyes, his fighting spirit came back. His whole body took a leap and fell with a thud on a pile of plates that stood still unwashed in a corner. A great clatter and the plates flew in smithereens.

Dobsche began to scream and the master's rage mounted. He made a sign to the journeyman and the apprentices. They took hold of Mottke. The apprentices sat on his legs, the journeyman held his hands, and Dobsche pressed his head against the floor. Then the old man tore down Mottke's trousers and the pigskin strap whistled on his naked flesh. Blue weals arose, then blood spurted out. . . .

Suddenly the door was torn open and Slatke rushed into the room.

"What are you doing to him, you murderers?" she screamed, flinging herself over Mottke to shield him.

"Aha! There you are! How do you expect him to be anything else when his own mother supports him in his ways?" cried old Berisch. "Give me back my rouble, pay me for what the rascal has eaten in my house, and take him away! I don't want him!"

"My husband is too weak to deal with such a hooligan. He would ruin us. He's gobbled up our hard won money. And then she comes here and sticks up for him! . . . Take him away!" Dobsche howled out of her clouts.

"Slatke, get out of this! Else I'll do for you!" shouted Blind Leib, stamping his feet with rage.

Slatke stepped aside, terrified.

"Don't you see what you've done?" Blind Leib went on. "Strangers have to step in to make a decent man out of your brat, and you come here and abuse them! You should thank them! Here, you can take your gallows-bird home with you."

"It breaks my heart when I see him being tortured. They were murdering him . . ." replied Slatke, bursting into tears.

"Reb Berisch, don't listen to this woman," cried Blind Leib. "Do with the boy what you like: thrash him, strike him dead if you like! You're feeding him, you're teaching him a trade, so you can deal with him as you like."

"No, Leib, you can take him back. I don't want to have anything more to do with him," replied the Master Cobbler. "Give me back my rouble and the money that the boy squandered, and take him back with you."

"You see now what you've done, Slatke! I'll thrash you half-dead, both you and the boy. Beg the Master Cobbler to keep him. Beg for your bastard, beg, I tell you!" Blind Leib shouted.

"I don't want this treasure of hers! She can keep him if she's so fond of him," replied old Berisch, laying the strap aside.

"We won't need to look far for another apprentice!" Dobsche said, licking her lips again.

"You see now, don't you?" growled Blind Leib, giving his wife a furious glance.

Slatke saw that she had acted unwisely. She felt ashamed of herself and did not know what to do next. So she clenched her fists and fell upon Mottke and began to beat him.

"You good for nothing, do you see what you've done, you bad, bad child?" she screamed. "I wish you had never been born."

"That's better. That's the way that a mother should talk!" said old Berisch, wiping the foam from his lips.

But Slatke did not hear him; she had drawn her cloak

round her and rushed away, not knowing where she was going.

After that old Berisch did not beat Mottke any more. The journeyman and the apprentices lifted him up, carried him into the cellar, laid him down on the damp floor, shut the heavy door and barred it from outside.

For a long time Mottke lay on the wet floor, not knowing whether he was alive or dead. His whole body was filled with pain and he felt his arms and legs were broken and that he would never be able to stand up again.

During his thrashing he had flung himself about and this had slightly loosened the rope. By straining his whole body he tried to free his hands. At last he managed it. Then he lay for a long time with his hands free, not daring to move them yet. Suddenly the black cat appeared beside him. The beast looked round and walked first to the corner of the cellar, from which the scrabbling and gnawing of mice could be heard; it suddenly fell silent. Next the cat turned round, went up to Mottke, sniffed him, and then started licking him with its tongue. Mottke kicked it away with his foot. This surprised the cat and it took itself off.

Then Mottke caught sight of a little window just underneath the roof of the cellar. A thought immediately occurred to him, but he was afraid to put it into practice yet, for he still felt too weak. But his strength was gradually returning. As soon as he thought that it would serve his purpose he crept on all fours to the wall, dragged over a sack of potatoes, got up on it and tried to stick his head into the window opening. He managed it. But he could not get any farther, for it was covered with wire netting. He took hold of the netting with both hands, pulled with all his might and wriggled his body into the opening. He felt neither pain nor anything else; his senses were too dulled. He put for-

ward all his strength to break the netting, pushed and pushed.
At last with a final push he slipped through and was lying
outside in the gutter.

As soon as he found himself in the open air and at liberty
he looked round and made sure that he had not been noticed by anybody. Then he picked up a sharp-edged stone,
crept to the window of the workshop and flung the stone
against it with all his might.

The glass smashed and fell clattering into the room. Shouts
and screams followed. But Mottke did not hear them; he
was off. Like a weasel he slipped through a gap in a fence,
ran through a dark passage into a courtyard, and hid himself behind a pile of planks that he saw there. Then he lay
without moving and waited.

He heard them rushing about the courtyard looking for
him, and recognized his master's voice and the voices of the
journeyman and the apprentices. But he lay quite still behind the planks and they did not find him. Once they were
quite near him, but they did not find him. He stayed in his
hiding place until the evening.

When night came he began to shiver with cold and hunger.
He considered where he should go. Then he remembered his
friend Burek, crept out from behind the planks and stole by
by-ways and through dark passages to Note's courtyard,
avoiding everybody. He crept into the dog's kennel.

Burek warmed him. He searched in the kennel for something to eat, but all he could find was the mess left on a
dish for the dog. He tried to eat it, but he spat it out in
disgust. Then he suddenly felt so weary and beaten that he
crept under the dog for comfort. Burek warmed him with
his breath and his coat and Mottke went to sleep quietly and
securely, for he was not among men.

After that he led a solitary and lawless existence.

CHAPTER IX

*

Mottke Chooses a Profession

IN the morning hunger drove Mottke out of the kennel. He carefully looked up and down the narrow street to see whether Berisch or his father was about. But he could see nobody. The sun had just risen; it shone encouragingly on the pavement, admonishing man to set about his day's work, and gleamed on the window panes.

Most of the people in the little street were not awake yet, and many of the shops were still shut. But Schloime the butcher was already striding to his stance, a shoulder of a calf slung over his back. Across the bridge came Chaiml the dairyman, returning with his cans from the villages. There was a smell of new rolls, poppyseed rolls and caraway seed rolls, outside the bakers' shops. Mottke stood in the street shivering with cold. He had been half-frozen all night in the kennel. Hunger cramps twisted his entrails. The smell of the new bread tormented him, and the smells of the butter, the milk and the raw meat on Schloime's shoulder soon became unbearable. He was strongly tempted to rush into a shop and snatch a roll. But the baker was standing in his doorway. With a shudder he remembered the thrashing he had got the day before, gave up his idea and made for the market place.

It was early autumn and everything in field and garden was hanging ripe; a Friday, the day of the weekly market. The peasants had brought in from the villages round about the best and juiciest things that they had for sale, and plump chickens were hopping with tethered legs round the wagons. The market place was filled with the cackling of fowls of every description. Feathers flew. In the middle of the square Selig the village Jew was sitting with his daughter Baschke selling live fishes that swam about in a tub. All round were piled green vegetables and ripe fruit; blue plums and red raspberries. And the rosy cheeks of the girl, coolly fanned by the morning air, were like the ripe fruit that she had brought with her from her village.

New wagons kept driving into the square, wagons piled with fruit and vegetables, and wagons filled with ducks, hens and geese; peasants with young calves for sale, potatoes, butter, eggs, cheese and milk. And the whole square smelt of fresh fruit. Then dogs appeared sniffing at all the wagons, their appetite whetted by the smell of so many things to eat.

And behind the hungry dogs came Mottke. Like them, he had been drawn there by the smell of food, and like them he wandered about hopelessly among the wagons. He looked round every moment, for he was terrified that his father or old Berisch might catch sight of him. He sidled up to the fruit stands and picked up the rotten apples and worm-eaten plums that the vendors had thrown away, but he could not eat them. He shivered with cold; his very bowels seemed to be frozen. Then the fragrance of fresh butter came to him; a peasant woman had taken a pat of it from her basket and set it out for sale. He went up and was just stretching out his hand to take it when he remembered his thrashing and turned away. His torments grew. For a little later the square began to smell of sausage and roast pork; the Christian butcher had opened his shop. The night before he had killed a pig for the market and now his apprentices were turning it into sausages. The dogs, with their finer sense of smell, had been the first to find this new attraction. They gathered before the butcher's, licking their lips and gazing with greedy eyes at the "trefe" meat, which the Jews were forbidden by the law to enjoy. Herr Scholz, the fat German butcher, stood in the doorway of his shop with a bloodstained apron round his belly. The dogs looked up at him with great respect.

The warm smell of new sausage was too much for Mottke. The sun was shining on the butcher's shop and the steps in front were warm. So he sat down on them, warmed himself in the sun and sucked in the odor of roast pork. His mouth watered and he felt a little better. The dogs looked at him with envy, because he dared to sit so close.

Gradually the square became filled with obese Jewesses come to shop, and in the air rose a confusion of human voices mingled with the cackling of fowls. Hens, ducks and geese were torn out of women's hands by other women, and the peasants cursed and swore; the feathers of the poor birds flew about everywhere. Amid all this din the German butcher Scholz calmly stood in his doorway, the German baker Konig facing him. The stray dogs, Mottke at their head, wandered in front of the two shops. But neither the butcher nor the baker paid any attention to them. In complete calm Herr Scholz and Herr Konig contemplated the life and bustle in the square, smiled quietly to themselves, nodded contentedly across at each other, and thought in their hearts that the Jewish Rabbi would presently declare all these hens, ducks and geese "trefe," and that thereupon they would both be able to buy up the whole lot, killed and dressed, for a mere song.

Suddenly, between the wagons, Mottke caught sight of his mother. At first he felt like rushing up to her. A deep feeling drew him towards her, but since she had beaten him like the others he had a sense of fear at the same time. And so he hastily ran away. The dogs followed him.

He turned into the Tempelgasse, where the cattle market was held. Peasants were standing there with their oxen, sheep and cows, and Jews were walking about feeling the beasts with their fingers to see whether they were well covered, milking the cows and tasting the milk, haggling with the owners, shouting, settling bargains with a handshake and paying out money. Mottke mingled in the crowd of men and beasts. Once he tried to get at a cow's udder to have a drink, but the peasant noticed him and drove him away with a cudgel. So he fared just as badly among the cows and calves as he had done in the market square among the women and geese.

The lame Jewish butcher Gedalje was driving his calves from the market, but could not keep them together. The calves ran in every direction, and each time Gedalje had to run after them. As soon as Mottke saw this he snatched a stick from the ground and began to help the man to keep his calves together.

"That's right! Help me to get them to the slaughter-house and I'll give you a roll for yourself. Do something, boy; give me a hand. Don't stand about like that!" shouted Gedalje. His red eyes were always watering and he was deaf in both ears. He was convinced that everybody else was deaf, too, and always shouted at the top of his voice.

Mottke liked this new occupation. He drove the calves together, twisted the tails of the ones that would not move, and helped Gedalje to bring the beasts to the slaughter-house. Some of the dogs joined him. He whistled to them, and the dogs ran to round in the calves.

At the slaughter-house a new world opened before him.

He saw things he never forgot all the rest of his life. Up till now he had never thought when he saw a butcher, such as Gedalje or Schloime, going past carrying hunks of meat, that this meat came from the same cows, calves and sheep that he had seen so often in summer returning through the streets from their pastures. Such a thought would never have occurred to him; he had always fancied that a living calf was something quite different from the cold chunks of veal that the butcher bore past on his shoulder. But now he could see Gedalje driving the calves together in the slaughter-house, choosing out one of them and binding its legs. The calf fell to the floor, and bellowed and glared with great terrified eyes. Thereupon a Jew in a blood-stained overall went up to it, carrying a huge knife whose blade glittered in the sun. The man put the knife between his teeth, and then with a razor shaved the throat of the calf till not a single hair remained. That done, he took the great knife out of his mouth and with one stroke cut the beast's throat. Blood spurted out. The calf turned up its eyes, gasped, and was dead. And nobody punished this Jew or Gedalje, either. Nobody shrieked at them, nobody gave them a hiding. Quite calmly they turned their attention to another calf.

When Mottke looked he saw that there were other men, too, with bloodstained overalls and great knives in their hands, stabbing and murdering. In one corner a huge ox was lying with its legs bound. A great powerful lad was holding its head down and paying just as little attention to its wide terrified eyes as another Jew standing over it with a still bigger knife, who presently cut its throat. At the other side of the slaughter-house a few Christian boys had bound a pig to a stake and were beating it over the head with heavy sticks. The pig squealed and wailed. And in a third corner another Jew was sitting with his knife be-

tween his teeth and a hen held fast between his knees. Its
eyes were glazed with terror. The Jew tore the feathers from
its soft neck and a strip of blue, young-looking skin appeared, covered with a fine network of veins. One gash,
the blood spurted out, and the man flung the hen away.
It fell to the floor, cackled confusedly for a while and went
on bleeding till its eyes turned up and it lay still. And then
Mottke saw that after killing it Gedalje hung up every calf
from a beam, slit open its belly, pulled out its smoking
entrails, its lungs and liver, and then flayed off the hide.
Blood ran from Gedalje's knife over his hands and his
caftan, and the eyes of the calf were still open and staring.

Wherever Mottke looked he saw nothing but blood and
slaughtered calves, and pigs with their throats slit. Oxen
bellowed in terror of death and made the air tremble with
their cries. The calves and sheep seemed to beg for mercy,
and lowed and bleated in weak and pathetic voices. Pigs
squealed, cocks and hens uttered terrified cries that were
like the puling of infants. But round them all stood men
with huge knives, their clothes splashed with blood, killing
all that remained alive, flaying hides and plucking feathers.
Mottke felt that after killing so many beasts they must presently seize some man too, fling him on the floor and slaughter
him. For in the slaughter-house everything was permitted;
they could strike, stab, kill as they liked and no one punished them. He had never known before that you were
allowed to destroy living things.

He was deeply excited by all the blood. At last he walked
over to Gedalje and begged him to give him a knife, so as
to flay one of the calves. Gedalje stared at him with his red-
rimmed eyes and said:

"You aren't up to that yet. You would only cut holes in

the hide. Look on first and see how it's done, and later you'll be able to do it, too."

Mottke watched attentively, eager to learn the art. Then his attention was caught by a lad who was tearing out a dead ox's lungs and liver and blowing up the lungs with a tube. The man who had killed the ox examined the lungs to see whether they were sound and whether the flesh of the ox was fit for human usage or "trefe."

Mottke began to make himself useful by pulling out lungs and livers, and his hands were soon covered with blood. Suddenly some one gave him a buffet on the ear from behind.

"Hullo, who's this that's begun shoving in his oar?" It was a tall lad known in the town as Nussen the Thief.

"Let him be. He's Blind Leib's son. A handy lad. We'll make a man of him yet, you take my word for it."

"Oh? Well, in that case, you run and get me a half-bottle of aquavita from Chane-Surele's and bring a roll and a pickled herring with you, too," said Nussen, turning to Mottke and giving him some money. "But come back straight! Do you hear? If you don't, I'll break your neck."

Mottke made no protest against the blow, and it never entered his head, either, to decamp with the money as he had done with the Master Cobbler's. He liked the slaughterhouse and he would do his best to please his new patrons. He flew to Chane-Surele's. And in a jiffy he was back again with the half-bottle of spirits that he had paid for as well as another that he had snatched up and stuck in his pocket. He wanted to distinguish himself before Nussen and, to tell the truth, Nussen was more than satisfied. The bread was all bloody with being carried in Mottke's hand. Nussen the Thief took the spirits, patted Mottke genially on the head with his hard hand and said:

"Well, you seem to be a proper lad! We'll make a real man of you yet!"

Mottke smiled with pleasure at such praise, and after that he was prepared to do anything that Nussen told him. Even if he had been asked to kill some one he would have done it without turning a hair. And when Nussen gave him a swig from the bottle and a chunk of the bloodstained roll, he was the happiest boy on God's earth.

He lifted a scrap of lights from the floor and flung it to the dogs that had followed him. The dogs looked up reverently and were pleased that their Mottke had distinguished himself so brilliantly.

CHAPTER X

*

The King of the Dogs

SINCE Mottke had found a home in the slaughter-house he had become the king of the dogs. A pack of them escorted him everywhere like a bodyguard and saw to it that nobody molested him. He had no friends among boys of his own age and the dogs were his sole companions. But Burek, his first friend, was his bosom crony. He made himself respected and feared with the help of his dogs. The boys of the town trembled at his approach. He only needed to wave his hand and set his dogs on them to put them to headlong flight, no matter who they were.

And when he wanted to have some sport he would take his dogs with him and make them lie down before the door of some little shop. The dogs would stay there until he ordered them to get up again. During all that time nobody dared to go in or come out. The children were terrified even of going near the beleaguered door. And Mottke stood by like a king and saw that his dogs obeyed their orders: they lay before the door looking about them with glittering eyes and greeted everybody who tried to enter or leave with a menacing growl, ready to fall on them if they did not scurry away at once. Then the shop-keepers would turn to Mottke and say pleadingly:

"Mottke, do take the dogs away! Mottke, what harm have I done you?"

Sometimes Mottke would relent, wave off the dogs and

raise the siege. But when he had a grudge against some shop-keeper he would leave his dogs lying before the shop door all day and see to it that nobody went in and nobody came out.

He gradually acquired power through his dogs, and people competed for his favor. One shop-keeper actually offered him money to besiege the shop-door of a rival. But Mottke did not use his power to make money, but solely to serve his ambition. Once on a Friday evening he actually besieged a whole congregation of Chassidim in their synagogue and refused to let them go home after the service, and he did that simply because Ojser the Chassid had once called after him that he had seen him stealing pears from a Christian's garden on the Sabbath. And Mottke didn't raise the siege of the Chassidim until he was tired of the whole business.

His power over the dogs hadn't been gained simply by flinging them chunks of old flesh and lights at the slaughter-house. The affection the dogs had for him came from a deeper source. They felt that in him they had a leader equipped with all the human instincts, reason included, a being endowed with the gift of speech and the capacity to walk on two legs. They knew that this being was prepared to use all his gifts for their good, and guide and rule them. Before him there had been nobody who wanted to be the leader and king of the dogs; but he gladly took up the rôle. The dogs recognized him as their master and obeyed him unquestioningly. Sometimes he beat them, forced them to sit up on their hind legs and beg, made them leap fences, climb roofs and even jump over houses. And the dogs did whatever he asked them. A dog only needed to sniff him to tell at once that he was king of the dogs.

As soon as he had gained power over the dogs he used it to

pay off his old scores against his enemies. And these were his father, Dobsche, old Berisch, and the "Dajan," Reb Leibusch.

Mottke had no deep grudge against old Berisch, who had thrashed him so mercilessly. He told himself that Berisch, who was a good man after all, had had a sort of right to do it. But as for that woman with the plugged ears, he hated her almost wildly. Whenever he saw her in the street he set his dogs on her. They fell upon her and tore her skirt right off her, while she shrieked as if she was being killed. And Mottke stood by and laughed for all he was worth. He simply wouldn't let the woman out of her house. Once the dogs snatched a pound of meat out of her hands and another time a basket of butter and eggs. And they tore off the black cat's tail, and scratched and mauled it until it hadn't a sound spot on its body. But Mottke's thirst for revenge was still unsatisfied and for a long time after that he wouldn't let the woman out of her house.

As for his father, Mottke still felt too weak, in spite of his dogs, to deal with him, and waited patiently for the day when he would be able to settle accounts with him without outside help. So he avoided him for the time being. And Blind Leib gave his son a wide berth, too, and didn't dare lay hands on him for fear of the dogs. If he caught sight of Mottke in the street, followed by his pack, he would gaze after him with his one eye and think to himself that his son would become something yet that would surprise people.

Mottke hated the Dajan Reb Leibusch without any real reason. Reb Leibusch was a little childless man with a face of stone, and completely hard-hearted. Every Friday afternoon he sat in the synagogue, his little knife in his hand, and decided whether this or that piece of meat was "trefe" or "kosher." And if a woman brought him a hen or a duck or a goose to be examined, the verdict was always the same; everything was unusable, "trefe." At the other side of the synagogue sat the second Dajan, Reb Jizchok, a tall man who was always smiling. If Reb Leibusch had no children, it must be admitted that Reb Jizchok had a whole swarm of them. And with Reb Jizchok every hen and duck and goose was always usable, always "kosher." Yet the women never went to Reb Jizchok but always to Reb Leibusch, and in consequence they had to sell to the Christians of the town for a mere song the fowls that he declared "trefe."

Mottke had hated this Reb Leibusch ever since his earliest days. His mother rushed about all week with her heavy baskets and worked herself to the bone so as to save enough to buy a hen or a duck for the Sabbath. Now it often happened that these fowls weren't quite without reproach; there were doubtful cases among them. So whenever Mottke was sent to the synagogue with a bird he always turned to Reb Jizchok. Then his mother instructed him to go to Reb Leibusch and nobody else. At the same time he knew beforehand that his mother would cry when she heard the result, and his sister be sent off with the "trefe" hen to sell it at a loss to the fat Germans; and after that they would all have nothing but dry bread for their Sabbath dinner. So ever since his early days Mottke had hated Reb Leibusch for his severe verdicts. And now he saw that the man declared everything "trefe" at the slaughter-house too. If Reb Liebusch appeared all the butchers hung their heads and trembled. They brought him the lungs and the liver of the slaughtered beasts. Nussen blew up the lungs and old Reb Leibusch examined them in great detail and then said briefly and finally: "Trefe." It sounded like a doom and Nussen would whisper softly every time:

"I knew that the old boy would say 'trefe.'"

"Is it any wonder? The man has no children, his heart is as hard as a stone," red-haired Schloime would reply with a sigh, and tears would start from his reddened eyes.

But when Reb Jizchok appeared at the slaughter-house everybody looked cheerful, and Mottke knew that after the examination he would be sent to Chane-Surele's to fetch some brandy.

For this reason Mottke hated Reb Leibusch and would have been only too glad to set his dogs on him, and gladder still to keep him shut in the synagogue for a whole day. But he was afraid to attack the man. Even Nussen the Thief was terrified of the old fellow. He swore at him behind his back, certainly; but when Reb Leibusch appeared at the slaughter-house Nussen trembled from head to foot. And old Schloime and all the other butchers behaved just like Nussen; and so Mottke followed their example. But he hoped that the time would come yet for a settlement with Leibusch, too.

Meanwhile he ruled the town with his dogs, and the dogs did whatever he asked them. They obeyed him as if he were a king.

At night, when everybody in the town was asleep, Mottke and his dogs would assemble beside the butchers' blocks in the market square. The moon shone. Mottke sat like a king on the tallest block and beside him lay his friend, the oldest among the dogs, Burek, who was shorn behind and had a lion's mane, Burek, who had helped Mottke when he was still small and weak and did not know how to defend himself against men. Burek remained his closest friend, and Mottke raised him to the position of senior dog. He always flung the best chunk of meat to him, he freed him from his chains and took him wherever he went. Sometimes Burek would lie on the butcher's block with Mottke and Mottke would play with him. His subjects, the dogs, leapt around him, stood on their hind-legs, and barked madly as if they were saying:

"Command us, command us, master! We will do anything, anything that you tell us."

CHAPTER XI

*

Blind Pearl

THERE was only one human being that Mottke respected and tried to imitate. This was Nussen the Thief, who earned his living by flaying dead beasts in the slaughter-house and afterwards hanging up their flesh for sale in the butchers' shops. But his chief source of income was theft. Nussen the Thief lived with his mother in a little wooden hut on the edge of the town, not far from the Schuster-gasse. The whole town trembled at the mention of that little hut. If a theft happened anywhere, if a few silver candle-sticks disappeared from some one's table or Leiser-Meier's warehouse was broken into and all the hides stolen, the injured person went straight to the wooden house before thinking of anything else. Nobody dared to enter, for that might very easily have meant getting slashed with a knife. So the injured man generally contented himself with walk-ing up and down outside groaning and clasping his hands, and trying every now and then to get a peep through the curtained windows. Then Nussen would appear in the door-way and ask mildly:

"What's up?"

"Nussen, for God's sake take pity on my wife and chil-dren! Give me back my hides!"

"What hides? Has somebody been stealing hides again? Well, I never! This is getting past a joke. Soon it'll be impossible to live in this town. Every night there's a new robbery."

"Nussen, tell me. How much do you want for the hides?"

"How much I want? Nothing! The thieves will want something, though. They came to me and told me everything. I understand that they'll be content with two hundred roubles."

Then they would haggle for a while and at last Nussen would divulge the place where the skins were buried, beside the pond in the meadow.

The guardian of law and order in the town was Janowitsch, the captain of the gendarmerie, called "Blind Pearl" by the Jews, because when he liked he could be just as blind as poor Frau Pearl, who begged in front of the synagogue. He shut his eyes if a Jew kept his shop open after twelve on Sunday; he shut his eyes if a calf vanished from under a peasant's wagon, or if some one calmly unyoked a horse from another man's cart and confiscated it, or if Nussen's gang broke into a warehouse and went away with all the hides. At such times he was "Blind Pearl" and saw and heard nothing. This Janowitsch could speak Yiddish, and whenever an investigation was on foot and the District Inspector wanted to scrutinize the manual workers' trade certificates he always let them know beforehand. Blind Pearl was just as indispensable to the town as the Rabbi and the women's baths were in another way. He reconciled the Jews of the place with one another. If a Jew reported another Jew for selling illicit spirits, Janowitsch would pass the news on to the man who was accused. Then the man would charge his enemy in turn with selling stolen goods. Thereupon Blind Pearl would lift a nice little bribe from both of them and, lo and behold, everything was settled and the public never knew anything.

During his rule no Jew had ever appeared before the court. And when Berl the informer once accused Blind Pearl to his superiors of bribery and corruption, Blind Pearl

appeared before the Rabbi among all the Jews and cried
in excellent Yiddish:

"Have you ever heard of a Jew giving away another
Jew? Is there no Rabbi in this town, may he live to be a
hundred and twenty? If a man has anything to complain
about he should go to the Rabbi!"

For a long time there had existed a feud between Nussen
the Thief and Blind Pearl, and they fought each other in
silence but very stubbornly. Like Nussen, Blind Pearl had
a whole robber band at his service, who handed over their
stolen goods to him and got him to negotiate for them with
the injured parties. These two bands were keen competi-
tors. Outwardly the two ring-leaders, Nussen the Thief and
Blind Pearl, behaved as if they were on the best of terms.
They talked together, drank a bottle of untaxed brandy
together every now and then at Chane-Surele's, but took care
that there were always other people there when they met,
for they were both afraid that one of them might sometime pull out a knife. And the glances that they shot at each
other gave their feelings away. There was a tacit agreement between them that the one wouldn't interfere with the
other's business. So whenever there was a burglary and the
injured man came running to the guardian of law and order
Blind Pearl was never at home: he simply hid and didn't
appear until the crime had been "cleared up."

In return, the leaders did the most they could to injure
the members of the rival gang. If ever Nussen the Thief
came across one of Blind Pearl's band in the streets he
gave the poor devil a thorough drubbing before letting him
go again. And since Mottke had been adopted by Nussen,
Blind Pearl had paid particular attention to him. On market
days he wouldn't let Mottke into the square, drove him
away with blows whenever he met him, and waited for the
day when he would get a chance to settle accounts properly

with the "little villain," as he called him. Mottke didn't complain to Nussen about this treatment, for he knew for one thing that it was in the order of things, and for another that he was still of far too little importance for his protector to embark on an open war with Blind Pearl on his account.

For Nussen the Thief, who had won such a strong position that Blind Pearl trembled before him and went out of his way, Mottke felt the deepest reverence. He absolutely worshiped him and would have gone through fire and water for him. Nussen the Thief for his part considered Mottke a dare-devil lad who might sometime come in very useful. So he made much of him, took him to the wooden hut, and even let him sleep there.

Nussen the Thief lived in the hut with his mother. He had one good trait; he honored his mother. And the town praised him for it. He actually drove away his wife because she couldn't get on with his mother and was always quarreling with her. He saw that his mother had decent clothes, got her a good seat in the women's row in the synagogue, and every Sabbath brought her the best meat and the most delicate fish that could be bought. After dinner on Friday he got her to put on her best dress and her best hood and went walking with her. And when the women saw how well the lad treated his mother they forgave him all his tricks and declared that he would go to heaven yet. People told that old Pesche—her husband had been a butcher—could still drink a half-bottle of brandy at one go, and added that she still let her son have the weight of her hand if he did anything that displeased her, and that, though he was feared by Blind Pearl himself, he submitted meekly to his mother's blows and never complained.

This old woman, almost eighty but still active, with cheeks red as a frost-bitten apple, gave Mottke a place in

the corner of her kitchen. She looked after him, washed his
clothes, and now and then gave him something hot to eat
as well. She became his foster-mother and scolded her son
whenever he dared to beat him. And when Nussen saw how
fond his mother was of the boy he changed his own attitude
to him and began to treat him like a younger brother.

One evening after Nussen and Mottke returned from the
slaughter-house, old Pesche set a great bowl of potato soup
on the table and then turned to her son:

"Nussen, it will be the New Year soon and we'll be
holding the Feast of Reconciliation. And I'm afraid the
boy doesn't even know the confession of faith."

"Don't you know the prayer?" asked Nussen, starting
on his soup.

Mottke, munching a hot potato, laughed and replied:
"No."

"What are you laughing at? The great holy days are
coming and you can't even hold a prayer-book in your hand,"
said the old woman.

Nussen gave the boy a buffet on the ear, but Mottke
didn't stop laughing.

"What are you striking him for? It's easy to strike a
boy! Better if you fetched out a prayer-book and taught
him to read," screamed the old lady. "You can read. And
he should learn to read too."

Mottke laughed.

After supper Nussen took his mother's prayer-book down
from the shelf where the Sabbath candlesticks stood, turned
the pages until he found some capital letters and began to
teach Mottke.

"Look here. This thing here is an 'H' and that thing there
is a 'B.' Say them after me: 'H' and 'B.' "

Mottke laughed.

"What are you laughing at, you fool? You seem to think this is funny!" cried Nussen, laying Mottke over his knee and walloping him.

"What are you doing? What's the meaning of this?" screamed the old lady. "Nussen, you thief, let the boy go, let him go, I tell you! You'll break his bones!"

And the old lady jerked Mottke from her son's hands.

Nussen began to teach him again and in a little the beatings began once more.

"I must say you're a fine teacher! Just look at this teacher—may his hands wither on his wrists! You can beat him, I can see that well enough, but as for teaching him!"—the old woman screamed at her son.

And Mottke laughed under Nussen's blows.

He felt that old Pesche meant well by him, and he wanted to show his gratitude in some way. But he didn't know how to do it.

So now and then he would bring her home a hen hidden under his coat or go to Chane-Surele's and swipe a bottle of brandy for her. But when he brought it home and offered it to her, the old lady would drive him out and yell at him:

"Get out, you young thief! Go to the devil with your stolen property!"

Mottke went. But when he saw that the bottle vanished under the old woman's pillow he laughed happily.

When Blind Pearl heard that Mottke had been taken into the house of Nussen the Thief and that Nussen thought much of him, he began to consider how he could get the little villain into his clutches. He made up his mind to pay off his scores on the boy and waited patiently for a favorable opportunity. And he didn't need to wait for very long: quite unexpectedly the chance came his way.

CHAPTER XII

*

A Jewish Pawnshop

THERE were a great number of cobblers in the town who made boots for the annual fairs. All summer they stored up these boots in preparation for the autumn, when the fairs began and they could sell them at their own stands. But very few cobblers managed to carry on until the time came to leave for the fairs with their boots. The majority found that they couldn't get through the summer without having to get rid of some of their goods, and before the fairs began the boots had wandered into the warehouse of Ephroim Geiger, where you got only a few roubles for them. Still, one needed money to live on, buy raw material with, and celebrate the holy days properly.

Ephroim Geiger was the profiteer of the town. On every rouble he lent he exacted thirty kopeks in interest, while he kept the boots as a pledge. When autumn came the cobblers would go to him and implore him: "Reb Ephroim, give us back our boots, so that we may sell them at the fair." But Ephroim knew that every cobbler was a boozer and that the boots would find their last home in a pub and never reach the fairs. And as these boots were no longer worth the money that had been lent on them, not to speak of the interest that had accumulated since, they simply remained in Ephroim's store-room, where they rotted away and never saw the daylight again. Ephroim never sold them. He had no need of money. With his wife Taubel, nick-named the

viper, he had lived for twenty or thirty years in perpetual
dissension and eaten nothing but dry bread and onions.
Now he found his only pleasure in contemplating his store-
room and seeing it growing fuller and fuller. After the Feast
of the Tabernacles was over, and the rainy season began,
almost all the town went about in torn shoes. The mire of
the streets pierced through the holes and rents in the
leather, while in Ephroim's warehouse the boots rotted that
the cobblers had made so that the populace might have
something to put on their feet when the rain came.

Ephroim was so miserly that he grudged his wife even her
dry bread. Every morning the street was roused by a wild
hubbub coming from the Geigers' house. And every morn
ing Ephroim dragged his wife to the Rabbi to get a divorce

"You come along with me to the Rabbi at once! At once!"
he would scream.

Once it actually happened that the Rabbi, weary of his
continual efforts to reconcile the couple, decided to grant
them a divorce.

"How much will it cost?" asked Ephroim.

"First of all you must have a declaration of divorce drawn
up, pay the clerk's fee and settle other expenses. After that
you'll have to pay for having the divorce officially ratified
at the district court. . . ."

"How much will that come to in all?"

"In all? Well, it will cost you something like twenty-five
roubles."

"Twenty-five roubles?" screamed Ephroim. "Taubel,
come home! Come home at once!"

With that he seized his wife by the arm and dragged her
home. And because of the twenty-five roubles that the divorce would have cost him he lived all his life with a woman
who was famed for her sharp tongue, a wife he was always

quarreling with, that he hated just as much as she hated him, and that he was always cursing, just as she cursed him in return.

Perhaps, indeed, he wouldn't have been such a bad fellow if it had not been for Taubel the viper. For she was certainly poisonous. She had no children, you could tell that by merely looking at her face. . . . Her features were like a man's except for the lack of a beard; but in compensation she had a whole lot of warts on her face equipped with long hairs, and she hated mankind. If she saw a child in the street she couldn't help giving it a cuff. And she drove away every living creature that came near her; she only had one answer for them: "Away you! Get out!"

On the summer evenings she would sit on the steps before her house, gasping for breath. For she suffered from asthma and was always wheezing. The cobblers' children brought the finished boots and shoes to Ephroim. The woman would grunt at them, take the boots, fling them into the store-room, and drive the children away, shouting at them: "Away you! Get out!"

Ephroim Geiger's sole pleasure consisted, as we have said before, in contemplating his store of boots. Sometimes he shut himself up all day in his warehouse and sorted out the boots; some of them had rotted there for years. The musty leather spread a horrible stench, but Ephroim breathed it in as if it were a precious perfume. He always left the room with a blissful smile. The smile shone in his eyes and was lost in his matted beard, whose hairs were stuck together with leather dust. But if he caught sight of his wife sitting before the door and looking about her with lowering eyes, his good spirits vanished at once. He would grunt morosely, curse his wife, fling on his long caftan, and rush to the synagogue.

Nussen the Thief had cast his eye on the store-room with
the rotting boots. He began by sending Mottke to Ephroim's
on some trifling pretext. The boy was to find out whether
the room had a window and where it lay.

When Mottke arrived Taubel was sitting on the steps
before the door breathing in the cool evening air. She received him with her usual: "Away you! Get out!" But
Mottke made no answer and walked straight past her.
Taubel asked him what he wanted, but he pretended not to
hear and slipped into the house. He pushed open the door
of the store-room, which was only ajar, and beheld Ephroim
Geiger surrounded by a whole world of boots. Mottke
started back when he caught sight of the man's eyes and
beard among the boots.

"Who's that?" shouted Ephroim, highly indignant that a
strange eye had seen him in his Holy of Holies.

"The master-cobbler sent me."

"What master-cobbler? What master-cobbler? Taubel,
hi, Taubel, where are you?" shouted Ephroim, leaping out
of his pile of boots, quite covered with dust.

But Mottke was gone.

From that day the window of the store-room was provided with a shutter and nailed up with boards into the
bargain. And the door to Ephroim's Holy of Holies was
furnished with two new locks, so that no strange eye might
in future see past it. And Mottke got a good hiding from
Nussen the Thief for his clumsiness.

Nevertheless he had managed to find out that the only
window in the place issued on to the roof of a neighbor
called Mandrik.

And soon a chance offered itself of getting in Ephroim's
warehouse. Although Geiger was so miserly, he wanted to
leave some memorial of himself behind him. For five years

he had been haggling with a clerk who was willing to write him a Torah roll for the synagogue where he worshiped. His wife Taubel begged him with tears in her eyes to have her name inscribed on the roll too, but Ephroim refused to listen to her. At last she said she was prepared to pay for part of the roll and fetched out fifteen roubles from a stocking, where she had saved it up kopek by kopek from her housekeeping money. And Ephroim at last gave his consent that the cover of the Torah roll, which showed the Tree of Knowledge in fine stitch-work, should bear her name as well as his.

Since Ephroim had married, his Holy of Holies had never for a moment been without supervision. Whether he himself was at home or at the synagogue, his wife always sat at the door like a faithful watch-dog and drove away everybody who came near the place with her usual: "Away you! Get out!"

But on the day when the new Torah roll was to be consecrated he went with his wife and all the other Jews to the synagogue and left the boots to their fate. In the prayer house the Jews rejoiced over the new Torah roll, and Ephroim and his wife danced with their "little one" (that is to say, the new roll) until late in the night.

On the same night Nussen the Thief climbed up on Mandrik's roof and broke open the shutter and the boards with a chisel. After that there only remained the iron bars over the window, and Nussen soon disposed of them. Then he waved to Mottke. The boy twisted like a cat between the bent iron bars, jumped into the room and began to throw up the boots to his master.

When two sacks had been filled Nussen commanded the boy to arrange the boots so that the theft mightn't be found out. Mottke did as he was told and squeezed out through the bars again. Nussen made everything look as it had been before, nailed the boards back again, and shut the shutter, so that nothing might be noticed and he might have a chance of paying another secret visit.

When Ephroim and his wife returned from the ceremony his first thought was of his store-room.

God, he had left it without anybody to look after it! And for the first time in his life! And trembling with anxiety he examined the locks on the door. Praise be to God! The boots were still there, the shutters closed and the iron bars unarmed.

"Thank God!" Ephroim Geiger sighed in relief. "What a fright I had! The room was left there defenseless!"

"God has been good to us because of the Torah roll," Taubel said.

"You're right, wife!"

And that evening husband and wife talked to each other quietly and peaceably for the first time since they had been married. They were still filled with the gladness that their "little one," the new Torah roll, had brought them.

After that, thanks to Mottke and his teacher Nussen, the boots began for a while to reach their proper owners for whom they had been made: that is, the people of the town. Lots of folks now had good strong boots for the rainy season. And as presently footwear became cheap, even the poor could afford to get a pair of boots for the New Year festival.

But this state of things soon stopped. The boots began to return to Ephroim's store-room again. How this happened you will see later. But the real cause of the change was that Blind Pearl, the guardian of law and order, was at his post and following with a vigilant eye the happenings in the little town.

*

Stop Thief! Stop Thief!

ONE fine morning a cry rang through the streets: "Help! Robbers! Help!"

Shutters were flung open. In the windows appeared white nightcaps and beards with feathers still sticking to them. The people looked at one another and asked:

"Where is the fire?"

Then they saw Ephroim Geiger standing at his door in his drawers and night cap. He waved his arms and screamed:

"Help! Thieves! I'm robbed! I'm ruined!"

Doors and gates flew open. Men in underclothes, women in nightdresses, young girls with wraps hastily flung round them, lads armed with sticks and axes, rushed out of the houses shouting:

"Where is he? What's happened? Who is it?"

"He ran past here just now and climbed over that fence!"

"No, he ran into that yard, Gombiner's yard!"

"I saw him myself running across the yard!"

"Come on!"

But they were all shouted down by Ephroim:

"He's murdered me!"

"Well, who was it?"

"There he is over there!" a boy suddenly cried, pointing at a chimney.

And, right enough, there on the roof just opposite the window of the boot store stood Mottke. He was partly hid‑‑

den by the chimney. But they could see his cap and his glittering eyes. He was half-standing and half-lying down. In one hand he was holding a pair of boots and looking about him desperately.

"There he is! There he is! Look!"

"It's Mottke! Mottke the Thief!"

"Blind Leib's brat! I always said that lad would turn out a rogue."

"Make a ring round the house!" they cried.

Through all this noise rang the piercing cries of the much afflicted Ephroim, and at last they brought the whole town running. From all the streets, lanes and by-lanes, men, women, girls and boys came rushing, armed with sticks, rolling-pins, brooms and axes. They all shouted:

"Where's the thief? Where's the thief?"

"We've got him already! We've got him!"

"There he is! Over there!"

All this time Mottke kept running backwards and forwards on the roof like a trapped rat. He was so terrified that he didn't think even of dropping the boots and wondered what was going to happen next.

"On the roof!"

"Who'll follow me on to the roof?"

One or two daring blades came forward and began to climb on to the roof to capture Mottke.

But when he saw the danger coming near he sprang right off the roof, and for a little while nobody could see him. But he soon popped up on another roof.

"Look! Look! There he is again! Over there!"

And the whole town, men, women, boys with sticks and girls with brooms, rushed after him.

Mottke leapt like a cat from roof to roof. Suddenly he slipped round a chimney, jumped over a house roof, flew

across the street, rushed into the carpenter's yard and disappeared behind a pile of planks and boards that was standing there.

The crowd, following him with sticks and brooms over
roofs and through yards, saw where he had come to ground.
And they soon filled the carpenter's yard to overflowing;
among them Ephroim Geiger in his night cap and drawers,
following up the rear and roaring:

"Help! The robber has murdered me!"

"Come, Reb Ephroim, let's pull down these boards and
capture him," cried Nuchem the cobbler, who all his life
long had made boots to see them disappear into Ephroim's
store-room. His sunken cheeks puffed and blew and he could
scarcely breathe for running.

"Stop! Stop! Here comes Blind Pearl!" the crowd
shouted.

"Make way! Here comes Blind Pearl!"

Everybody stood back. In full uniform, with his sword
and his revolver by his side, Blind Pearl stepped into the
yard. His red neck swelled over his tight collar. His eyes,
still sleepy, glittered as if he were drunk, and his hair stood
on end with rage.

"What is this, Jews?" he asked, stroking his long mustache with his great hand. That was always a sign of anger
with him.

"Oh, Panie, he's murdered me! He's fair killed me!"

"Posmotrim! Posmotrim!" Blind Pearl suddenly fell into
Russian, a sure sign with him of towering rage.

He stepped up to the wood pile, tapped on it with his
sword and shouted:

"Hi, you rascal! Come out of there!"

Mottke lay behind the planks and boards, peeped through
a hole and saw the Jews with their sticks and Blind Pearl

with his sword. He was not trembling. He wasn't afraid. Calmly he stared at his persecutors and waited for what was to happen.

"What's the matter?" asked Nussen the Thief, suddenly appearing among the crowd.

The others looked at one another and replied with an uneasy smile, as if they wanted to disavow the affair:

"Nobody knows rightly. Everybody ran, so we ran too."

"But what's up? Who is it? A thief?" Nussen persisted.

"Posmotrim!" shouted Blind Pearl again, with a side glance at Nussen. Then he struck the boards with his sword a second time, and shouted at the top of his voice:

"Ho, you rascal! Come out!"

Nussen merely gave him a glance and stepped over among the others to see how things would jump.

As Mottke made no reply to the second summons, Blind Pearl turned to the crowd and commanded them in Yiddish:

"Here, Jews, shift these boards away, will you?"

The men flung themselves on the boards and planks, eager to carry out the order. The cobblers who had pledged their boots with Ephroim were the most enthusiastic of all. They flung the boards to the side and Mottke fled from one hiding hole to another.

Then a piercing scream rang over the yard:

"I won't allow it! I won't! I won't!"

It was Slatke, once more come to the rescue of her son. She planted herself before the wood pile and would let nobody go near it.

"You get out of this! And right away!" cried Blind Pearl. "I command you to go!" he added, tapping his sword.

But Slatke stood in front of the wood pile and refused to budge. She screamed:

"I won't go! I won't go! You'll murder him!"

"Take this woman away!" cried Blind Pearl. "Otherwise I won't be responsible for the consequences!"

The crowd made for Slatke. But she drove them back with her hands and feet, scratched their faces raw and went on screaming:

"I won't let you get at the boy! You'll murder him!"

And Nussen whispered to the more ardent helpers of Blind Pearl, quietly but distinctly:

"I'll split your head for you!"

The men looked at Nussen and stopped. They didn't know whom to obey: him or the police.

When Blind Pearl saw that the Jews were giving way before Slatke he threw another glance at Nussen the Thief, then stepped up to the sobbing woman himself, struck her with the sheath of his sword and shouted:

"Get out of here, you whore! All you can do is spawn thieves for us!"

That was too much for Nussen. He walked over to Blind Pearl, seized him by the collar, held his fist under his nose and yelled:

"You would beat a woman, would you? I'll bash your jaw in!"

Blind Pearl started back, snatched his revolver and shouted:

"Get out! Or else I'll shoot you like a dog! Don't dare to interfere with an officer in the course of his duty!"

Things were becoming distinctly nasty and Nussen thought it best to give way. When Blind Pearl saw that he had the upper hand he turned to the crowd, pointed at Nussen and said:

"Seize him! He has resisted the law."

Nussen grew pale and with a nasty smile seized the

knuckle-duster that he used whenever there was a shindy. No one dared to go near him.

Blind Pearl saw now that he could not expect any support, so decided to capture Mottke himself. Pushing Slatke aside, he called on the crowd to remove the boards.

But nobody helped him. Perhaps they were afraid of Nussen, perhaps the fact that Janowitsch had struck a woman turned their sympathies in Mottke's direction: however that may be, Blind Pearl had to clear away the planks himself. This made him so hot that the sweat ran in streams down his fat neck and he got redder in the face than ever. He kept on cursing the Jews and their Rabbis. But the people stood about the yard looking on with a smile at Blind Pearl doing some hard work.

At last with a final effort Blind Pearl got the planks cleared away.

Suddenly Mottke jumped out of his hiding hole and with one spring was among the crowd. Nobody tried to stop him. Some of the men actually did their best to hide him behind their long caftans. Having drawn a blank, Blind Pearl dived into the crowd after Mottke. But Mottke was too quick for him. He flew into another courtyard, jumped over a fence, and made for the open, hoping to reach the river. Blind Pearl and Ephroim Geiger were the only two to follow him. All the others, all the men and women, lads and girls with their sticks and brooms, stayed where they were and watched Blind Pearl with his sword in his hand and Ephroim Geiger in his drawers and nightcap pelting after the boy. Mottke flew like an arrow over fences and roofs. Blind Pearl panted and gasped behind. And everybody laughed.

At last the guardian of law and order grew tired of the chase. He stopped, rammed his sword back into the sheath, spat, and said, turning to the spectators:

"Well, what does it matter to me if you want to harbor a thief among you? I have other things to bother about!"

His glance fell on Ephroim standing beside him in his drawers and still bawling at the top of his voice: "Help! He's murdered me!" Then all his rage turned on him. He mimicked him furiously:

"Help! He's murdered me! You're to blame for everything yourself! Who asked you to keep all these boots in your house? Give their goods back to the shoemakers, then nobody will steal from you!"

But then there were signs of excitement at the end of the little street. A crowd of boys flew by shouting: "We have him! We have him!" They were followed by the Christian butcher and his apprentices. They had Mottke by the arms and were dragging him along with them. They had caught him in their yard as he jumped into it. The boy followed them with lowering looks. But he was quite calm, except for a glitter in his eyes.

Blind Pearl drew himself up, pulled out his revolver and released the catch. At the sight of this weapon the crowd started back in fear and gave way. The butcher handed Mottke over to Justice, and Justice in the person of Blind Pearl received him with grave official formality, covered the boy with the revolver and marched him to the police station.

CHAPTER XIV

*

In the Lock-up

THE police station was in the market square, and occupied part of one of the finest and most commodious houses in the town. The windows looked straight out into the square, so that from the police-station you could see everything that was happening there, with the result, however, that from the square you could see all that was going on in the police-station as well.

Whenever anybody broke the law he was locked up in the police station. For instance, if a Jewish shopkeeper sold some article too near twelve o'clock on Sunday, when the church bells were ringing, the police in the person of Blind Pearl appeared and took down his name. The court thereupon sentenced him to a fine of twenty-five roubles with the option of five days' imprisonment. Usually the offender chose to save his twenty-five roubles and sit his five days. And his acquaintances heartily wished that he might earn as much money every week.

But that sort of thing happened only in Blind Pearl's first phase, just after he came to the town. At that time he had not yet tumbled to the situation, and every offense he came across vexed him so much that he immediately took it down in his book and gave the offender in charge. But presently he began to take things more easily, shut his eye now and then, and finally came to an agreement with the Jews, as a result of which he became the richer by a rouble and a half

a week, supplemented with a pound of tea and three pounds
of sugar.

It was the Temple attendant who collected this weekly
tribute. The householders contributed ten kopeks each and
the housewives had to make up the dole of sugar among
them. Since this arrangement had been made, decent householders had come in conflict with the law only on exceptional
occasions, as for instance when the District Inspector from
the nearest big town came to examine the back yards and
see that all the hygienic regulations were being complied
with. After that inspection almost every householder got
five days, but that could be avoided by paying five roubles
per day instead. For the synagogue attendant, old Moische-
Schloime, with whom another agreement had been made,
always took his place in the lock-up instead of the real
offenders and served their sentences for them. He even reduced his terms, for instead of five roubles he only demanded
one rouble thirty kopeks per day, and so the law-breakers
came out of it very well.

And in the police-station Moische-Schloime by no means
wasted his time: during his captivity he prepared himself
for the next world by reciting the Psalms. And Blind Pearl
saw to it that he had a regular income and was constantly
employed, for which Moische-Schloime was very grateful to
him. He sat all week in the lock-up, but on Fridays Blind
Pearl let him out, for he knew that every Jew liked to be
with his wife and children on the Sabbath. So he gave his
prisoner leave of absence on Friday evening in time to light
the Sabbath candles. And on Saturday evening, when all
Jews return to their daily occupations, Moische-Schloime
punctually reported himself for "duty" at the lock-up.

Once it actually happened that Blind Pearl forgot Moische-
Schloime and let a few weeks pass without taking down the

name of any of the better off householders. Then Moische-Schloime went to him in person and asked:

"What about me? Amn't I a man like anybody else? Don't I have to live, too?"

Blind Pearl told himself that the man was quite right, and needed money for his wife and children. After that he saw to it that some householder or other got his five days' sentence, not because he had committed any offense against the law, but simply to provide employment for Moische-Schloime and keep the lock-up occupied. Sometimes a householder, accused without any reason, would make a fuss and cry out at Blind Pearl:

"What are things coming to? What about justice? Don't you get your rouble and a half every week? What do you take down my name for?"

In such cases Blind Pearl would reply in Yiddish:

"There's another man in this town who has to live just as much as you. Hasn't Moische-Schloime a right to live?"

Moische-Schloime was in the lock-up, sitting at the window with his huge glasses on his nose and a prayer-book in his hand, reading. Suddenly Blind Pearl, armed to the teeth, entered with a new prisoner, the twelve-year-old Mottke. When Moische-Schloime caught sight of this hardened criminal come to bear him company, he cowered back, coughed, sighed deeply, shook his head and murmured the Psalm:

"Well for him who walketh not in the way of the godless, nor treadeth in the path of the sinful."

Blind Pearl pulled out his revolver. This weapon, which had never been loaded and had long since grown rusty, put Moische-Schloime into such terror that he shut his eyes and roared: "Hear Israel!" as if he had gone mad. But the

revolver was not directed at him. Blind Pearl held it close
to Mottke's face and shouted:

"Say that Nussen the Thief put you up to it, say that
you stole the boots at his orders, say that he took them over
from you! Come, say it! Do you hear? At once!"

But Mottke was not alarmed by the revolver. His eyes
gleamed, but then he looked Blind Pearl calmly in the face.

"I'll shoot you down like a dog!" shouted Blind Pearl.
"Say at once that Nussen put you up to it, or I'll shoot
you dead!"

"Oy!" cried Moische-Schloime from his corner.

Blind Pearl gave him a look. Moische-Schloime stuck his
nose in his book and began to recite lugubriously:

"For the Lord knows the way of the righteous, but the
way of the godless is dark."

When Blind Pearl saw that Mottke couldn't be brow-
beaten he gave him a buffet on the ear.

But Mottke remembered that he could still scream, and
he began to bawl till everybody was soon in front of the
lock-up.

Blind Pearl fell into a towering rage. He flung poor
Mottke on the floor and began to kick him and beat him
with the sheath of his sword, not caring where the blows
landed.

But Mottke refused to be silent. His yells summoned all
the people in the town together like a fire-bell. The crowd
in front of the police-station grew bigger and bigger, and
there were shouts of:

"They're half-killing Mottke in the lock-up! They're
half-killing the boy!"

From afar Slatke had heard her son's cries for help coming through the barred window of the lock-up. She hastily
flung a wrap over her head and rushed to the police-station.

There she wrung her hands, wept and cried till the tears ran in rivers down her face, and howled like a beast robbed of her young:

"Help! He's killing my boy! Help me, Jews! Help me!"

She tried to climb up the wall to the barred window, beat her head against the locked door, and kept on screaming:

"Jews, have pity! He's murdering my boy!"

Her hair was flying, her eyes were wide open with terror, and with her lean cracked hands she kept shaking the door of the police-station and beating against it with her head, crying:

"Jews, help me!"

When Mottke heard his mother's voice he began to bawl more loudly than ever. The cries of mother and son mingled and made the clear sunny day horrible. At last the crowd could stand it no longer. The first to follow Slatke were the Jewesses and the peasant women. They rushed at the locked door, beat on it with their fists and shook the handle. Lads with sticks and spanners followed them and at last they managed to break open the door. The crowd rushed into the lock-up.

Mottke was lying on the floor covered with blood and Blind Pearl was still standing over him, red with fury and beating him with the sheath.

Red Slatke flung herself over her son and shielded him. The women and lads seized Blind Pearl and dragged him away.

"What justice is there in this? Don't you get your rouble and a half every week? Your bloody rouble and a half?" they screamed.

When Blind Pearl saw the excited faces and outstretched fists of the Jewesses and the peasant women, when he saw how wrought up the men were, he felt scared and cried:

"But he's a thief! A thief!"

"Who's a thief? There are no thieves among us!"

"Thief yourself!" cried the women. "Ho, look at the saint!"

"So you want the thief back? All right! I don't care! It doesn't matter to me!" shouted Blind Pearl at last, flinging Mottke out of the room and slamming the door behind him.

"Take him, take him, if you're so fond of him!" he said to finish the matter, and then turned and looked severely at his remaining prisoner. But Moische-Schloime had retreated trembling into his corner.

Slatke wrapped Mottke in her shawl and took him home. He could hardly walk, so she had to support him. The tears flowed down her cheeks on to his head and face. She cried:

"My bad boy, what will be the end of you?"

CHAPTER XV

*

Mottke Sticks Up for His Mother

SLATKE brought Mottke home and laid him on her bed. His face was covered with weals, his body showed blue stripes, his clothes were in tatters with his beating and filthy with the dirt on the floor of the lock-up. His mother took off his clothes, washed his bloody face with a wet rag, then covered him up under the bedclothes, all the time admonishing him:

"Mottke, my unhappy boy! What a state you're in! What will be the end of you? Mottke, my unhappy, bad boy!"

Mottke scowled and let his mother run on. He muttered something or other to himself. But after she had taken off all his clothes, laid him in her bed and covered him up, he felt more comfortable than he had ever felt before in his life. And then he had the strangest feeling, he felt ashamed of himself and wanted to jump up and rush out just as he was.... He felt ashamed for his mother, too, and then something came up into his throat and seemed to be choking him. He rolled himself in the clothes, curled himself up in one corner of the bed and covered his head with a shawl that he found lying beside it. He lay like that for a little while, and then all at once he felt something streaming from his eyes and something bursting from his throat.

Slatke heard Mottke's stifled sobbing and was terrified; it was the first time that she had heard her son crying like that. He did not cry out, he made no noise, but sobbed quietly to himself, and that stabbed her to the heart. She went over to the bed, tried to pull the shawl from his face and asked:

"What is it, Mottke? What are you crying for, child? O God! O God! What have they done to you?"

That made him feel still worse. He would not let her pull away the shawl, pushed her away with his feet, and struck out at the wall, the bedclothes, his mother, not knowing what he was doing. Then he leapt out of the bed and made for the door, naked as he was. Slatke managed to hold him back. She kept crying:

"What is it, Mottke?"

"It's nothing, nothing, nothing!" shouted Mottke, and he snatched up his coat and trousers and began to put them on. "I'm going ! Let me go!"

"Where can you go? Out there to steal again? To get another beating? To lie out in the streets again?" retorted Slatke, planting herself in the doorway.

"I'm going! Let me go!"

"Mottke, for God's sake think! Where can you go now? You're knocked to pieces, you're all black and blue!"

"That's nothing to you. I'm going, and that's that!"

"Why do you want to run away from me, my boy? Why?" Slatke began to cry.

"I must go, mother. . . . Let me go. . . ."

"Wait till I've mended your trousers anyway. You can't go out in the street like that! The people will laugh at you. And at me too."

Slatke fetched a pair of Blind Leib's trousers out of a chest and began to make them over for Mottke. When he saw her sitting down to work at the trousers his throat contracted and he began to cry again, but more softly this

time. He sat down in a corner of the cellar, naked, and
cried quietly to himself.

His mother said nothing more. She bowed over the
trousers and began to sew.

Mottke went on crying until he felt better. His mother
thought he had gone to sleep, got up and threw an old coat
over him.

But Mottke was not sleeping. He lay under the coat and
stared at his mother sewing away at the trousers. He examined her attentively. Her cheeks were gray and fallen,
and her great long nose stood out white from her ravaged
face. Her eyes were half-shut now like those of an old hen.
She reminded him more than anything else of the hen
that he had once seen between the knees of one of the men
in the slaughter-house. The poor fowl had turned up its
eyes and it seemed to him that it was begging him to save
it. He still remembered how near he had been to flinging
himself on the man to set the hen free. But Nussen the
Thief had held a fist under his nose and threatened to bash
him, so he had started back and given up his intention. It
seemed to him that his mother was in just as dreadful a
state now as the hen was then, and he thought that it was
for him, for him that she was turning up her eyes. He
wanted to get up, go across to her and kiss her hands, her
eyes and her old gray face; but he felt ashamed.

In the evening Blind Leib came home. He had already
heard all that his son had been up to. His chums, the market laborers, had shouted after him: "Run and save your
Mottke! Blind Pearl is half-killing him!" But he had sent
a silent curse after them and come home, so as to give vent
to his full heart and take it out of his wife for having borne
him a son that all the town was talking about. When he
entered the cellar Slatke was still sewing away at the

trousers. The sight displeased him. He stared at her suspiciously with his single eye and asked:

"Who are you mending the trousers for?"

"For nobody."

This answer did not satisfy him and he began to look
round him. He saw something in a corner covered up with
a coat and asked:

"Who's that lying in the corner?"

Slatke jumped up and said violently:

"Nobody!"

Blind Leib wanted to see for himself, but Slatke rushed
across, planted herself in his way, and cried:

"I only let him in for a few minutes so that he could
warm himself. What are you going to do to him?"

Blind Leib got angry. His face grew dark red and his
blind eye popped out, as if it wanted to see too.

"You've let that gallows-bird into the house? He must
get out of this in a hurry!" he shouted. "Or else I'll kill
him!"

"You won't touch him. If you do, I'll kill myself!" retorted Slatke, planting herself before Mottke.

She flung herself upon her son, clasped him in her arms,
kissed him and pressed him to her breast.

"My poor, poor unhappy boy!"

Blind Leib stood irresolutely where he was.

But Mottke had heard everything; he freed himself from
his mother's arms, snatched up the trousers and cried:

"Let me go! I won't stay here another minute!"

He slipped hastily into the trousers, flung on his jacket,
took his hat and made to rush away. But before going he
stepped up to his father and held his clenched fist under
his nose:

"I'll give you the best hiding you ever had if you ever lay a finger on my mother."

"What's that you say? You damned upstart!" yelled Blind Leib, snatching up a stick.

But Mottke did not retreat. He stood his ground, picked up an iron saucepan that was standing within reach and said quietly:

"I'll split your head for you if you ever touch my mother!"

Blind Leib turned white and flung a furious glance at Slatke, who stood looking on, terrified to death.

"O God, O God! That I should see this day! Mottke, would you lift your hand against your father?" Slatke burst into tears.

"I know no father! But I'll strike him dead if he touches a hair of your head!" retorted Mottke, shaking his fist in Blind Leib's direction and leaving the cellar with a defiant look.

Father and mother gazed at each other in silence.

CHAPTER XVI

*

First Spring-time

MOTTKE had no desire for human company now. The summer had come, the fields were dry and it was lovely to lie out in the soft grass. In the little gardens of the houses in the town onions, radishes, tomatoes and carrots were growing, and the new potatoes were almost ready. What more did he want? He spent his days in the meadows beside the river, and in the evening he slipped into the shed of the market gardener Selig. Selig was a red-bearded Jew who, after his term of military service, had settled down outside the town and started a market garden. The decent burghers of the town jeered at him:

"The idea of a Jew taking up such a silly job!"

But Mottke lived all summer on Selig's vegetable garden. Red Selig dealt with the soldiers from the garrison, which was only a little distance from his garden. In the evenings the sergeant and the trumpeter of the solitary company quartered in the town would come over to drink tea with him. And while Red Selig was enjoying himself with his friends Mottke would slip into his wooden hut, creep into a corner, cover himself up with a few bast mats and sleep for an hour or two. But long before daybreak, as soon as the sky began to grow bright, he was off again, taking as many onions, tomatoes, carrots and potatoes as he needed, and set out with them for the river, where his hiding-place was. There he gathered some dry twigs and withered leaves

and made a fire in a cave. The wind carried the smoke far
over the river, the potatoes cooked on the ashes, and Mottke
warmed himself at the fire and whistled to himself.

These were the happiest days of his boyhood.

In the meadows Matschuk, the old herdsman, tended the
cattle of the town. He was lame and left the herd to the
protection of his dog Kudlak, on whom he could always de-
pend. But Kudlak had been a friend of Mottke's ever since
the time when they were both young and Mottke was king
of the dogs. And through Kudlak Mottke became king of
the herds. Whenever he was thirsty he lured a cow aside,
crept under her and began to suck at her udders just as if
he was a calf. As soon as he had enough he would creep
out again, wipe the traces of the milk from his lips, and
give the cow a friendly clap on the back in thanks for her
kindness to him.

And the cows seemed to be pleased to let him have their
milk, for as long as he lay beneath them they never stirred:
usually they stood quite stolidly, gazing into the distance
and giving a grunt of contentment now and then as if they
thought it a great honor for Mottke to drink their milk.

Sometimes old Matschuk caught sight of him milking the
cows in this illegal way. Then he would start to run as fast
as his lame leg would let him to rescue the cow. But long
before he could get near Mottke was far away.

But Matschuk did not always run after Mottke when he
saw him milking the cows. Very often he actually invited
him to milk one of them. But he only showed this friendly
disposition when he was sitting at Mottke's fire eating baked
potatoes. Then he felt obliged to respond to the potatoes
and carrots by an offer in kind.

From Matschuk Mottke heard for the first time that the
world was a very big place, that there were many other

towns in it beside his own, and that the greatest city in the world was Warsaw, where the people lived in great houses and ate white bread and meat every day. And from Matschuk he learned, too, that there were women in the world so wonderful that, if once you fell under their spell, you could never get away from them again. "A man has to be on his guard against women of that kind," said old Matschuk, and then went on to tell of countless other things. And Mottke listened greedily, lying in the warm sun. He spent whole days by his camp-fire beside the river, baking potatoes and eating them.

About this time a thing happened to him which he could not understand. Once as he lay by the river watching it running past he saw a young peasant woman wading across it barefoot. She lifted her skirt so that he could see her naked white thighs reflected in the water. Usually when he saw such sights he paid no attention and didn't bother his head about them; at most he would fling a stone into the water out of mischief so as to splash the woman. But this time he had a queer feeling. His heart beat against his ribs as it had done that time when he had lain behind the wood pile and the Jews were flinging aside the planks to get at him.

He crouched down on the river bank, so that the peasant girl mightn't see him, and stared intently at the water rising against her naked thighs. Then he gathered a few small stones and flung them into the water, not out of mischief this time, but to make the girl lift her skirt higher. At first he felt like jumping into the river beside her. But then he saw that he could watch her better from the bank. His eyes were fixed on the girl's white, gleaming legs, and his heart beat fast.

Then he crept to the edge of the water and lay down in

the white sand; it was almost too hot, the sun had beat so strongly on it. He felt the warmth under him and over him, soothing him. Then he flung off his clothes and lay down again, quite naked, in the sand. The rays of the sun fell straight on his body and seemed to make every drop of blood in his veins tingle. The sun covered him like a warm blanket. And then it seemed that the sun was lying beside him and upon him like a living warm body, and warming him like his friend Burek in the kennel, or like his mother much much earlier, when he lay beside her through the cold winter nights among the cloths and rags. Except that now his heart was beating so strangely, and the warmth that he felt was strange too.

Then he pressed himself close against the ground and clasped the soft warm sand as if it were Burek.

The sun slid over his body and caressed him, and he felt that he had made a new discovery and that from now on everything would go well with him. And then he felt as if he had lost something, and all at once he had a feeling of misery and forsakenness such as he had never known in his life before. He began to pity himself and kiss and stroke his own hands and body, and such a longing for kindness came over him that he was almost on the point of weeping.

He had nobody in the whole world. Under him was the warm sand, over him the hot sun, and a deep love for them awoke in him, and he kissed and stroked the ground where he lay.

*

Mottke Takes Revenge

IN summer the women and girls of the town came to bathe
in the river on warm afternoons. Mottke would lie hidden
near by and wait for them. And as the women were undressing he would creep up and suddenly step right in among
them. The naked women would shriek: "A man! A man!"
Some of them would jump into the water in their chemises
and duck until only their heads showed. Others would throw
themselves on the grass and try to shield their nakedness
from him with their hands. And they all shrieked as if some
one were trying to murder them. And Mottke stood there
and laughed and laughed.

But these pranks didn't always end so harmlessly. For
sometimes fat Pesche, the wife of Feivel the butcher, came
to bathe, and she was neither ashamed of anything nor afraid
of Mottke. One day she sprang naked out of the water,
seized him by the leg and dragged him just as he was into
the water. Thereupon all the women, old and young, fell
upon him and tried to duck him under the water. He gasped
and panted and struggled for breath, but the water poured
into his mouth and nose. He got away from them more
dead than alive and after that took care not to surprise the
women when fat Pesche was there.

One fine afternoon about two o'clock, when the sun was
at its hottest, he was lying half naked on the bank of the
river gazing at the water. A soft breeze ruffled the stream

and now and then he could hear a curious trilling sound. It sounded like subdued laughter.

He peered about and saw not very far away two young girls undressing. They did not appear to have noticed him, for they were quite unconcerned and one of them had just taken off her chemise. The wind blew it out in her hands and played with her hair; her slim young body gleamed in the sun. Mottke's heart began to beat fast; he turned pale and his limbs trembled. Very softly he stole towards the girls, creeping on his belly through the grass. Then he remained lying, holding his breath so that they might not hear him, and looked at the girls. The one that was already undressed was Chanele, the grand-daughter of the old Shochliner. His mother had nursed her and she was of his own age. The second girl—she was sitting on the grass pulling off her stockings—was Chanele's bosom friend. Chanele ran laughing to the edge of the water, stuck her foot into it, then withdrew it and squealed:

"Ow! It's cold!"

"You must jump in. With one jump!" cried her friend, hastily taking off her clothes. "Just wait till you see me!"

"Oh, yes, we'll see!" retorted Chanele. "It's terribly cold!"

She stretched out her foot again, hardly touching the water with her toes. The cold gave her gooseflesh, and her back shivered so violently that it seemed on the point of breaking.

Mottke followed every movement of the girl, and his heart beat faster and faster. He felt in some way close to Chanele. Whether it was because he had seen her so often with his mother or because they had drunk the same milk is hard to say: at any rate, he gloated on the warm light that radiated from her body and felt that that body was so incontestably his that he could touch it and caress and kiss it without any one denying him.

But he stayed quietly where he was.

"Now watch me! Look!" said the other girl, jumping into the water.

Then Chanele's body gleamed in the sun, the water splashed up and he heard her shrill laughter.

He could hardly keep from crying out.

The two pairs of arms and legs splashed about, and the girls' voices rang over the water like silver bells.

Mottke quietly undressed and jumped in too.

The girls shrieked.

But when Chanele saw that the "man" was Mottke she was a little reassured.

"Mottke!" both girls cried together, taking each other by the hand and crouching down until only their heads appeared above the water, their plaits waving in the wind.

Soon they recovered from their first shock and looked at each other. Their hearts were still beating violently, but their eyes were sparkling and they could hardly keep from bursting into laughter. At the same time they felt ashamed and a little frightened. So they covered their faces with their hands and tittered.

"Let me stay with you! Then we can jump into the water together," said Mottke, laughing and showing his white teeth. He stood up quite naked; the water reached only to his knees. His dark vigorous body looked as if it had been cast in bronze.

"That would never do. You're a boy!" replied Chanele's friend. Chanele herself still kept her hands over her face and giggled.

"Well, what about it if I am?" replied Mottke, biting his tongue and putting on an innocent expression.

They stayed like that for a while: the girls hidden under the water and Mottke stark naked.

Everything was still. The sun poured down on the meadow and the river. Flies buzzed. In the distance a cow lowed, calling to her calf. Nobody was in sight. The meadow, the river and the whole world lay outstretched in the sun, which poured down its heat upon them.

Suddenly Mottke disappeared under the water and came up again close beside the girls.

They began to tremble; they felt like screaming and pressed closer to each other, locked their arms together and gazed into each other's eyes, as if they were trying to read there what was going to happen.

Mottke stood quite still for a while and looked at the girls awkwardly. Then he came closer to Chanele.

The girl started back and sprang away.

Mottke stopped and examined Chanele's friend for a moment; she stood her ground. But then he suddenly sprang on Chanele and flung his arms round her.

"Mother! Mother!" shrieked Chanele.

Mottke let her go, terrified. Chanele rushed hastily out of the water.

"Chanele, don't scream for God's sake! You'll bring all the town here and they'll give us a beating," cried Chanele's friend.

Chanele pulled herself together. And as she was afraid, like her friend, of the scandal if people came, she felt alarmed now at her own screaming.

But when she saw Mottke standing on the bank she remembered that she was naked, so she hastily flung herself down on the sand and covered her face with her hands.

Mottke soon got over the fright that Chanele's screams

had thrown him into. He ran over to the girl and sat down beside her.

Chanele was trembling from head to foot. Her heart beat with furious speed; she still held her face in her hands.

Mottke moved still nearer and began to stroke her smooth wet back.

When Chanele's friend—she was still in the water—saw Mottke sitting beside Chanele and stroking her back she began to giggle.

Chanele heard her friend laughing and couldn't restrain herself any longer. Her fear vanished and she burst into a peal of laughter.

Then Mottke flung himself upon her and when she tried to move she found that his body quite covered hers.

She tried to cry for help, but Mottke closed her mouth with his and pressed his face, his hands and his body firmly against hers.

Soon she didn't want to cry for help any longer. The only feeling that she had left was fear, and she snuggled completely under Mottke, as if she were seeking protection.

Her friend stamped with mirth in the water and laughed and laughed.

But in a few minutes Mottke got up and rushed away, still naked, his clothes in his hands. He ran off across the meadow and away from the river.

Under a hill he hastily slipped on his trousers and his shirt. Then he stole into a wood and set out by by-ways on his search for the great city that Matschuk had told him of, where all the people lived in big houses and ate white bread every day.

He was fourteen when he started on the road that led him out into the wide world.

BOOK II

CHAPTER XVIII

*

"Hell"

FOR a long time Mottke followed the road that was to take him to the "great city." The sun burnt his face, hunger and thirst racked him, but he went on and on. He avoided the people that he saw on the way and stole like a thief past the villages so that nobody might see him. On and on he went, but the great city was still nowhere to be seen. At last he grew so tired that he sat down on a heap of stones beside the road. He was hungry and his mouth watered at the thought of food. He swallowed down his spittle, but his throat was quite dry. Then he caught sight of a little brook, crawled over to it, ladled the water into his hat and drank. He tried to eat some ears of corn to satisfy his hunger. But they weren't ripe and he couldn't eat them.

When it began to get dark he became afraid. He looked around him. Everything was strange. In the distance he could see a wood that seemed to stare at him out of the darkness. This wood wasn't in the least like the one that he knew outside his town: it looked strange and hostile. The fields were strange, too, and the lights in the houses glowered at him like the eyes of an enemy. He sat down on a milestone and decided: "I'll stay here, whatever happens!" When it grew quite dark he began to shiver with cold. The naked flesh showing through his rags and tatters seemed to freeze.

114

He began to stroke and kiss it. Then he burst out crying.

In the distance he heard voices. The gravel of the road crunched. As he heard the footsteps coming nearer, he began to cry louder than ever. Then a peasant man and a peasant woman loomed out of the darkness. At hearing Mottke's cries they stopped.

"Where have you come from?"

"The town."

"Why are you crying?"

"They beat me. . . ."

"Why did they beat you?"

Mottke thought for a little while.

"Because my father and mother are dead. . . ."

"Where are you making for?"

"I don't know. . . ."

The peasant whispered something into the woman's ear, then turned to Mottke again and said:

"If you like, you can come with us."

Mottke rose and followed the peasant. In a little while a hand reached him a slice of bread and a chunk of cheese. He seized them and bolted them at once, but didn't stop crying.

The darkness grew still deeper and they all strode on without speaking. Then Mottke caught sight of the chimney of a big house; flames and smoke were bursting from it. He thought the house was on fire and became excited. But then he saw that neither the peasant nor his wife seemed to pay attention to this strange sight, so he composed himself and quietly went on. They came to a village and passed a long row of little wooden houses. Peasants sat before the doors smoking. A few were asleep on the doorsteps of their houses, others were lying with their heads on their wives' laps. From a hut came the sound of a mouth harmonica. The

wind blew about the smoke from the big chimney, so that
the sleepy peasants seemed to be in the middle of a cloud.

"Evening, Anton, what's new in the town?"

"Nothing new at all, Stepan," replied the peasant that
had taken Mottke in tow.

"Who's the lad?"

"I found him crying on the road. He says his father and
mother are dead and he has no home."

"What are you going to do with him?" asked Stepan,
getting up from his doorway and walking over to have a
better look at Mottke.

"I'll put him in the glass shed. He can sleep there all
night and keep warm. We'll see tomorrow what can be
done about him."

"Perhaps you'll manage to make a blower out of him.
The boy looks strong enough. He may turn into a good
worker," said Stepan, clapping Mottke on the shoulder.
"Seeing your own lad is dead...."

"I would like to teach him, but I'm afraid the foreman
won't allow it, for I hardly fancy that the boy has a pass.
Have you a pass?" he asked, turning to Mottke.

"But this boy is one of the foreman's own people, you
can see for yourself that he's a Jew boy. Your foreman
won't turn away a Jew," retorted Stepan, returning to his
house again.

"Good night."

"Good night."

Mottke followed his rescuer.

The nearer he got to the house with the flames and the
smoke the more scared he became. Everything round the
house was dark. He could not see the night nor the stars in
the sky; he walked through thick clouds of smoke. But
now and then he could see by the flicker of the flames single

figures working at something or other with their arms bare.

Then the fire died down again and everything was wrapped in smoke. Mottke followed the other two, jumping over puddles, piles of coke and asphalt and huge heaps of refuse and splintered glass. With his bare feet he walked over whole little ranges of glass splinters, smashed bottles with sharp edges, and all manner of broken glass, but they didn't cut him, for his soles were so hardened by use that they were as tough as leather. At last, following Anton, he entered a great shed. Here it was bright as day, for great tongues of flame kept shooting up from a furnace.

It was warm here too, and after the cold night air the warmth did Mottke good. He looked around him. There weren't many people in the shed. He saw a few peasants stripped to the waist standing before a great cauldron of fire and stirring something in it with long pointed tongs. Now and then one of them opened the sliding door of the furnace and then the flames burst out as if they wanted to lick up the whole shed and everybody in it. But the door was shut again at once and the flames driven back.

Mottke stood in a corner and gaped at all that was going on; he was quite terrified. But Anton went over to the men working at the furnace and began talking to them. After a little while a few of the workmen walked over to Mottke. Their naked bodies gave out a heat like an oven. They stared at Mottke and then asked Anton:

"Where did you find him?"

"He was sitting by the side of the road crying."

"A thief, I suppose?" said one of the peasants.

"Are your father and mother alive?"

"Dead," replied Mottke briefly.

"Why did you run away from your town?"

"They beat me."

"Who?"

"Everybody."

"Have you a pass?"

"No."

"Let him sleep here for the night," said Anton.

"A fine idea! If the gendarme comes and finds him here we'll all be hauled to court."

"But you can't drive him out again in this cold!"

"He can return where he came from!"

"I'll hide him. You come here, boy!" cried one of the men, and he led Mottke to a corner of the shed.

"Lie down there and see you don't move from the spot!"

"Here's a sack, throw that over him. And scatter some glass dust over him so that the gendarme won't notice him."

"I'll give him something to eat. Here's a bite for you," said the peasant who had wanted to fling Mottke out, and he took a slice of bread and a piece of sausage and handed them to Mottke under the sack.

At once Mottke fell into a dead sleep.

"To think of a child of God wandering about the world like that, just like a stray dog!" said the bad peasant, spitting and returning to the furnace to bank up the fire.

"We're all in the same box. If they sack you from this place tomorrow you'll have to wander about the world like a stray dog too."

"And you wanted to fling him out just now because he was one of 'their people'!"

"Oh, to hell! Our people, their people! There's only one devil!" retorted the bad peasant, spitting into the fire.

Next morning Mottke was awakened by a long piercing wail; it was like the howling of wild beasts. He sat up, looked around him and couldn't make out at first where he was. People were bustling round him and it was so hot in

the shed that it seemed as if the thin walls would burst.
Anton was standing beside him. The boy had a good look
at him now for the first time. He was an enormous peasant
with great powerful arms.

Anton winked at him and said softly:

"Lie where you are till the foreman has gone."

Mottke threw him a glance and stuck his head under the
sack again.

"Here, eat this!" Anton pushed a slice of bread and cheese
under the sack.

The shed was growing fuller and fuller. Mottke peeped
from under the sack and saw that he was in a great long
building of wood. In the middle stood an enormous furnace;
it was red hot and sent out such a heat that you might have
thought it would melt everything round about it. Then he
saw that a number of children had come into the shed;
there were both boys and girls. They all stripped to the
waist and then stood round the furnace. The door of the
furnace was thrown open and fire poured through it and
down from it like water.

Anton gave a sign and Mottke followed him. As he approached the fire he thought that the heat would burn him
up; but when he saw children younger than himself standing
beside it he made up his mind to show that he had just as
much pluck as they, and went and stood beside Anton.

Two boys were standing there already, and a little girl.
All three stared at him with great curiosity. Anton flung
the door of the furnace open and such a heat beat upon
Mottke that he thought he was going to fall to the floor.
But he felt ashamed in front of the children and held his
ground.

Anton took an iron tube and drew a lump of fire out
of the furnace with it. Then raised it up, blew into the tube,

turned it round and round for a little while, until the lump
of fire began to take on a definite shape, then handed it to
Mottke and ordered him to blow through the tube:

"Hard!"

Mottke blew for all he was worth.

"Harder!"

Mottke blew still harder.

"That's right! And now give it to him," said Anton, pointing at one of the boys.

Mottke did as he was told. The second boy blew into the
tube and then handed it to a little pale girl, who went on
blowing until the lump of fire looked like a great balloon.
Then Anton took it from the girl and stuck the fiery globe
into a mold. A minute later Mottke saw with astonishment
a great bottle there instead of the lump of fire.

"Ooh! Look!" he cried.

"Try and see if you can hold it," said Anton.

Mottke put out his hand but drew it back again with a
howl.

"Ha, ha, ha!" the children laughed. "Look at the great
big boy blubbering!"

"It isn't hot at all!" said the girl—she was only nine—
taking the bottle in both her hands and walking about
with it.

"You see! That's how you must accustom your hands to
the heat. If you want to be a glass-blower you must learn
how to take hold of the fire with your bare hands."

"And I will, too!" cried Mottke, ashamed that the little
girl had beaten him. He jumped up and seized hold of the
bottle again, firmly this time.

His skin couldn't bear the heat and came out in blisters.
The places that had been burned the first time felt as if
long needles were being stuck into them. His eyes filled

with tears, but he held on to the bottle. But when he tried to set it down it stuck fast to his hand and strips of skin were left on the glass.

Mottke didn't cry. He only became as white as a sheet and the tears rushed out of his eyes.

"You're a brave lad. You'll be a fine glass-blower yet. You've had your first baptism. Any one who wants to be a blower must learn to put his hand in the fire," said Anton, clapping Mottke on the shoulder.

Then the man pulled another lump of fire out of the furnace, and yet another, blew into them and gave them to Mottke. His burnt hands could scarcely hold the tube. Whenever his raw fingers touched the hot iron they stuck to it, leaving another strip of skin. He bit his tongue with the pain but didn't make a single sound of complaint.

The heat near the furnace grew unbearable; Mottke's head burned as if it were on fire, and his throat was dry. He flung off most of his clothes and stood stripped to the waist like the others. And when he saw that they were all pouring whole canfuls of water into them from the buckets that stood close by, he began to do the same. But the heat soon made the water evaporate, and the naked bodies of the glass-blowers smoked and sweated so hard that they looked as if they were covered with dew. The water boiled in their bodies and turned to steam.

"Let's see who has drunk most water, me or you," said the little girl, pointing at the bucket she had been drinking from. "Look, there's none left in mine, and he's got a whole half-bucket yet!"

Mottke felt ashamed to be beaten by a girl and drank more water.

"Look, look what a great big belly I've got with drinking water!" the girl cried, and she beat on it with her hand.

"Me too!" said one of the boys, pointing at his belly; it was smoking like a chimney.

Mottke was the only one who couldn't brag about his belly. He had drunk too little water.

"Children, keep blowing! You can show your bellies to each other later!" cried Anton.

Mottke wasn't amused any longer by this game with the fire. He thought of the meadows he had lain in at home, of the river where he had bathed, the cows he had milked, the vegetable gardens where he had stolen carrots and onions, the sun that had warmed him, and compared all these things with the red hot furnace and the flames bursting from it, the darkness of the shed, and the sweat pouring from these people's bodies. And he couldn't understand why people did the things they did here. He simply couldn't see why these people were standing here with their children, letting themselves simply be roasted as they blew into the lumps of fire, while outside the sun was shining. Why didn't they walk out into the fields, why didn't they live on the bank of the river and kindle camp-fires for themselves as he had done? He saw that he had got among bad people who tortured themselves and others before a flaming furnace, and told himself that he must fly as soon as he could and live in the fields near his own town again, as he had done before.

But he went on willingly with his work for the time being, for he felt ashamed before the little girl, who blew so much better than he did and could drink so much more water.

Anton was very pleased with Mottke and decided to teach him the trade and make a capable glass-blower out of him. A little Jew with a round hat who kept scuttling about the shed stepped up to Anton. He was the foreman. When he saw the new assistant he asked:

"Who is he?"

Anton replied:

"He's a boy from the town, his father asked me to teach him. He's staying with me and I'll put him up to the work."

"Has he a pass?"

"He's only a boy! He doesn't need any papers yet."

"Everybody must have a pass. You know what the gendarme's like! Every worker in this hut must have a pass. Anybody that wants to work here must show that he's entitled to do it," said the foreman decidedly.

"All right, I'll make it my business. I'll see that the matter is put in order," replied Anton, hoping that he would manage to square matters with the gendarme.

The clock struck twelve. The siren shrieked, and the workers streamed out into the yard. Their wives were waiting for them there with their dinners all ready. The various families withdrew into different corners of the yard and began to eat. Mottke followed Anton, whose wife had brought an extra spoon for him. He ate with Anton's children out of the same pot.

"Do you know," Anton turned to his wife, "this lad will be a good blower yet. In a short time he'll be a great help to me, as good as our poor Jascha, God keep him." Jascha was Anton's oldest son, who had died of consumption, as most of the lads and girls did that worked in the shed.

While the children proudly showed their bellies to their mother and bragged of the water they had drunk, Mottke sat gazing longingly at a wood that rose a little distance away like a black wall. He blew on his burnt hands and wondered to himself how he would get away from this hell that he had wandered into.

CHAPTER XIX

✱

Mottke Saves Himself from Hell

EVENING. The peasants sat before the doors of their houses breathing freely at last, after having panted all day in the scorching heat of the furnace. The older ones were quite done in; they never stirred and gazed with dead eyes into the distance. But the younger ones, though they had toiled from morning till night, swallowing the burning air and filling their bellies with water, flew about happily and had both the energy and the inclination for play. Their childish laughter was like a gleam of sunshine in the long row of smoke-blackened houses, which looked like dull and gloomy coffins for living corpses. The older people smiled contentedly as they sat before their doors.

Mottke wandered about like a stranger, for he didn't feel at home either among the children or the grown-ups.

The young lads drank beer and played tricks on the girls. But they didn't take Mottke into their circle and looked down on him, calling him contemptuously "the vagabond," although he was wearing a new suit that Anton had got for him on tick from a Jewish shop. And Mottke didn't want to make friends with the children, for he felt that was beneath him as the oldest glass-blower. He had hated the factory from the very start. He couldn't understand the life there. At first the shed and the furnaces and the strange people interested him and he looked on the work as a kind of game. But when he found out that every day was the same as the last, that every morning you had to go to the shed and blow glass and do nothing but blow glass, he became disgusted, and made up his mind to run away. But up till now there had been no chance, and besides he was held back by a strange fancy.

Anton had a little daughter about eight or nine, or she may have been a little older. The poor thing was a cripple and couldn't walk. Her legs were as thin as sticks and couldn't bear her weight, so that she could only sit with them tucked under her. Everybody swore at her. Sometimes she would sit all day on the same spot, for she couldn't move by herself and nobody took the trouble to lift her and carry her somewhere else. She was in everybody's way and if anybody trampled on her she got a scolding, as if it were her fault. The girl would smile awkwardly, as if to excuse herself. And this crippled girl was the reason why Mottke couldn't make up his mind to leave Anton's house.

This was how it came about: after Anton decided to keep Mottke as a glass-blower he took him home with him. Bedtime came and there was neither bed nor blanket for the new member of the family. So Anton's wife sent him to sleep beside the cripple girl; she lay in a corner by herself, for the other children refused to sleep near her. Mottke cast a suspicious glance at the corner, where a heap of skin and bones seemed to be lying under a coat. But at last he lay down in the corner, too. For a long time, filled with a vague fear of his unfamiliar surroundings, he stared at the holy pictures lit up by little red lamps, and made up his mind to steal away as soon as everybody was asleep. He looked at the things lying about and tried to decide whether he should pocket some of them or pinch the money out of Anton's pocket. Then he felt something pressing close to him and a hot face snuggling into his and thin arms taking him round the neck.

He started back, shivering with disgust, and pushed the cripple away. Then he looked at the child. With her head to one side she was gazing into the distance, a smile of happiness on her face.

"I say, do you know that there's a stream in the wood where men and devils bathe together? Do you know that?" she asked, suddenly turning to Mottke.

He put out his tongue and turned his back on her.

But the girl wouldn't let him go to sleep.

"I say, will you take me to the woods with you and dip me in the stream?" she went on.

Mottke gave her a push with his foot.

The girl didn't cry out. But all at once Mottke felt a curious warmth on his body. She was pressing quite close to him with her head, her arms, her legs and her body, and stroking him: he felt as if a dog were licking him.

He lay without moving.

Since that night he had had a strange feeling for the cripple. He couldn't ignore her, he couldn't bear to see her looking enviously at the other children playing while she sat by herself. So he would take her in his arms and carry her out into the street to the other children. After doing that once, he had to keep it up. So he carried her from place to place and became a sort of father to her. He hated her, and sometimes he beat her when nobody was looking, or dug her in the ribs; but whenever the girl looked at him with her sad eyes or smiled at him with her thin lips, that strange feeling came over him again like a spell. He hardly ever left her, he didn't even go strolling in the woods or join the lads of his own age in their walks, but stayed with the cripple, looked after her and carried her from place to place.

It was this that kept him in Anton's house. Often he felt tempted to carry the girl to the woods, push her into a hole there and shovel earth over her, and then fly from this life that he hated so much. And he would have done it, too, if he hadn't been ashamed to carry the girl through the whole village on his shoulders.

In the office of the factory there was a sort of shop for the workers. The peasants employed in the place didn't get their wages in cash but only in promissory notes; in return for these they were given food and clothes at this store. The owner of the factory delegated a part of his authority to members of his family, and an uncle of his had set up this shop, where he sold goods to the value of eighty kopeks for every rouble inscribed on the workers' slips. The men and their wives gathered on Sundays in his shop, and received their letters and held divine service, for the shop served them as a church as well. They were Roman Catholics, and the Russian police forbade them to build a church for themselves. For fear of the police they didn't dare to worship in a private house, and so they gathered in the Jew's shop, which was not so likely to come under suspicion. There they set up an image of the Madonna on a meal-sack and prayed to it. Mottke usually stood guard and kept a look out for the police inspector. As soon as the inspector appeared the workers hid the Madonna and began to weigh out flour, measure out paraffin, and drink beer. For to encourage drunkenness was to the inspector's mind a far less heinous offense than to hold divine service.

As Mottke kept watch for the workers during their worship, he soon rose to a position of respect among them. Besides, for some time there had been going on a silent but stubborn struggle for him between the Christians in the factory and the Jews in the shops. The Jews knew that Mottke was of Jewish birth and looked upon it as a scandal that he had fallen "into the hands of the Goyim." But the workers, much as they felt down-trodden by the Jews, were proud that there was a Jew among them all the same, and they made up their minds to save Mottke from the devil and regarded him as belonging to them. For the time being both parties were chary of calling in the police inspector to decide the matter. Mottke knew all this very well and exploited the situation as much as he could. Now and then he would stroll over to a shop, and when he found the owner's wife sitting behind the counter reading psalms he would try to frighten her:

"You know that I'm a Jew?"

"Oy, Oy!" the woman would sigh. "To think of a Jew living among Christians, eating unclean meat and praying to idols! Oy, Oy!"

"Give me something nice to eat and I won't kiss the Cross any more."

"Oy, Oy, that my ears should hear such words!" cried the woman, giving Mottke a handful of sweets.

"Say a blessing before you eat them," she said.

"You expect me to say a Jewish blessing for this? Throw in three rolls and I'll do it."

The woman haggled with Mottke for a while and they compromised at last on two rolls, in return for which he had to say the Jewish blessing.

Everything that he squeezed out of the Jewish religion in this way he shared afterwards with the cripple.

All the same he stuck to the God of the Jews, and though Anton often threatened him with the strap, and the boys and girls chaffed him, they could never make him kiss the Cross or recite "Blessed be thy name, Holy Virgin" after them. Once when Anton's wife made the sign of the cross on his brow he spat, rushed to the well and washed.

It was a curious feeling that made him act in this way. Whenever Anton's wife made the sign of the cross over him he saw before him his mother, Red Slatke. He saw her sitting sewing his trousers with the tears running down her cheeks, and himself crouching naked in the corner of the cellar looking at her.

Besides, everything in this place was beginning to disgust him; the blowing of the molten glass, the flaming furnaces, the everlasting flakes of soot in one's food at meal times, the blackened street and the holy images in Anton's house.

He had been in the factory now for two years and the fires of the furnace seemed to have steeled him for all that the future could bring. His arms had grown thick and powerful, his hands had got used to dealing with the fire. His face was manly, burnt brown, almost sharpened; his body, which had borne so many things, was supple and strong. He had accustomed himself to breathe the fire. Nature herself seemed to have fitted him for this ordeal, and to have sent him into this hell that in its fires he might come to power and maturity.

And soon the chance he had been looking for arrived.

The Christians and the Jews in the shed were at last preparing for the decisive battle over him, when he suddenly left them both in the lurch. It happened in this way.

As the workers were returning from their work one evening there appeared in the street that ran through the working quarter a big caravan with windows and a chimney all complete. It looked like a long house and was drawn by two mules. Behind on a halter trotted a little ass, a dog and a goat. A girl was looking out through the window. A tall lad with ear-rings and a whip in his hand brought up the rear. From inside came the twittering of strange birds.

When the children in the working quarter saw the caravan and the mules and the goat they began to shriek with joy till the whole village rang and everybody rushed out. Mottke, who had just carried the cripple girl outside, was cast into raptures by the unusual sight and the twittering of the invisible birds. So he ran after the caravan, too. Then he heard some one calling his name (or had he merely imagined it?). Looking round he saw the cripple. She had been left behind, quite alone, in the middle of the street. Without stopping to consider, he hoisted the girl on his shoulders and ran after the caravan, which was making in the direction of the wood. The other children stopped at the edge of the wood and screamed after him:

"Mottke, Mottke, come back, it's getting dark!"

But Mottke had no thought of turning back. He followed the caravan, carrying the cripple girl on his shoulders; she clasped him firmly round the neck. He made up his mind that he would never go back to the shed again, that he would follow the caravan with the little donkey and the parrots instead, spend the night where they halted and never leave them again. But what was he to do with this girl on his shoulders? He didn't want to carry her back to the village, for then he mightn't find the strangers again. Coming to a sudden decision he lifted her from his shoulders, set her down on the ground and ran away. But he turned back several times. The girl sat with her thin legs drawn under her and looked at him without speaking. Her eyes had grown bigger; they glittered feverishly and were filled with terror. And the bigger her eyes grew the more furious Mottke felt with her.

He gave her a few hard buffets and turned to run off again. But every time he ran off it seemed to him that she was calling him. Then he took her in both hands and squeezed her thin throat. She made no sound, but merely smiled at him. Then he let her go. He would have liked to set fire to the wood, so that everything in it, the cripple included, might be burnt to ashes; but he had no matches. The caravan was leaving him farther and farther behind. As if he had gone mad he gave the girl a bang on the ear and screamed at her: "Cry, can't you? Cry! Howl!" Then ne rushed away after the caravan.

But the cripple girl neither cried nor made a sound. The darkness grew deeper and deeper. It seemed to Mottke that the great unhappy eyes of the girl were following him through the darkness. He could feel them on his back.

CHAPTER XX

*

The Tumblers

THE CARAVAN went on and on. Mottke ran behind it like a dog, without heeding where he was going. The lad with the ear-rings noticed him at last and asked what he wanted. Mottke made no answer. When the caravan stopped he stopped too, and when it went on he went on with it. Late in the evening the tumblers halted on the edge of a wood near a village. The tall lad unyoked the mules and tethered them with a rope to the wheels of the caravan. Then he went into the wood and gathered twigs and made a fire. Mottke stole up with an armful of dry branches and helped to blow the fire. The tall lad seized him by the arm:

"Who are you?"

"I don't know."

"How is that?"

"I have no father or mother."

"Where do you come from?"

"I've followed the caravan."

"Where have you been living?"

"With the Goyim in the last village. I worked in the shed. The Goyim wanted to baptize me. They beat me because I wouldn't kiss the cross. So I ran away. I was just starting when I saw your caravan and so I followed it."

"What do you want?"

"Take me with you, I can help with the horses, I know all about them. I'll do anything you like—I'm a good worker. Take me with you."

Mottke said these words so imploringly that the tall lad pulled a burning twig out of the fire and held it up to his face so as to see him more clearly. Then he shouted:

"Hi, Old Terach! Come out here a minute and look at this!"

Several faces appeared at the windows of the caravan, which were feebly lit.

"What's up?"

"Here's a young rascal begging us to take him with us."

"The devil run away with you! You put me all in a sweat! I thought one of the beasts had died or the police were on our heels. Tell the bastard to clear off, else we'll have all the Goyim in the village after us. He's a little spy sent by them, take my word!" cried a voice from one of the windows.

"He seems a bit of a greenhorn, as far as I can see..."

"What does he want? Bring him in. I'll have a look at him."

The tall lad pulled Mottke through a little door in the back of the caravan.

When Mottke saw the inside of the caravan he gaped with amazement.

He was in a long narrow room separated into several compartments by curtains. In a corner burned two paraffin lamps and their light, falling on the red curtains before the beds, gave the place a warm comfortable look. In the middle of the room hung a great cage, in which a red parrot was sitting on a little perch. The bird was shouting "Old Terach" in one long breath. That was the nickname of the oldest tumbler, the owner of the caravan. Old Terach himself lay fully dressed on a heap of rugs, cushions, and gypsy blankets: he wore ear-rings like the tall lad, but they were much larger and of pure gold. Round his great head, which was covered with gray curly hair, ran a strip of clean shaven skin that encircled his brows, temples, and skull like a fillet. His thick eyebrows looked as if they were powdered, they were so gray, and they almost covered his eyes. His broad flat nose, from which long bristles stood out, worked like a bellows and made a snoring noise even now, though he was awake. The air sent out through his nostrils made the bushy mustache over his thick lips wave to and fro. A sign with his hand, which held a burnt and much chewed old pipe, and a wink of his eye indicated that Mottke was to be brought nearer.

The tall lad—he carried a whip in his hand—seized Mottke by the scruff of the neck and pushed him forward.

The old man looked at Mottke without stirring and growled:

"Heda, you witch, bring the lamp here!"

Some one came out of a corner bearing one of the lamps. All that Mottke could see of her was a mane of long black hair with gray strands in it, and a patch of skin·burnt quite brown gleaming through the rents of her blouse.

The old man took the lamp in his hand, turned its light on Mottke and asked:

"Who are you?"

Mottke made no answer. He listened in delight to the chirping of canaries coming from every corner of the room and the screaming of the parrots. He felt he had wandered into another world. Everything here pleased him so much that he would have given his life to stay.

"Who are you?" old Terach asked again in his powerful deep voice.

"I'm an orphan, I have no father or mother," said Mottke, reciting his piece in a voice half-tearful and half-defiant.

"I know that story all right. You're lying. Have you a Ksibel? Give it here!"

Mottke looked at him blankly.

"Have you a pass? Show him your pass," the tall lad translated.

"I have no pass. The peasants took it away from me."

"What peasants?"

"The peasants that caught me and wanted to baptize me. But I refused, for I'm a Jew. And that's why I ran away."

"Who do you think you're telling these fairy-tales to? You're a runaway. The coppers are after you. Keep hold of him, we'll have to hand him over to the police."

Mottke was a little frightened but smiled all the same, for he knew that before they could do that he would manage to run away. Then he saw a sight that quite took his breath away. A curtain was pushed aside and a girl appeared. She was wearing a red tricot that clung so tight to her legs that you might have thought it was a second skin. Her breasts and arms were scarcely concealed by a thin silk blouse. Her long black hair fell loose over her back and her face. When she pushed it away with her hand he could see her great black eyes, her red rouged cheeks and lips and a pair of great gold ear-rings. The girl held a mirror in one hand, a high comb was sticking in her hair and on her shoulder sat a blue bird with a gilded beak, which it opened and shut menacingly. Mottke was so amazed by this sight that he quite forgot the old man's threat and the heavy hand of the lad on his shoulder, keeping him prisoner. He looked at the girl. A smile lit up his face and he felt like falling at her feet.

"Say freely who you are and then I'll let you go. You're a runaway, aren't you? Escaped from jail? If you don't tell me the truth I'll hand you over to the police!" the old man said.

"Who is this?" asked the girl in a sweet voice.

"A thief come to steal our horses," retorted the old man.

"I'm not a thief, I'm not a runaway, and I'm not afraid of the police. Or of you either! I'm afraid of nobody!" cried Mottke defiantly, but then he blushed to the roots of his hair. For he felt ashamed in front of this girl with the blue bird.

"What? You aren't afraid? Not even if we give you a beating?" asked the old man, laughing.

"I'll strike back! I'm not afraid!"

"Well then, strike back!" said the tall lad, giving him a whack with his whip from behind.

Mottke flew round, clenched his fists and made to rush at his attacker. But from the lad's face he saw that he had won his place and that this whip blow made him one of the band.

"May your hand wither!" screamed the old woman that Terach had called a witch a few minutes before. She leapt out and gave the tall lad a buffet on the ear. "Here's an orphan that has neither father nor mother and you strike the poor lad! Don't you pay any attention to these savages! The only thing they can do is eat, the lazy gluttons! I'll see to you, I'll look after you. Don't you pay any attention to them, but stick to me!"

"No harm meant, old lady, no harm meant. If the brat wants to be an artist he must be able to stand a wallop now and then."

"Come here, you young ruffian!" cried old Terach. "What's your name?"

"Mottke."

"We'll call you little Schmadnik. You hear?"

"Yes."

"Do you want to be an artist?"

"Yes."

"Pull off my boots."

Mottke at once set about his task. He summoned all his strength so as to show off before the girl; but it took him a good while before he managed to pull off old Terach's top-boots, for the long shafts stuck on the layers of rag that were wound round the old man's legs. All the same he did well, for he was quicker at getting the boots off than the tall lad had been, who up till that evening had had the job. Old Terach winked at the girl and asked:

"Well, how do you like our new lad?"

"Better than you two old gluttons!" retorted the girl, disappearing behind the curtain.

CHAPTER XXI

*

Mottke Becomes an Artist

As soon as the first light appeared they made ready to start. Mottke had spent the night outside along with the mules, and he looked imploringly at old Terach. He was still afraid they might leave him behind. The old man was in "full uniform": a showman's cap with gold braid, a whip with a finely woven lash and his indispensable pipe. He let fly his whip at Mottke and shouted:

"Hi, you rascal, gather the straw together, the beasts have scattered it everywhere, and fling it into the caravan."

Mottke had only been waiting for the order. He willingly did as he was told. The tall lad—the old man called him Kanarik—yoked the mules in the caravan.

Mottke looked at him longingly to show that he was eager to help.

"Hi, you rascal! Yoke the brown beast, will you? What are you standing there for with your hands in your pockets?"

The whip fell stinging on his shoulders.

But never had a blow made him so happy. For old Terach himself had given it. Mottke felt like kissing the hand that had struck him, and set about yoking the brown mule.

Soon the caravan was ready for the road. Then one of the windows flew open and the girl appeared in the red silk blouse that had filled him with such rapture the evening before. She combed her hair and sang a Russian song:

"A thousand I've loved,
A thousand I've forsaken,
By one alone
My heart is taken. . . ."

Mottke was deeply moved by the song, and didn't know where to look. He still couldn't believe that they were taking him with them. His friend—the fat old woman, the "witch," who had made herself responsible for him the evening before —wasn't to be seen. But the smoke rising from the chimney showed that she was inside somewhere.

And soon her face appeared at the window. Her black hair was still uncombed and she had a dirty cloth round her head, so that she looked like a real witch. She waved to old Terach, a tender smile passed over her fat old face, and she asked:

"Are you going to start on an empty larder, old Terach? Where am I to get your dinner today?"

"Well, you've taken on a new apprentice! Let him show what he can do!" retorted the old man, pointing at Mottke with his whip.

"Hi, sergeant-major! See what you can get from the village for our breakfast!" cried Kanarik, blinking at Mottke with his red eyes. His red hair, damp with sweat, clung to his freckled forehead.

"And for dinner and for supper, too, while you're at it!" added old Terach. "See what you can get from the peasants' back yards. We'll wait for you at the edge of the wood on the other side of the village."

Mottke made his way to the village to get their breakfast and their dinner and supper. The only thing that he was afraid of was that the caravan might go on without him, and that the errand might be only a pretext to get rid of

him. He threw an imploring glance at the "witch," begging
her to take his part and wait for him. He didn't dare to
glance at the window where the girl was. So he consigned
himself to God and took the road to the village.

Come what might, he made up his mind to do the best he
could. Quiet as a cat, he crept along the backs of the village
houses. And while the peasant women and their children
were out on the road gaping at the caravan and the tumblers
and the strange birds passing by with a great clatter and din,
he inspected the back yards. In a sack he had brought with
him he flung several hens and ducks, first twisting their
necks to keep them from betraying him with their cackling.
Then he captured one or two young geese, twisted their
necks, too, and threw them into the sack. Soon the sack was
so full that he could hardly carry it. He crept over fences,
crawled through thick bushes and clumped through bogs, to
avoid meeting any one. The caravan was actually waiting for
him at the edge of the wood. In great elation he ran up to
it and emptied his sack.

The old woman danced for joy and then turned jeeringly
to Kanarik:

"Well? Do you think you could have done as well? You
can eat, the pair of you, but as for working . . ."

Old Terach said nothing, so as not to make Mottke con-
ceited. He lowered his eyes as if he were contemplating his
mustache, and fell into deep thought. Clearly he had plans
for Mottke.

Kanarik made Mottke a sign to get up on the caravan, and
then they went on.

The caravan went on and on, the bells tinkled, and at
every village they came to the people ran out of their houses
to see the wonderful sight. Mottke was happy, for he was
traveling with the tumblers. All the way the girl kept singing:

"A thousand I've loved,
A thousand I've forsaken,
By one alone
My heart is taken...."

Mottke tried to picture the "one" to himself. Who could
it be, the one who had taken her heart? Certainly nothing
lower than a cavalry officer, with a horse of his own and
boots with spurs on them. Mottke envied him. Perhaps he
was sitting now in an inn playing cards, with a glass of beer
in front of him, quite unaware that his sweetheart was sitting here at the window singing a sad song about him.

Old Terach lay comfortably outstretched on some rugs,
chewing at his pipe and listening to the song. The old woman
stood by the fire roasting the hens and geese, and red-haired
Kanarik was asleep. So Mottke seized the reins and drove.

About midday they stopped near another village, on the
banks of a stream. There they unyoked the horses, fed them,
and then sat down to eat. Mottke wasn't invited inside to the
table, but the old woman brought him out a slice of bread
and a leg of chicken, and he ate them with great enjoyment.

After this meal they set about teaching Mottke his
"work," and put him through his first rehearsal. First of all
the old man ordered him to stand on his head. Mottke did
so, but couldn't keep it up for long, for the blood ran to his
head and his legs grew weak. He made to lower them, but
at either side of him stood old Terach and Kanarik with
whips in their hands, and they forced him to keep up his
legs. But it wasn't the whip blows that made him keep his
legs straight. For he saw that the girl was standing at the
window watching him; and whenever the others flicked him
with the whip she laughed. And he made up his mind to
show her that he could do tricks, too, and so he held out

although his head was going round and his back felt as if it were breaking. He stood on his head until old Terach counted a hundred.

Then they tried out an act that Mottke was to do along with the mules. The brown mule was chosen as his partner. For every creature that went with the tumblers had to do some trick and earn its living by real work. The very beasts that pulled the caravan had to know their tricks. The brown mule, for instance, could sneeze like a human being; and when old Terach pulled it by the tail it would waggle its ears, a trick that always gave great pleasure to the audience. Now old Terach thought out a number for Mottke and this mule: Mottke, dressed as a clown, was to stand on his head on its back, while it trotted in a circle and waggled its ears at the same time.

The brown mule was of good stock. Old Terach had got it from a circus owner in exchange for two dogs who could walk the tightrope. In former days the brown mule, groomed and beribboned, had performed in a circus. At that time it bore the proud name of Nero, had bells round its neck and was ridden by the world-famous "Spanish" dancer and acrobat Sabina. Now, in its old age, it belonged to old Terach and answered to the name of the brown beast, because it had two bright brown patches on its belly. And it was the old man who had taught it to sneeze and waggle its ears.

So now the poor beast had to balance forlornly on its forelegs with a red circus jacket round it, while a mere lad stood on his head on its back, and it sneezed and waggled its ears.

But Mottke's chief turn was to be a wrestling match with Kanarik, in the "Spanish" style at that. Mottke must beat his opponent; that is to say Kanarik had finally to touch the mat with both shoulders, for old Terach considered that the combat would be far more effective if the "little one" beat the "big one." And so Mottke became "the world-famous Spanish Champion Severin Severus" and wore a row of medals on his chest which he had won in Constantinople.

To heighten this impression his body was rubbed with fat and his arms and legs tightly bound with cloths. This was supposed to make his muscles swell and produce the impression that his biceps were terrific.

The cloths cut painfully into his arms and legs, but he bore joyfully all these tortures, since they were necessary to make him an artist. The girl with the long black hair was always standing at the window singing her sad song:

> *"A thousand I've loved,*
> *A thousand I've forsaken,*
> *By one alone*
> *My heart is taken...."*

And Mottke kept thinking and thinking who that "one" could be and where he lived, the one that had taken her heart.

CHAPTER XXII·

*

Mottke Becomes a World-Renowned Spanish Champion

SOME time had passed now since Mottke joined the tumblers. He had to go through all the circles of the hell that gapes in front of the career of an "artist"; for old Terach kept beating him with the whip until he became a capable performer and could appear in the troupe.

From early morning the market-place had hummed like a hive. The peasants in their wagons and the landowners in their carriages had poured all day into the town to see the celebrated tightrope dancer. It was said that even people from the surrounding towns had come to behold the performance of this renowned artist. A tightrope was stretched across the square from the butcher's shop to the church. A stage was being hastily hammered together out of boards and planks, on which the "famous wrestlers," Kanarik and "the young Spanish Champion Severus" (our friend Mottke), were to measure their strength and perform all sorts of feats. But at present Mottke was strutting about in a grotesque pair of trousers reaching from his shoulders to his knees, on the back of which was painted a clock. And everybody who saw him simply rocked with laughter when he turned his back view to them and showed them how late it was.

Kanarik was going about in strange clothes too. And to heighten the effect he had rubbed his face with soot. With his red hair and red eyebrows, that made him look like the devil in person. Old Terach alone was attired as beseemed a real artist; he wore red tights, his arms and legs were bare, and a belt of red velvet was bound round his waist, on which tinkled medals and orders from all the countries of the world. He had cribbed these distinctions from old soldiers, and some of them were as big as plates. In this rig the tumblers knocked together their stage in the market square and fixed up the tightrope, while all the town stood round gaping at them.

At four o'clock in the afternoon, when the worst heat of the sun was past, the performance began. First of all old Terach, Kanarik and the Spanish champion strutted round the stage cracking their whips over the heads of the "ladies and gentlemen," and clearing a space round the arena, so that everybody might be able to see the performance at their ease. The very first number roused great enthusiasm. Our old friend the "witch" appeared, but now she was changed beyond recognition. For she was wearing a short red tricot, padded enormously before and behind, and her arms, hands and legs were so thickly powdered that you would have thought she had just come out of a flour-mill. The impression was heightened by her red chemise being covered with powder as well. On one of her wrists sat the blue parrot who was always screaming: "Old Terach!" But now as it perched on the old lady's hand it screamed: "I love you" instead in Russian, in reward for which she kissed it on the gilded beak. Then she set it on her shoulder and lifted towards it a pretty little box in which there were slips telling the "fate" of the various members of the audience. For five kopeks the bird would pull out a blue slip in which any one could read all the good fortune that would befall him to the end of his days. The paper told how often he would marry, how big a dowry he would get each time, how many legacies

would be left to him, if he would die in his own bed, that a
letter with very important news was on the way to him, and
other interesting information of a similar kind.

As soon as the "witch" had left the stage, old Terach
appeared with all his medals and orders on his belly. He
announced the next number. His speech was made up of a
mixture of Russian, Yiddish and Polish, among which appeared as well all sorts of words belonging to some incomprehensible language that sounded like Hungarian or Turkish. From his announcement it appeared that the renowned
Spanish champion was now about to come on, a lad who, in
spite of his tender years—he wasn't twelve yet, the old man
swore—had beaten thousands of great athletes and was
already world-famed. This young Goliath would measure his
strength in a wrestling match with the equally renowned,
more, world-renowned Hungarian champion Kanarik-
Kanarinado. But before the combat began the famous champion, who was still a mere child, would display to the public
some feats of strength.

Old Terach made a sign with his hand, whereupon without
more ado Kanarik kicked Mottke on to the stage.

When Mottke saw the crowd before him he was filled with
terror and didn't know what to do. But the crowd gaped at
him with open curiosity. He was wearing short black pants
to make him look younger. The old woman had seen to his
appearance before he went on, and his hair, which had never
known a comb before, gleamed raven black with the grease
she had smeared on it. He wore a velvet jacket too, which
had once belonged to Kanarik. In this and the short trousers he actually looked like a very young boy, and this
impression was heightened still more by the fact that he
stood there, terrified and awkward, not knowing what to do.

Old Terach took him by the hand and, pointing at him, said to the people:

"Do you see this boy? He isn't twelve years old yet. A mere child. Yet this child will lift a weight of two hundred pounds with his teeth before your eyes. After that he will hold back two grown men with one hand. There's nobody in the whole world as strong as this boy. He's already beaten twenty champions, and the King of Spain himself gave him this medal in recognition of his prowess." Old Terach pointed at a round piece of lead that Mottke wore on his chest. "His father was the world-renowned champion Severus, and his mother weighed four hundred pounds. She was the heaviest woman in the whole world. That's why he's so strong. Just look at his arms," the old man went on, pointing at Mottke's muscles, which had been worked up for a fortnight by being bound in tight bandages. "Just look at them. Look at his muscles, Why, I'm scared of him myself!" He jumped back from Mottke, pretending to be frightened, and the audience roared with laughter.

Mottke still didn't know what to do. His panic grew and he felt ashamed at being stared at by so many people. But all the same the old man's words and the way that the crowd swallowed them made him want to laugh, and he had to do all he could not to burst out laughing.

"Bow to the people, you fool! Smile! Smile! May the devil run away with ... What are you standing here for like a Golem?" the old man whispered into his ear, while he tenderly stroked his hair to impress the audience.

"He's only a child yet, his mother gave him to me to look after for her. Gratana, gratana chocoladana," the old man said in a quite unknown language, suddenly turning to Mottke. Then he explained to the crowd: "I asked him if he would like a piece of chocolate. The boy doesn't understand our speech, and so I have to speak to him in Spanish. Gratana, gratana chocoladana? Here you are!" The old cheat stuck a piece of sugar into Mottke's mouth as if he were feeding a bird. And then he whispered:

"Will you bow to the people, you rascal? If you don't smile this minute I'll break every bone in your body! Bow, I tell you! Bow!"

Mottke couldn't contain himself any longer. The laughter had risen in his throat and was almost choking him, and yet he was afraid of bowing or smiling or changing his attitude in any way; he was frozen to the spot. But now he couldn't keep himself in any longer, and he began to splutter and roar with laughter.

The crowd joined in and began to laugh too.

For a minute the old man was quite at a loss, but he soon found a way out of his predicament:

"He wants you to clap. Will you kindly oblige? Like this!" Old Terach turned towards the audience and began to clap his hands. "In Spain you laugh if you want the audience to clap you."

The crowd began to clap madly, and old Terach whispered to Mottke:

"May the cholera gripe you! You just wait, you bastard, I'll soon teach you to laugh on the stage!"

Then he said in a loud and tender voice to impress the audience:

"Now lift this two hundred pound weight with your teeth, my boy!"

Mottke did so. The old man showed the crowd how heavy the weight was and the crowd applauded again.

Thereupon Kanarik made his appearance. He also wore short black pants and a velvet jacket, and his chest, too, was richly decorated. With professional grace he bowed to

the public, smiling graciously, shook back his red mane and
squeaked: "Igra, igra, igra!" which was intended to sound
like Hungarian. Then he whispered to Mottke: "Did you
see that, you silly fool? That's how you make your bow to
the public. Do you hear?"

Then the two gladiators put on their belts and the combat
was ready to begin.

But before it started old Terach turned to the audience
with the request that it should choose a jury to come on the
stage and see that everything was fairly and squarely done.
But nobody in the crowd seemed very eager to feature in a
jury. At last two men were found ready to undertake the
work: Chaim, the assistant at the baths, who was a lover
of sport (he was a member of the local fire brigade too) and
the Polish cobbler Kozlowski. They seated themselves on
the stage to decide which was the victor. (For their hardi-
hood they won from the townspeople the nickname of "the
performing twins," which stuck to them all their lives.)

Kanarik took a firm hold of Mottke and made up his mind
to show the brat that he was the stronger and could do with
him what he liked, in spite of their agreement. But very soon
he saw that Mottke wouldn't let himself be easily beaten;
the presence of so many people fired the boy and he made
up his mind to show his strength. Besides, he told himself
that if he beat Kanarik in a fair fight he would go up in
the eyes of old Terach and win a claim to the favor of the
tightrope dancer, just like Kanarik. Kanarik saw through
all this, and a silent and stubborn battle began between the
two lads. Mottke brought up all his strength, and before
Kanarik knew where he was, before he knew what had happened, he was lying with his shoulders on the mat.

The crowd, worked up to great excitement by the struggle, yelled with rapture and wildly applauded Mottke, who,

as the younger, already had their sympathy. They whistled, clapped and shouted for the "Spaniard." But the only combatant to appear was Kanarik; he kept on bowing, while Mottke hid himself, ashamed of appearing before so many people. But the crowd wouldn't be appeased until old Terach appeared on the stage leading the "Spaniard" by the hand. The old tumbler pointed now at himself, now at Mottke, and bowed with great dignity. Nobody could make out what he could mean by pointing at himself.

However that may be, from that day Mottke was a great favorite with the public, a genuine artist who knew how to set to work. Old Terach himself saw this and began to treat him differently. And Kanarik found himself faced with a rival.

After the wrestling match there was silence for a little while. The barrel-organ stopped playing. The star turn in the program was now to appear: the world-renowned Spanish dancer (all that was world-renowned with the tumblers had to be Spanish), the lovely Mary was about to display her skill. The crowd waited breathlessly. Mary was actually renowned throughout the whole neighborhood; it was said that great lords followed her from town to town to admire her art, and that lots of rich men were madly in love with her. The rumor went that they had forsaken their wives and children to follow her, but Mary had refused them all and preferred to devote herself to her art..

And now she appeared before the audience. Old Terach led her on. She wore a red dress touched up to make it look Spanish, and trimmed with coral beads and all kinds of tinsel. Her neck, arms, and legs were powdered pink, cheeks and lips slightly rouged, her hair curled and hanging loose, so that long black locks of it fell down her back and over her bosom. Mary bowed to the crowd, seized a little silk parasol, and planted her foot on the back of the old tumbler, who with a graceful gesture knelt down before her. Then with her free hand she clutched the cord that hung down from the tightrope and in a moment swung herself up, light as a bird, and stood up there trim and secure, throwing kisses to the breathless crowd. But nobody smiled; all waited tensely for what was to come. Mary put up her parasol and began lightly as a butterfly to glide to and fro on the rope. With her parasol she regulated the balance of her body, and up there, in the sunlight, she didn't look like a woman any longer, but more like a splendid red bird with a human head, soaring above the crowd. From below old Terach, Kanarik and Mottke followed every movement she made, their arms outstretched and their eyes anxiously fixed upon her, ready to catch her if she made a false step.

But the girl seemed to have no fear of that. She felt just as safe on the rope as she did on the ground. She leapt and danced on one leg, whirled round, threw the parasol from one hand to the other, and displayed the lightness of her movements, the pliability of her body and the beauty of her arms and legs. And everybody who saw her, old and young, fell in love with her. Even the women were carried away by her, and didn't dare to speak or even to breathe, for fear the girl might be startled and fall from the rope.

And Mottke was more deeply in love with her now than ever and ready to die for her. His heart beat with fear; God, if she were to fall! Tears came into his eyes. And when Mary climbed down from the rope, quite unharmed, and the dammed-up enthusiasm of the crowd broke out at last in wild applause, Mottke almost went off his head with joy. He danced on one leg, wept with happiness and rushed after the old man, who had hoisted Mary on his shoulders and was walking with her through the crowd. She put up her parasol again and the public began to fling money into it. Everybody gave as much as he could and many more than they could afford. The neighboring landowners flung silver coins into the parasol, and the lords who were supposed to have left wife and family for her actually flung roubles to her. The girl caught the coins in her parasol, and what escaped her and fell to the ground was picked up by Mottke. Usually it had been Kanarik who did this, but this time a concession was made to the sympathies of the public, for old Terach fancied that the people would give more if Severus were on show.

And Mottke was happy and in love.

CHAPTER XXIII

*

Starlight

ONE night shortly after this Mottke was sitting by a merrily leaping fire in an open field keeping watch over the horses. Near him Kanarik lay fast asleep, wrapped in a blanket. Mottke listened to his snoring. Woods rose in the distance like a black wall. The ground was wet with dew. Mottke couldn't sleep. He kept staring at the caravan standing a little distance away; in the dark it looked like a deserted house with the windows nailed up. He kept his eyes fixed on a little window that showed a faint chink of light, and he thought he heard a child crying in the caravan. He crept nearer, listened, and tried to look through the chink. He could see nobody, there was no sign of life in the caravan. He lay down on the ground again and dreamt and listened into the night. Everything was strange to him, and he reflected that he was a great distance from his own town and probably would never return there again. These people that he was living with had put a spell upon him, yet he felt something almost like fear for them. Then he thought of Mary and that first evening, when he had seen her coming from behind the curtain. She was so lovely and so unlike anybody that he had ever known before in all his life. He would give anything to see her now, but the mere fact that she was near made him happy.

He crept over to the caravan again; but he couldn't see anything this time either. Yet he felt so happy that he

153

wanted to shout for joy. He managed to restrain himself. He returned to the fire again, threw some more twigs on it and sat down.

Then his mood changed and he felt cold and forlorn. He thought of his mother. He saw her sitting in the cellar sewing his trousers and gazing silently at him. He saw her rushing to the police-station to save him from Blind Pearl. And he made a vow that when he had made his pile he would return to the little town, draw up in his carriage before the cellar, call out his mother, seat her beside him and drive with her through the town, so as to show the whole world that this was his mother. And he would give her costly jewels and expensive clothes. But he would only be good to her; he would give his father nothing, refuse to let him drive in the carriage and not even speak to him.

He believed firmly that he would become rich sometime and call for his mother in a fine carriage. And the fact that he had hit upon the tumblers and learned from them how to "work" strengthened him in his belief.

Through all these pictures of the future shone more and more brightly the figure of the girl that he had seen on that first night in the caravan. In some way or other all his hopes and wishes for the future were involved with Mary; but why that was so and what made him think it was so he did not know and he did not try to find out.

Then one of the windows opened and Mary stuck out her head. By the light of the fire he could see her gleaming hair and pale face. His heart beat faster, he jumped up, then sat down again, trembling with joy and yet afraid to look at the girl. Then he heard a soft: "Hst! ... Hst!" He crept up to the window again.

"Is Kanarik sleeping?"

Mottke nodded.

"Hush! Don't speak! Bend down!"

Mottke bent down. A light foot touched his back. He felt a bird had settled on him for a minute.

"Let's go farther away, else they'll hear us," whispered Mary, taking his hand.

They hurried off in the direction of the wood. Their footsteps made no sound on the wet grass. At the edge of the wood they stopped and sat down.

"Don't make any noise. If they catch us they'll kill us both!" the girl whispered in his ear, putting her hand over his mouth. She was afraid he might cry out with joy, for she felt the happiness in him.

Mottke winked at her to show that he understood.

They sat side by side like this for a while without saying anything. Mottke's heart beat fast, and he wondered whether this was reality or a dream. Then he grew hot, felt he couldn't look the girl in the face, stared into the darkness, and let Mary do with him what she liked.

"Come. Let's go farther into the wood," she whispered to him.

Mottke followed her, his heart hammering.

CHAPTER XXIV

*

The Imperial Hotel

A FEW weeks later the tumblers arrived at a little town where they were to give a show. Here they left their caravan and went to stay at an inn which bore the proud title of The Imperial Hotel. The proprietors were Chaim Spassvogel and his daughter, the fair Dwoirele, a young bouncing wench. Nobody knew whether she was a widow or a divorced wife or whether she had simply run away from her husband; the only ascertainable fact was that she had once been married and that there was no sign of a husband now. Travelers and business people liked to put up at her place when they were passing through the town. But it wasn't strangers only that frequented The Imperial Hotel; in the long winter evenings the rich young people of the town sat there too, playing cards. Occasionally the little town would be shocked by the news that some quite respectable young man had played away his wife's dowry at Dwoirele. Then the women would whisper: "Dwoirele has plucked another fool, it seems."

This was the place patronized now by old Terach, the witch, Kanarik, and the tightrope dancer. Mottke had to sleep outside in the caravan and watch over the horses.

The show was over and the tumblers were sitting in their room in the inn. The window of this room looked out on a little garden at the back of the hotel; it was always curtained. The inn people called this room "the dark chamber." For in this room occurred the dark deeds that made Dwoirele so much talked about.

Old Terach was highly pleased with the show. The takings had been excellent. And whenever the old man was pleased he always drank oceans of tea out of a samovar that he kept in the caravan. He had taken off his top-boots and was half sitting and half lying on the bed, to which the table had been drawn up. From the tea before him rose huge clouds of steam that almost completely hid him. His forehead was covered with sweat. He smoked contentedly at his pipe. With the mouthpiece he now and then dug the old woman under the arm at the same time throwing a glance at Mary and Mottke. The girl was sitting in a corner rubbing her legs with oil after her performance. Mottke stood beside her pouring the oil on her hands out of a bottle.

"A handsome couple! We should be able to make something out of them yet," said the old man slyly.

Then Kanarik came in and cursed at Mottke for having left the caravan and the horses to look after themselves. The old man and the old woman took Mottke's part and said that he could stay; the horses were in the stable and nobody would steal them.

"Do you know what, Mary? The gentleman that took such a fancy to you in Plozk has followed you here!" said Kanarik.

Mary flushed.

"How do you know? Have you seen him?" asked old Terach with great interest.

"I saw him in the market square. He got off at the hotel here."

"You don't say so."

"Yes, it's quite true," replied Kanarik, nodding at the

old man and making a sign that he couldn't say any more before Mottke.

"Come, you young rascal, get off to your horses," said old Terach almost tenderly, turning to Mottke.

"Why should you send him off to the stable? He'll be much better in the bar-room, he'll manage to scrounge a glass of beer there maybe. There'll be lots of people drinking and he will be able to turn a penny for himself," said the old woman.

Mottke looked round him, threw Mary a glance, took his cap and left the room.

But instead of going into the bar-room he slunk behind the house and into the garden and from there looked for the window of the "dark chamber." He soon recognized it by the gray curtain. He took a run, swung himself on to the ledge, grasped an iron stanchion that he found there, and tried to peer into the room and listen through a chink in the shutters.

What it was all about he couldn't tell, but he guessed; his heart told him. He saw Kanarik letting fly at Mary with his fists, heard her crying out and the old man and the old woman talking kindly to her and trying to persuade her to do something. He saw them showing her money and Mary shaking her head and stamping angrily with her foot.

Then Dwoirele stepped into the room, followed by a little Jewish-looking gentleman wearing a short jacket and carrying a little stick in his hand. The newcomers began to whisper in a corner with old Terach and Kanarik. When they were finished Dwoirele went across to Mary with a sweet smile, stroked her hair, kissed her and pleaded with her. While this was going on the old woman combed Mary's hair and slipped a new blouse over her head. The girl let them do what they liked with her. Her face was flushed a dull red. Kanarik put the room to rights and pushed the bottle of oil into a corner. The man with the walking-stick smiled on the company and disappeared. Mottke knew quite clearly what was afoot. His heart beat madly, his arms and legs trembled, something seemed to be choking him and squeezing his heart together. Then he was suddenly tired of everything; and if the whole house and everybody in it had sunk through the ground taking him with it, he felt he wouldn't have stirred a finger to save himself. He was merely curious what would happen next.

Presently the man with the walking-stick returned, smiling expansively, this time followed by a tall Pole with a huge mustache, elegantly dressed. He seemed to be very embarrassed, kept on bowing, and greeted everybody in the room. Dwoirele begged him to sit down at the table. In honor of the visitor old Terach donned his coat again; Kanarik smiled obsequiously. But Mary kept aloof and stayed in her corner. Then Dwoirele led her, protesting, to the table where the Pole was sitting. The Pole made a disarming bow and held out his hand to Mary. Then Dwoirele sat down at the table, and beer was brought and poured out into glasses. Some one pulled out a pack of cards and the company began to play.

Mottke was so agitated by all this that he wanted to spring into the room. But he mastered himself, climbed back into the garden and went up to the room again. He knocked and said to himself: "Now for it!"

"Who's there?" cried some one.

"Me! Mottke!"

There was a sound of whispering in the room, then the door opened.

Kanarik stood in it. He barred Mottke's way and asked in a severe voice:

"What do you want?"

"You'll soon find that out!" Mottke retorted, flinging him aside and stepping past him into the room.

"Oho, so this is the young Spaniard that won the wrestling match! Splendid! Splendid!" cried the Pole with the huge mustache, clapping his hands.

"I intend to take him to Warsaw shortly to challenge Byshko," said old Terach.

"What have you come here for? Somebody may be stealing the horses this very minute!" he whispered to Mottke.

"Let *him* go to the stables for a change!" retorted Mottke, pointing at Kanarik. "I'm going to stay here."

"Let him stay," said the old woman.

"Perhaps our young Spanish friend would drink a glass of beer with us?" said the Pole, pouring out a glass for Mottke.

Mottke felt awkward, made a gesture of refusal with his hand, but then drank up the beer after all.

"Why, he's only a child still! Just look what pretty hands he's got!" said Dwoirele, stroking Mottke's hands and throwing him an inviting glance.

This flattery was sweet as honey to Mottke. He blushed and answered Dwoirele's glance eagerly.

The others went on with their game of cards without taking any notice of him.

Dwoirele's glances made him feel quite drunk now, so that he forgot both the Pole and Mary, who was sitting at the table absently following the game. He swallowed up Dwoirele with his eyes and tried to get another glance from her, but she seemed to have forgotten him completely and to be quite absorbed in the game.

Then he glanced at Mary. But she was cross and refused to look at him. He realized that she had caught the play between him and Dwoirele. Then he saw that Mary was pressing closer to the Pole, slipping cards into his hand and behaving as if she was quite gone on him. She kept stroking his hands. The sight roused Mottke to fury. He wanted to fling himself on the Pole and strangle him. He glared at Mary, but she didn't seem to know that he was there. So he tugged her by the sleeve. She looked round in annoyance, threw him a furious glance, then turned back to the Pole and gazed up at him with adoring eyes. Mottke felt he was going to die.

In the middle of the game Dwoirele suddenly jumped up as if she had remembered something and said that the people down in the tap-room were waiting to see the "artists," they could earn a mint of money down there; the customers, she went on, had sent her up to beg them to come down, but in the excitement of the game she had completely forgotten about it. Old Terach got up, took up a tambourine and made a sign to Kanarik.

"Come, there's money to be made. Mottke, you come too."

The old woman got up next. "I'll come, too. But the child," she pointed at Mary, "had better stay here. She's tired. The poor girl has worked hard today."

She took up a wrap and they all made ready to go. The Pole and Mary stayed at the table and went on playing. But Mottke stopped at the door.

"Come, you young rascal, come, there's money going!" cried old Terach, taking him by the shoulder.

Mottke shook himself free and stood his ground.

"What's gone wrong with you?"

"Nothing!" retorted Mottke.

Kanarik winked at him:

"Come on, you fool! You can see for yourself that the two of them want to be left alone."

"I won't!" replied Mottke.

"What?"

The old man turned round. He wanted to avoid any scandal. Then Dwoirele slipped her arm under Mottke's, stroked his cheek, looked deep into his eyes and said again with an inviting smile:

"He doesn't want to go with you; but he'll come with me. What have you got to show him? But I can show him something. He knows that too."

She said this with a glance that quite convinced Mottke she was going to accord him her favors at once. And he couldn't resist the temptation.

He answered her smile hardily and left the room along with her.

Behind him he heard the Pole and Mary locking themselves in. He felt a little frightened at that, but the buxom young woman was beside him and that made him forget everything.

But as soon as Dwoirele got him safely into the taproom she forgot all about him. She avoided his glances and he couldn't get near her among all the travelers, butchers and wandering peddlers who had been impatiently waiting for her. She doled out glasses of beer to them and slices of roast goose, and stroked their hands; she gave them tots of brandy which they gulped down hastily, pinching her bottom afterwards, as dessert, so to speak. Mottke looked on and saw everything and got so confused that he scarcely knew where he was. Then he remembered the Pole and Mary locked in the "dark chamber." He pushed his way out of the crowded taproom and rushed upstairs; but the door was locked. He could see nothing through the keyhole, for the key was in it. He hurried down into the garden, climbed up to the window again and found the chink he had spied through before. But the blinds were drawn now. He let himself down again, looked round for a piece of wood, stuck it through the chink, pushed the blind aside and saw what was happening.... The blood flew to his head. He couldn't tell what was happening to him. He pulled with all his strength at the window and easied it up carefully so that they shouldn't hear him. Then he flung the window open. With one leap he was in the room.

Mary was half-undressed and lying on the bed with her hair down; she jumped up in alarm. The Pole, who had nothing on at all, stood by awkwardly and seemed to be ashamed of his long hairy legs before Mottke. There was a disarming smile on his face; a smile half of past enjoyment and half of shame. Mottke all at once felt sorry for the man and stopped in confusion, not knowing what to do. The Pole hurriedly began to look about for his trousers and his jacket, so as to cover his nakedness.

Mary made to go up to Mottke. He looked at her naked brown shoulders showing through her torn blouse. Then he let fly and struck her in the face. The girl didn't cry out or even step back. He felt her hand snatching at his and pushing something into it. By the faint light of the paraffin lamp, which was turned down, he saw that it was something made of leather. He realized that it was a purse and instinctively pocketed it.

"Hide it ... Get away before they find out.... The Goy will kick up a row."

Mottke heard her whisper, but he didn't grasp what it was about, and still didn't know what to do. The Pole looked miserable with his bare legs; he was still looking for his trousers. Mary tried to reassure him:

"Just stay here, you just stay here! He's going again at once." And then she whispered to Mottke: "Get off and hide it!"

Mottke felt the soft pocketbook in his hand. A warm excited feeling rose to his heart: "Money!"

He made off with the pocketbook.

CHAPTER XXV

*

Mottke Comes Into Money

HE ran to the stable and looked at the pocketbook by the light of the lantern. When he opened it he went rigid with fear: it was stuffed with notes. He couldn't think what to do with it. Then he remembered a trick of Nussen the Thief. He took down a horse-collar that was hanging on the wall, found a hole in it, pushed the pocketbook deep in among the straw, and hung the collar up in its place again.

That done, he stretched himself out on a heap of straw and began to think. He was suddenly filled with rage and felt he wanted to beat himself. He was angry with everybody, but most of all with himself. But a still deeper feeling, a feeling that nothing mattered, came over him then, and he did not care in the least what was going to happen. He was prepared for anything. Then a strange thought came into his mind: he would take out the pocketbook again, climb into the room, and fling it into Mary's face. But then he considered whether it wouldn't be better to give the money to Dwoirele, in such a way that Mary would see him doing it. But thereupon he told himself:

"It would be a pity to waste the money. Let it stay hidden."

He felt completely indifferent to Mary now. And to Kanarik too. All at once his life with the tumblers seemed stale and he began to think of ways of escape.

But then his blood boiled and he was furious at himself. Should he go up there again, give her a thrashing, bash her face till it bled and then go off? It wouldn't be worth while. He had no interest in her now. But the money counted for something. "It's a good thing to have money," he told himself. "If you have money you can go where you like and buy what you like."

And suddenly the money in the horse-collar became very precious to him. He wanted to take it out again, look at it and count it. But he was afraid some one might come upon him, so he restrained himself. And then there woke in him, just as suddenly, a curiously strong feeling for Mary; but it was quite different from his former one. Now Mary was only an object through which he could get hold of money. And he was surprised that he had never realized that before.

Then he thought how differently he and Kanarik were dressed. Kanarik had beautiful top-boots with patent leather uppers, and a velvet waistcoat too, while he wore old torn shoes that had once belonged to the witch and trousers with a tear in the bottom. Kanarik drank beer and ate ices whenever he took a fancy for them, and he, Mottke, never had a groat to bless himself with except when he pinched a kopek now and then out of the money that was thrown to him when he played the barrel-organ, or when the old woman gave him something for scratching her back before she went to sleep. And he marveled that he had never noticed all this before and never felt ashamed of going about in women's shoes and torn trousers.

"First of all I'll get myself a pair of top-boots that squeak when you walk, and a pair of black velvet trousers like old Terach's. I'll carry a long whip in my hand, and I'll wear my hair long in front and part it. I'll show them how an artist should look!"

The longer he pursued these thoughts the dearer Mary grew to him; for she had given him the possibility of fulfilling all his desires and would certainly get more money for him when the next chance came. And suddenly he felt that she was his, that she belonged to him just as a cart or a horse might belong to him. Of course she belonged to him!

All that he marveled at now was that he had never realized this before and had let her give all the money she earned to Kanarik. "That'll have to change! This money belongs to me. I'll fight Kanarik for it."

Then a great din rose outside. There was shouting, screaming and sounds of dissension. Loud steps came towards the stable. A beam of light appeared through a crack in the wooden door. But Mottke felt quite indifferent. At the moment he had no wish but to fight with somebody. He shut his eyes and waited. Then some one knocked on the door.

"Open, you little fool, open the door!"

Mottke remained calmly lying where he was.

"Open the door, you fool, open!"

Mottke recognized old Terach's voice. He was fond of the old man and grateful to him for having taken him into the troupe and teaching him the work. He actually felt something almost like reverence for the old boy. So he got up and opened the door.

"Where have you put the purse the girl gave you?" Kanarik shouted at him.

"Don't shout like that. Let me talk to him," said the old man soothingly. "Listen, you young rascal," he said, turning to Mottke, and his voice sounded almost indulgent. "Give the purse back. The Goy is making a row, he says he's going to call in the police and then we'll all be in the soup."

"A purse? What purse?" asked Mottke with surprise.

"The purse that Mary stole out of the Pole's pocket and slipped to you," retorted Kanarik.

"She never gave me any purse. I know nothing about it," replied Mottke shortly.

"All right, you come inside with us," they cried, dragging him along with them.

Dwoirele was standing in the "dark chamber" wringing her hands. The tumblers would bring her to ruin, she kept on crying, the police would be there in a minute and shut up her hotel.

Mary stood in the middle of the room in her petticoat, her hair in disorder. Her arms and neck were bare, and her breast gleamed through her thin chemise. She was quite calm and bore carelessly the glances which the wagoners, the fish-vendors and the butchers flung at her. They had crowded into the room when they heard the Pole shouting that he had been robbed of eighty-five roubles. The Pole himself wasn't in the room; he had gone to the police-station to fetch the inspector.

"She's worth the money, as true as I live!" said the butcher, who had been staring at the girl for a long time with the air of a judge.

"Hm, I'd rather get myself a new horse with all that money. But I would like fine to give her a little treat," said Jankel the carrier.

The others laughed.

Then the old tumbler and Kanarik entered, dragging Mottke after them.

"Here he comes, the right one!"

Old Terach drove out the strangers, shut the door behind them, and turned to Mottke:

"Listen, you young rascal, give over that money or else I'll hand you over to the police, as sure as I'm a Jew! I'll tell them, too, that you ran away from jail. You haven't a pass and I don't even know who your father was. Give back the money and then everything will be as it was before. If you don't it will be worse for you."

"You just hand me over to the police! I don't care! If you do I'll tell them that you stole the girl from her boozer of a father, and beat her when she won't do what you ask her. And I'll tell them that you deal in stolen goods and that you've let Dwoirele have the silver candlesticks the people gave us in Schochlin to keep for them, and that we're only stopping here because you're waiting for a dealer from Warsaw that sells things that go on two legs. And I've more to tell them still, and after that we'll all find ourselves in the lock-up. It'll be pleasanter if we're all there together."

"What are you talking about? What story is this you're inventing? Who would believe what you're saying?" said the old tumbler, trembling from head to foot. He was amazed that Mottke should know all these things, when they had always been careful in front of him and thought he had seen and heard nothing.

"What silver candlesticks do you mean?" cried Dwoirele, who had turned pale. "Who told you that story? My brother sent me fish from Schochlin, but I've never even heard of your candlesticks. Just come into my room and then you'll see for yourself, the box is still standing there!"

"Fish! I know what kind of fish it was!"

"Mottke, what are you saying? That I should hear such

words from you! Who's been telling you all these lies?" said the old woman, clasping her hands.

Mottke looked her in the eye and couldn't help laughing.

"And you've taken up with this little rascal, this public nuisance who can do nothing but twist hens' necks, eh, you tightrope dancer, you fine artist? You steal money and then slip it to him behind my back, eh?" said Kanarik. He walked up to Mary, glared at her furiously, and raised his hand.

The girl shrank back in fear, her eyes blinking in expectation of the blow.

"You touch her! You just try! I would like to see you doing it. You wouldn't do it again!" shouted Mottke, holding his clenched fist under Kanarik's nose.

"What? You'll forbid me, maybe? Well, there's one for you." Kanarik struck Mary in the face. "And there's one for . . ."

But before Kanarik could bring down his fist, Mottke sprang on his shoulders and began to throttle him. He bit into Kanarik's throat with his teeth until the veins swelled and swelled so that they looked as if they were going to burst. Kanarik tried to free himself but collapsed with the pain and fell to the floor. Mottke lay on him, still sticking fast to his throat with his teeth and beating him on the face with his fists. The women began to scream and tried to separate the gladiators. But whenever they came near they were struck by the men's feet and had to retreat again. The old tumbler snatched up his whip in desperation and belabored Mottke with it. Beneath the blows Mottke's hands and face began to swell up, but he felt nothing. He stuck to Kanarik with his teeth. Then Kanarik began to rattle in his throat and almost stopped breathing. At last Dwoirele, who had been looking on helplessly, tore open the door and shouted for her friends the wagoners:

"Murder! Murder! They're ruining me! The police are coming!"

The wagoners rushed in and separated the two lads with their cudgels. Kanarik was bleeding from several wounds and Mottke's face was black and blue.

During the whole battle Mary had stood calmly at the window looking on. No feeling could be seen in her face. But when Mottke flung Kanarik to the floor and began to belabor him with his fists an almost imperceptible smile appeared on her lips. She knew that as a result of this fight she would change her masters, and she was glad of it.

After that, Mary was Mottke's uncontested property.

CHAPTER XXVI

*

Where Is Your Pass?

Soon afterwards the police inspector appeared along with the Pole who had lost his purse. That gentleman—in his agitation he had forgotten to put on his collar and tie—told the police with tears in his eyes of the calamity that had befallen him; a purse with eighty-five roubles in it had been filched from his pocket, and he pointed at Mary and Mottke. The inspector, a squat little man in the sixties, with a red neck, an enormous belly and a long fair beard ending in two sharp points, listened calmly with a pacific smile. The whole business seemed to leave him cold. Then, still with the same indulgent smile, he turned to Dwoirele:

"What! Panie Spassvogel, so you're in the wars again? Whenever anything happens in this town it's sure to be at The Imperial."

"The Imperial? But Herr Commissar!" cried Dwoirele in assumed amazement, smiling coquettishly at the inspector. "You will have your joke. Good heavens, what a fright I am!" she said, raising her round arms seductively and patting her hair. "What can I do if this gentleman"—she pointed at the Pole—"insists on hobnobbing with the artists and getting one of their girls to love him? My hotel is open to everybody. I can't forbid a gentleman to enter if he wants to. What can I do?"

"We'll look into that later. First of all, I want to see everybody's pass. Herr Showman, bring me your pass and the passes of your troupe."

"At once, Herr Commissar, at once!" replied the old man.

"But the Herr Commissar mustn't sit here! It's so un-
comfortable and so untidy. Will the Herr Commissar be
good enough to come with me to my room at the back? He
can listen in comfort there to everything that has happened,"
said Dwoirele, taking the Herr Commissar by the arm.

"Oh, one can do one's duty here quite well, one's duty
to the law," said the Herr Commissar, but he got up, made
a sign to the old tumbler and said: "You follow me."

In the dark passage there was a whispered conversation
between Dwoirele and the inspector:

"Frau Dwoirele, it won't do, I really can't. You know
yourself—the law! The gentleman is a personage, he'll complain about me. It might cost me my post."

Dwoirele replied briefly:

"Herr Commissar, you're the boss in this town. What you
say goes. I don't need to tell you that. I leave myself entirely
in your hands."

As she said this something gleamed in the darkness and
vanished into the hand of the Herr Commissar. He felt it
with his fingers to find out how much it was. When he was
convinced that the coin was adequate to his rank and station
he declared once more that he could do nothing and dropped
it into his trouser pocket.

They entered Dwoirele's room, which was neat and clean.
Against the wall stood two beds with white coverlets; there
was a mahogany table in the middle of the room and a
cupboard with glass doors in a corner containing silver nick-
nacks. Here the Herr Commissar felt much better. He seated
himself comfortably at the table. Dwoirele begged him to
try a bit of newly cooked fish. The Herr Commissar de-
clined:

"The law requires me! The law comes first."

Dwoirele opened the door and shouted to her father:

"Father, bring the Herr Commissar a real tasty bit of that carp."

In a jiffy Chaim Spassvogel elbowed his way through the crowd that filled the room and set something that steamed on a plate before the inspector.

"Ah! It's Herr Spassvogel! How are you? I haven't seen you for a long time," said the inspector.

"Herr Commissar, I advise you to try this fish. I bet you've never eaten anything better in your life. It melts in your mouth!" said Chaim Spassvogel, smacking his lips.

"Very well, we'll try it, Herr Spassvogel, trying can't do anybody any harm," said the inspector, pulling the plate nearer to him. "Really excellent!" he said appreciatively, and fell to with gusto.

All this time the artists stood with uncovered heads by the door; old Terach held the papers ready in his hand. The Pole stood by the window and waited. They all looked on while the Herr Commissar ate his fish, and their mouths watered.

After the fish Dwoirele brought in fried giblets and Chaim Spassvogel followed her with all sorts of tit-bits. The tumblers swallowed with emotion at this sight, and the wagoners in the taproom next door cursed enviously over the Herr Commissar's banquet.

"Well, now, let me see your papers," said the inspector, when he had finished off the fish and prepared to start on the giblets.

"Here is the pass for me, my wife and my two children. I'm Gedalje Schabassnik, this is my wife Chaje Schabassnik, and this is my daughter Chane Schabassnik, nineteen years old," old Terach pointed at Mary. "And here," pointing at Mottke, "is my youngest son, Note Schabassnik. And this is the pass of my premier artist, Aaron-Meier Kanarik."

"Aaron-Meier Kanarik. Hm.... Good, very good." The Herr Commissar contentedly turned to his giblets, smacking his lips voluptuously. "Good, very good. Aaron-Meier Kanarik. All right. Everything in order. And what is this here?"

"This is the permit to display my art publicly, signed by the Herr Government Secretary in Warsaw," said the old man, pointing at the signature with his finger. "It cost me a mint of money, but I got it from the Herr Government Secretary's own hand!"

"Good! Very good!" said the Herr Commissar, looking at the paper without letting himself be disturbed in his enjoyment of the giblets. "And what else have you got?"

"This here is a letter from a colonel. The signature means 'Russian Imperial Colonel.' He wrote to my daughter. 'Dear Mary,' he called her. He writes that he has fallen in love with her art and completely lost his heart to her. He says that he'll get an order of merit for her from the Ministry," said old Terach, handing the letter to the inspector with a proud gesture.

"From a real colonel! An important document!" The inspector pushed his plate away and held the letter up to the lamp. "Right enough! 'Russian Imperial Colonel!' Keep that carefully, it's an important document." He handed the letter back to the old man. "So he's going to wangle an order of merit for her, eh?" he asked, pointing at Mary. "Bravo! She deserves it. Good. Everything in order. What have you got against these people, sir?" he asked, turning to the Pole, who was standing meekly in a corner to show that he had good manners and didn't interrupt people when they were conversing or eating. "What have you got against them? They're decent people. Have you seen this letter that the girl got from a Russian Imperial Colonel?"

"But they've robbed me! Sneaked eighty-five roubles from

me! It was these two!" screamed the Pole, pointing at Mottke and Mary.

"First of all, what business had you with these people?" said the Herr Commissar, getting up and walking up to the Pole. "How dare you approach a lady that gets love letters from a Russian Imperial Colonel? Did the Herr Colonel give you his permission? Or had you mine? In the second place, you've insulted a lady, an artist who has imperial orders and corresponds with highly placed personages. Do you know that they may bring you before the court for doing such a thing? In the third place, you say your money has been stolen. Who stole it? This lady perhaps? No! I could never believe such a thing! A lady who gets letters from a colonel steal a strange man's money out of his pocket! Or did that lad over there do it?" He pointed at Mottke. "Why, he's only a child! Have you seen his pass? He's just sixteen past. Do you mean to tell me that he violently wrested the money from you, a strong and powerful man like you? You needn't tell me such fairy-tales! But we'll search him if you like. Come here, boy," he said, turning to Mottke.

Mottke walked up to the inspector, smiling and assured.

"Well, look in his pockets, feel his clothes!" said the Herr Commissar, beginning to rummage in Mottke's pockets. "Well, where has he got your money? He never stole it. You've falsely accused innocent people, whose papers are quite in order."

"And fourthly," he continued in a lower voice, "when one visits a whore one doesn't take a well-filled purse with one. Besides," he added in a louder voice, pointing solemnly at the old tumbler, "these people's papers are in order. Now what about yourself? Show me your papers. Who are you, anyway? Have you got a pass?"

CHAPTER XXVII

*

Mottke Makes War on the World

MOTTKE was lying in the caravan watching over the horses. It was a clear starry summer night. He couldn't sleep. A feeling of dejection filled him, a feeling he had never known before. As he lay there all his life went by before him. He saw himself as a little boy being chased for stealing something or other, lying behind the wood pile, and then living alone in the fields like an animal. He regretted nothing and he didn't fear what the future held for him. Things were as they were and so they would remain. But now he suddenly began to wonder about the meaning, the goal of life. For the first time he thought of the future, and decided that it mustn't roll by as the past had done, but must be guided by him. Was it the money in the horse-collar that put him up to such thoughts? No, not so much the money as the pass that Kanarik had shown to the police inspector. That pass made Mottke brood over the purpose of life. That pass of Kanarik stuck fast in his memory. There in black and white were the words "Aaron-Meier Kanarik," and because of them Kanarik was a free and independent human being. But what was Mottke? Where was his place in the world?

He envied Kanarik his pass with which he could go where he liked, because of which he could leave the old tumbler whenever it pleased him. But he, Mottke, was bound hand and foot. If he ever dared to leave the old man, the first policeman he met could ask him for his pass and have him arrested. Old Terach had him in the hollow of his hand, and yet nobody could say anything to him if he gave him the sack.

"You haven't even a pass...." He saw through the old man's words perfectly. Old Terach could even have him arrested as a vagrant!

"I must get a pass! Without a pass you're nobody!" he decided.

But where was he to get one? If he went back to his own town he would simply be arrested. It was possible, of course, that they weren't looking for him still, but it was equally possible that they were. In any case, he was convinced that if he ever returned they would put their hand on him at once. Even if he had nothing to fear—what he had done to his foster-sister Chanele before he left didn't seem serious enough for them to put him in prison for it—even if his conscience was clear, he told himself that they were bound to arrest him straight away and chuck him into prison. They didn't need any particular pretext to do that! And he himself had no real objection to their doing it. Things were just like that....

He found himself in a state of war with the whole world. Consequently he believed that he had the right to do anything he wanted or was able to do against the world, without further excuse. But he allowed the same right to it as far as he was concerned. He had no intention of coming to terms with the world. "That's how things stand, and that's how they'll always stand."

While he was lying on the straw, thinking such things, he heard some one stealing up to the caravan. Something white gleamed in the starshine. He recognized Mary. He lay still and waited.

When Mary had climbed into the caravan and he could

hear the rustling of her feet in the straw, he called out roughly:

"Who's there?"

"Hush, don't shout, Mottke! They might hear. It's me, Mary."

"What do you want?" asked Mottke.

"Mottke, why, don't you know me?" asked Mary awkwardly.

"No. Go to your Kanarik, he'll know you all right."

Mary stopped as if some one had hit her. Ever since she had handed the money to him and he had fought with Kanarik for her, she had not exchanged a single word with him. He avoided her and never looked at her, although he forbade Kanarik to touch her, and made it clear to him that Mary was his property now. Yet he paid no attention to her and didn't even speak to her. This completely puzzled Mary, so that she didn't know where she was. She thought it queer that Mottke should forbid Kanarik to touch her and yet never came near her himself. On the top of this she had fallen madly in love with him after he beat Kanarik. Now she, who had been run after by him, came running after him, and this was her reception! She turned to go. For a few minutes she fought with herself, but her "homelessness" since he had taken her from Kanarik held her fast.

"Why are you like this to me? I gave you all the money I stole from that man. Why do you drive me away?"

"And what about it if you gave me all the money? Do you expect me to thank you for it? You should have given it to Kanarik. He would have loved you for it. But if you want it back, it's over there in the horse-collar. Take it and go to your Kanarik!"

Mottke's feelings towards Mary were very curious. Since

he had surprised her with the Pole she attracted him more than ever, but his love for her was suddenly gone, leaving in its place a desire for revenge, an angry passion that he hid from her. But, since she had given him the money, he was her master and he looked on her as his property. She looked on herself as that, too. That seemed to her a matter of course.

Mary was silent for a while, and thought to herself how she could win him back to her. He did not look at her, but whistled to himself. Then she said:

"Kanarik is always following me about. He wants me to go back to him. He says he'll do anything for me and give me anything if I'll only take him back."

"You just try, and I'll give you both a proper tanning with the whip."

"He keeps watching me all night to see that I don't go to you. I would have come to you long ago, but he won't leave me alone. He's threatened to beat me."

"What? He won't let you alone?" Mottke jumped up. "Well, we'll see about that in a minute!"

"Yes, he keeps watching me. With his whip in his hand! He's been trying to get me to leave the troupe with him. He wants me to go to Warsaw with him. He knows of a place there where we could make a lot of money."

"Run away? And what did you say?"

"You see for yourself that I wouldn't listen to him, seeing I've come to you and told you!"

Mottke thought for a while. Then his voice changed; it became softer and more thoughtful.

"Come here."

With a leap Mary was beside him. Mottke seized her and pressed her to him. Then by the dim light of the stars he looked deep into her eyes.

"Since I saw you with the Pole I haven't been able to bear the sight of you!" he cried, but then drew her gently on to his knees.

"Come, Mary. There! Just sit and don't say anything. I've something important to tell you. Listen and don't say anything. Will you run away with me? Why should we waste our time here slaving for the old man? You make all their money for them and you haven't even a decent dress. Just look at what you're wearing now."

"Mottke, Mottke, my life, my only love!" There were tears in Mary's eyes. She took his hand and pressed it to her lips.

"Be quiet. Listen. I've thought it all out. I'm going. If you like you can come with me. You'll be with me and I'll see nobody touches you. Nobody."

"Listen, Mottke, I want to tell you something," she whispered. "There was a dealer from Warsaw here a little time ago. He gave me his address. He's been trying for a long time to get me to run away and come to him in Warsaw. He's got a business there, and if I go he says I can make a lot of money. Here's the address, I've been wearing it next to my skin."

She pulled a crumpled visiting-card out of her blouse.

"Keep it safe, Mary, keep it safe! It may come in useful. And now listen. Hold yourself ready to run away with me. I've only got to wait for one thing now. Do you hear?"

"Yes, Mottke, dear, dear Mottke. I'll do anything you ask me, anything."

CHAPTER XXVIII

*

Judgment on Mottke

A FEW weeks later—it was towards the beginning of autumn
—old Terach with his troupe went to Lowitch for the great
annual fair. There were a great number of other tumblers
in Lowitch at the time, and they all camped in a big meadow
behind the cattle market, in tents or in their caravans. The
horses grazed together near a neighboring wood. Fires burned
in front of the tents. And in the smoke from the caravan
chimneys and these camp-fires, half-naked children played
about, and all sorts of outlandish animals nibbled the grass.
The old and respected proprietors of the shows sat about
bargaining with one another. Horses, circus animals, and
sometimes even human beings who could go through certain
tricks were bartered and sold there.

At Lowitch Mottke came to know the whole artist world,
and the various companies and showmen. And they all examined this new addition to their number with great
curiosity.

But Mottke showed very little interest in his professional
colleagues. He had made up his mind to leave and turn his
back on them. But Kanarik was acquainted with them all,
and on intimate terms with many of them, and drank with
them in the local pub.

On the first day of the fair, before old Terach's troupe
had even appeared before the public, Mottke presented himself in a new outfit from head to foot. He had got himself

new boots, a white flannel suit and a cap with a leather
peak.

All the artists came over to admire him, and tried to
reckon what the outfit had cost. They asked themselves in
whispers how he could have got hold of so much money,
and old Terach sighed loudly and said, so that everybody
could hear:

"All with my money, my hard-earned pennies! The boy
simply stole the money and kept it to himself."

Soon it was no secret that Mottke had got eighty-five
roubles out of Kanarik's "girl," which she had earned
from a Pole in Schochlin. So everybody was agog to see
him in the new clothes that he had bought with the money.
The young blades winked at Kanarik and chaffed him.

"All with your money, Kanarik, what?"

"A fine figure you cut, Kanarik! Your girl works for you
and another fellow pockets the takings."

"Stand a round of beer, you dandy!" cried one of the lads,
turning to Mottke.

Mottke smilingly pushed his way out of the circle and
shouted for Mary. She threw a wrap round her shoulders
and he went off with her towards the market-place.

Kanarik turned pale and bit his lips with rage. His throat
was dry. He had hated Mottke ever since Mottke had filched
Mary from him, and kept thinking and thinking of some
means to unseat the "rascal" from his place of power.

But he could do nothing against him. Old Terach secretly
supported him, first because he expected great things of
him, and secondly because the boy cost him nothing in
money. He looked on him as his property, for he knew
that without a pass Mottke was powerless. Kanarik, on the
other hand, drew his wages and could leave him at any time
and set up as a rival.

With a sore heart Kanarik looked on while Mottke supplanted him. He saw Mary stealing every night to the fellow, but he dared do nothing, for she was under Mottke's protection. And Kanarik was afraid of Mottke.

Yes, he had to admit it, he was afraid of Mottke. And Mottke had flouted him before all his friends, though they knew him and prized him as a capable artist. This young greenhorn had come and snapped his girl away from him before the whole world. He would have liked to rush at him and batter him senseless, but he controlled himself, for he had made up his mind to set a trap for the rascal.

"What's up with you? What game is this lad playing with you, Kanarik?"

"And you let a smout like that trample on you! Why don't you let him have it?" cried Welwel the conjuror, by profession a knife-swallower and fire-eater, the star turn in the troupe of Schloime the Bastard.

"Be a man! Have a go at him, anyway."

"If you want to risk your limbs, then do, certainly. You'll find yourself on your back as soon as you smell his fist," said old Terach proudly.

"What! That smout?"

"Yes, that smout!" retorted the old man calmly, with a dignified air.

"Where did you pick him up? Is he really a good worker?" asked Schloime the Bastard. He was blind in one eye and was greatly respected by all the artists.

"The boy is a discovery of mine. I happened to hear of him when he was quite a little chap, and said to myself, this boy will be an eye-opener, I'll take any bet you like that he'll put down Byshko, the Polish strong man. I'm taking him to Warsaw to put him up against Byshko," the old man bragged, passing one hand over his oily gray hair, while the other played with the gold chain that dangled on his fat belly.

"A nice fairy-tale to tell people! Why, the brat came running after us only a year or two ago; he's a bastard, a stray dog, a runaway, a nobody!" shouted Kanarik.

"Well, I'll knock the stuffing out of him some day, you wait," said Welwel the conjuror.

"Did you see the sniffy way he goes about with his nose in the air? He'll have to be given a good dressing down," said another lad belonging to Schloime's troupe; he was the "musician," that is, he carried a barrel organ on his belly and a drum and cymbals on his back, and by moving his foot rang a peal of bells that was fastened to his hat.

"He'll get his, you wait!" said Welwel with a final gesture of his hand. Then he drew Kanarik aside and consulted with him in a low voice.

"We'll see what you can do! But I fancy he'll be too much for you," said old Terach, who was proud of his Mottke.

All this time Mottke was innocently strolling through the fair with Mary. He stopped before a stand that sold colored ribbons. Mary picked up one or two and looked at them. She liked them.

"Have them, Mary, have them! There, have this, too." He pushed an apron into her hands and turned to the woman who owned the stand: "How much?"

Mottke never haggled. He pulled a handful of silver out of the pocket of his new suit and gave it to the woman. Then he led Mary to a stand where there were colored silk scarves.

"Well, Mary, how would you like this one? Take it, it suits you down to the ground." And he promptly paid for it.

Mary threw it round her shoulders and laughingly fol-

lowed him from stand to stand. Then her eyes were caught
by a pair of shoes with red heels.

"I say, Mary, how would you like these shoes?"

He bought them and went on. He led her over to a booth
where coral necklaces were sold. The annual fair at Lowitch
is renowned for its beautiful necklaces of red stones, amber
and Venetian glass; they are worn by the girls of the place.

Mottke hung several of these chains round Mary's neck
and then led her over to a stand of colored woolen stuffs.
In the evening they made their way back. He was smoking
a cigar with his hands in the pockets of his new trousers;
his patent leather boots shone. Mary was nibbling chocolates
and had both hands full of packages. The lads of the guild
were waiting for them. As soon as they saw Mottke they
hastily closed round him.

"Will you stand a round of beer, you fine dandy?" asked
Welwel the conjuror.

"None of us know whether you're a real artist that can
do an honest bit of work, or a dud. We hear lots about you
but never see you," added Schloime the Bastard.

Mottke smiled good-naturedly.

"If you're thirsty, come along to the pub."

"That's the way to talk! That's a lad!" cried Schloime,
and he clapped Mottke with his open hand, which was hard
as a board, on the top of the head.

Mottke looked at him in surprise and couldn't make out
whether the blow was meant in jest or in earnest. But as
Schloime was smiling, he smiled too, although the blow was
painful.

"Perhaps a tankard of beer will make you dizzy?" asked
Welwel the conjuror.

Mottke saw now that they were up to some trick with

him, but he was ashamed to retreat in case they should
think he was afraid of them. So he answered:

"Don't you worry about me! If you have a thirst, come
along to the pub."

And he went ahead with long strides.

"Mottke, don't go, don't go! They'll do something to
you!" cried Mary, running after the men.

"See how anxious his girl is about him! Don't you fear,
my duckie, who wants to hurt him?" replied Schloime.

"Go home, Mary, don't you worry about me, don't you
worry! They won't do anything to me," Mottke shouted
at her.

He saw that he had fallen into a trap, but it was too late
now. He couldn't turn back. He daren't show at any price
that he was afraid. So he prepared for battle. First he
looked in his pockets for something that would do as a
weapon but he found nothing, and that saddened him.
All the same he didn't lose courage, and he shouted angrily
at Mary, who was still following him up:

"Go home. Go home this minute! Else I'll smash your jaw
for you!"

"Good lad! That's the style! That'll teach her to interfere in men's affairs!" cried Welwel.

When they reached the pub outside the town Schloime
led them into a private room. The first thing that Mottke
saw there was Kanarik sitting at a table along with a few
other young lads. They were drinking beer and talking
loudly.

As soon as Kanarik and his friends saw Mottke they fell
silent and stared at him. In a cheerful voice he ordered
three glasses of beer and sat down with his escort at another
table. Nobody spoke. Then some one shouted from Kanarik's
table:

"So that's the fine customer that pinched his friend's girl! That's him, eh?"

"Yes, that's him!" replied the others.

Mottke glanced round for some handy weapon. But the table was bare. The beer he had ordered hadn't arrived yet. He thought of dashing over to the counter to arm himself with a tankard for all eventualities. But before he could get to his feet a tall lad with red eyes and a freckled face stood before him. He had never seen him before in his life.

"Listen, you little smout! Did you have the nerve to pinch an artist's girl?"

"What do you want? What business is it of yours?" asked Mottke calmly, but he grew pale. His hands were trembling, for he had nothing in them to defend himself with.

"What do I want? I've got a watching brief."

"What's that? A watching brief?"

"What is it? That!"

And before Mottke had time to see what was happening he got a terrific blow that covered his face with blood. His eyes and ears seemed to be filled with blood, so that he couldn't see or hear. He prepared to rush at the tall lad, but everybody in the room fell upon him at once, and blows rained down on every inch of his body. At first he struggled in silence, for he was ashamed of crying out. But when he saw that he was in a hole he began to yell in a terrific voice, so that he could be heard far and wide.

Then they took him and flung him in a corner. There he lay as if he were dead. He made no movement, but only gasped and panted. His face, his suit, and the floor under him were covered with blood, so that you could hardly tell one from the other.

The lads stopped beating him then, but Kanarik still

went on belaboring him and after that pulled his new boots off his feet. He prepared to take the new suit as well, but it was completely ruined with blood. He looked in Mottke's pockets and found about twenty roubles; he divided this among his friends. And so he had his revenge for his insulted feelings and got rid of the rage that had boiled in him for so long.

"Let him be now. He won't forget his lesson!" said Welwel the conjuror, dragging Kanarik away.

Mary was standing at the door. When she heard Mottke's shouts she began to scream still louder:

"Help! Help! Murder!"

"Haul her inside or else she'll bring everybody here."

Two of the lads rushed at her, dragged her into the room and closed her mouth with their hands.

Mary struggled and tried to free herself. They tore her clothes from her back, reduced her blouse to tatters and banged her on the head.

Then Schloime the Bastard took her hand, looked her up and down and flung a filthy term at her. Thereupon he led her across to where Mottke was lying in his corner like a heap of bloodstained rags and said:

"Do you see him? Do you want the same thing to happen to you? Go to Kanarik, and in future give him the money that you make. He's your master and you're his property. You'll give him all you make, if you don't want to get the same dose as him!"

But Mary wasn't listening. As soon as he let her go she flung herself down beside Mottke. With her new silk wrap —it was torn to tatters now—she began to wipe the blood from his face.

"Mottke, dear, darling Mottke, what have they done to you?" she sobbed.

"Go away... Go..." Mottke muttered, grinding his teeth.

But he had no need to tell her to go. One of the others took her by the hair, pulled her to her feet and with all his might flung her at Kanarik, who was gloomily sitting at a table. But Kanarik flung her back again. And then she got two hard bangs on the head from behind,

CHAPTER XXIX

*

Mottke Leaves the Tumblers

As Kanarik had prophesied, they brought Mottke back on a stretcher and laid him down on it before old Terach's tent. The old man was furious and cursed and swore at them for settling their score with the boy just before the fair; but that meant a loss in the takings. But he could do nothing: for the time being Kanarik had the upper hand. Actually Mottke's misfortune didn't move the old fellow very deeply.

"The rascal deserved all hè got. Some one had to teach him to be respectful to his elders. Now he'll know that it isn't the thing to pinch a girl from an older lad."

Mottke lay where he was without stirring. His faint breathing showed that he was still alive, but that was all. They were afraid of sending for a doctor. The tumblers didn't like strangers to be mixed up in their affairs, which they liked to keep to themselves. But the women, led by the witch, took pity on Mottke, washed the blood from his body, anointed his head wounds with a healing salve, and rubbed his bruises with a home-made drench that they used for their horses.

For several days Mottke lay where he was without stirring. The women brought him milk and water. Sometimes he drank, but generally he wouldn't look at anything they brought him, and it seemed doubtful whether he was going to live. Old Terach threatened the offenders with the police,

saying that they had ruined his best performer out of professional jealousy. But Kanarik paid no attention to these
threats. For since he had given Mottke his lesson he was
not only absolute lord of Mary again, but the most in-
fluential member of the troupe, and old Terach was secretly
terrified that the lout might seize control of the company
and reduce himself, in his old age, to the status of an em-
ployee.

But after a few days Mottke rose from his bed, and without any one's help crept into the caravan. After that he
anointed his wounds himself. But he was still very weak,
and so he had to submit to Kanarik and do everything that
Kanarik told him. He saw Kanarik ordering Mary about,
saw him forcing her to go with him and beating her when
she refused.

Mottke held his tongue. But he studied Kanarik's face as
if he wanted to imprint it deeply on his memory. He followed every movement of his enemy as if he wanted to
counterfeit him later, perhaps when he was no longer alive.
He drank in all that he could see and hear of Kanarik.

Meantime he was getting better and better. Soon he was
able to go about again and took little strolls in front of the
caravan. Kanarik swore at him for idling.

"Take a barrel organ and go out on the roads."

The witch put in a plea for the boy:

"Leave him in peace! Why, he can hardly move yet!"

"The devil run away with him! Are we to feed the idler?
He's got to earn his keep."

Mottke turned pale, shrank aside as if he were afraid
of a blow, but said nothing, and simply kept looking into
Kanarik's face.

At night, when Mary stole to him and clasped him in her

arms and kissed him and dropped tears on his wounded head, he whispered to her:

"Go away, Mary! Go! Kanarik may find you."

"He can kill me if he likes! I shan't leave you."

"I'm no use now. They've done for me."

"I'm yours, whatever becomes of you."

"If that's true, then listen carefully," he began suddenly, and his eyes glittered. "Get Kanarik to run away with you. . . ."

"Kanarik? I don't want to run away with him, I want to be with you."

"Do what I tell you. Get Kanarik to run away with you. Tell him that you love him only, and that you'd like to go away with him. Don't ask me any more now. I want you to do this."

"All right, Mottke."

"And when he agrees, tell me."

"All right, Mottke."

"But don't say a word about it to anybody, if you want to save us both."

"All right, Mottke."

"Go now. And don't forget what I've told you."

"I won't forget."

Autumn was over. The tumblers could not travel from town to town in their caravan now: it was too cold. Old Terach decided to spend the winter in a little town with a showman he knew. The great fair at Lowitch, the last of the season, hadn't come up to his expectations, for Mottke lay sick and Mary performed badly. She had fallen once or twice from the tightrope and didn't want to appear at all. So old Terach crossly packed up his things and left Lowitch earlier than usual, for he wanted to try one or two smaller towns before the coming of winter.

In one of these small towns Mary told Mottke that Kanarik had instructed her to smuggle a basket with their clothes out of the caravan and give it into his hands. Mottke was greatly elated by the news. The moment had come at last. He helped Mary to get the basket out of the caravan, and asked her to steal after Kanarik to see where he hid it. Kanarik took the basket to a village near by and gave it into the hands of a peasant, engaging a horse and cart at the same time. Then he arranged with Mary that as soon as she heard his whistle that night she was to climb out of her window. He would be waiting for her in the main road. From there he would take her to a peasant's house, and the peasant would drive them to the nearest railway station.

That day Mottke took a walk to the village. He impressed the road on his mind, and a stream that ran through a little wood near by; its banks were overgrown with shrubs. He stopped there for some time and thought deeply. He chose the place where the shrubs and bushes were thickest, and cut a notch on a tree to mark it. For a long time he gazed at the tree, the stones, the road, then went over to the stream again and glanced down into it. The bottom was covered with mud and slime, and long thin reeds rose above the green surface. He saw that the bank was almost covered with burdocks and thorns, and his thoughts took a direction that could not be called edifying. He whistled to himself and returned to the caravan, bending forward, looking feeble and sad, as if he were still suffering from his wounds. When he came to the caravan he scratched his head and muttered something to himself.

"What's up, you young bastard?" asked old Terach. He

was sitting before the caravan on a chest warming himself in the October sun.

"I must leave you," said Mottke in a low voice.

"Wha—at? Where are you going?"

"I can't do the work here any longer. They've done for me. I can't sit at your table and eat you out of house and home. I'd rather go."

"But where? Who'll take you in in your state? Look how these villains have ruined the boy!"

"I want to go to the town. I'll learn a trade there. I want to be a cobbler like my father. I can't stay here any longer, anyway."

Soon everybody knew that Mottke was leaving the troupe. The witch crept out of the caravan; her face and hands were covered with soot from the kitchen fire. At hearing that Mottke was going she burst out crying and wiped her face on her dirty apron; it only rubbed the soot in still deeper. She cursed Kanarik and the other maltreaters of her Mottke and wept as bitterly as if the boy were dead.

Old Terach grew quite sad. He saw the end: Kanarik would either wrest control of the troupe from him or go away and leave him to destitution in his old age. He saw no way out. He didn't want to quarrel with Kanarik on Mottke's account; besides, he still hoped that after Mottke was gone Kanarik might settle down, and Mary too, and then everything would be as it was before.

So the old man began:

"If you want to go I can't keep you. But I haven't a pass to give you. I need it for the hand I'll have to take on in your place. I can't give you any money either. You've cost me a lot as it is. I had to pay up the eighty-five roubles that the girl stole. But I'll give you a little pocket money, so that you may have something to tide you over for the first few days. After that you'll have to look after yourself."

He pressed a few coins into Mottke's hand.

Mottke took the money and went into the caravan to gather his things.

"Hi! old girl, give him a couple of old shirts," old Terach shouted to his wife. He felt sorry for the boy.

Kanarik was highly pleased when he heard that Mottke was going. It fitted in splendidly with his plans. For now old Terach wouldn't know which of them Mary had run away with, and which to follow. So he shouted into the caravan in a condescending voice that couldn't hide his satisfaction:

"Give him one of my shirts, too. And a pair of old trousers, the devil take him!"

Mottke rolled up the things the old woman threw to him.

Mary sat before the mirror combing her hair and humming the Russian song:

> *"A thousand I've loved,*
> *A thousand I've forsaken,*
> *By one alone*
> *My heart is taken. . . ."*

Mottke crept out of the caravan, his bundle on his shoulder. He crawled along as if he were still very weak, his head hanging dejectedly. The old woman stood on the steps of the caravan crying and looking after him. The old man blinked his eyes to keep back a tear, and said with a sigh:

"That's what happens in our line, Mottke. Go back among ordinary folk, learn cobbling, perhaps you'll be a decent man yet."

Kanarik flung a silver half-rouble at him and shouted superciliously:

"Here! Catch!"

Mottke let the coin fall on the ground and stared intently at Kanarik's face for a last time. His glance was very serious. He seemed to be thinking deeply about something. Then he took the way to the town.

But when he was out of sight of the caravan he branched off in the direction of the wood.

CHAPTER XXX

*

Mottke Becomes Kanarik

MOTTKE walked to the wood, found the tree that he had marked, and lay down near it. The setting sun gilded the branches and threw a red film on the water of the stream. He began to feel queer. He thought of many things, but none of them had any connection with what he was to do that night. He longed for his mother, and wondered how things were going with her now. The grass, the wood and the stream called back to his mind the time when he had lived beside the river outside his own town. And he was happy, thinking he was free again and no longer a member of the troupe. He had completely forgotten the thing he was about to do, and felt he was back again in the days when he was a boy. He ate the bread the old woman had given him and enjoyed it. He would have liked to make a fire, but decided not to for fear it might be seen. Then he went over to the stream, intending to have a bathe. But when he looked down into it and saw the mud and slime a distant memory seemed to stir within him. All desire to bathe left him. He went into the wood and hid among the trees.

Darkness fell. The ground grew damp and cold. And in the dark he began to think of Kanarik and Mary. He grew very serious. He saw that he had no home and no place of refuge in the whole world. The only way out for him was to kill Kanarik that night. He did not hate Kanarik now, but simply looked upon him as an object that legitimately be-

198

longed to him and that he must use in such a way that it would get him a home and a roof for himself, instead of this dripping wood.

Kanarik himself was of no account, completely unimportant. As unimportant as if he had never known him, never seen him, never fought with him. Kanarik was a thing that must be thrown into the water with stones to keep it down, so that nobody might ever know where it lay. And to keep Kanarik from crying out and summoning people, a knife must be driven into his ribs under his armpit, quickly, so as to give him no time. All this must be done silently and skillfully, so that nobody would ever hear of it or know of it. The old tumbler and the witch must think that Kanarik was still alive, that he had decamped with Mary for good—oh, the old woman would fairly curse and swear! And all the time Kanarik would be lying deep in the water here among the mud and slime, and he himself, Mottke, would be on the train to Warsaw; he would have the girl and lots of money as well, and a genuine pass, and call himself Kanarik.

He shivered and felt that it must be very late. The October night fell in a cloud of dense moist darkness. It seemed to him that the wood was filled with prowling monsters. But he paid no attention to them and he felt no fear, only exasperation that the time dragged so slowly and that the pair never came. He was angry with Mary particularly, for he felt that she was to blame. The idea that Kanarik might be responsible for the delay never entered his head, for in his thoughts Kanarik had ceased by this time to exist as a living creature who could cause anything or be blamed for anything. He walked across to the road once or twice to have a look. The sky was overcast. Only when there was a rift in the clouds and a few stars gleamed through could he see the road at all. But the greater part of the sky was covered and the air seemed to be filled with some curious stuff that hid everything. Nothing to be seen on the road, neither man nor beast. It was a rough gravelly country road, a side road leading to the village.

Then his heart beat faster: he heard hasty steps and raised voices. He hurried back to the wood and stepped behind the tree he had marked. He listened. The voices came nearer and nearer through the misty darkness. Soon he recognized Mary's voice; she was talking loudly to announce their coming. Then he could distinguish Kanarik's voice as well; it was low and apprehensive:

"Don't talk so loud, we might be heard!"

Mottke was surprised that Kanarik could still speak. Hardly breathing, he stood behind the tree. The voices and footsteps grew louder and louder. Then a black patch flitted past him and the air seemed to stir. He had quite forgotten what he had to do, but now he remembered again.

The shadowy shape cried out:

"Help! Mother!"

Mottke shuddered at the word "Mother." He was amazed that this shadow could call out "Mother." But the shadow had him by the throat. That gave him the courage and strength to fight with it.

Then some one flung a cloth over the head of the shadow. The cloth and the trees stifled its cries. And when it stopped crying "Mother" in a human voice, and merely gave out a gurgling noise like an animal, Mottke at last summoned the strength to drive his knife into it as if it were a piece of wood. The only thing that surprised him was that something warm and sticky poured out of it and ran over his hands. It was a curiously pleasant sensation. But he had no time to think of that and the sensation passed away like a dream.

At last the black shadow stopped making a noise, fell down,
writhed for a little and was still—a dead object.

At that Mottke came to himself. He felt for the bundle
that Kanarik had on his back and handed it to Mary. Then
he took Kanarik by the feet and dragged him to the stream.
There he went through his pockets, but he found nothing.
He tore the cloth away, taking care not to look at the face,
and then tore off the shirt too. A little purse was bound
round Kanarik's neck, and inside was some money and a
pass wrapped up in paper. Mottke was greatly pleased with
the pass. He pocketed it and then fetched some stones that
he had laid ready. He wrapped Mary's cloak round Kanarik,
put the stones inside, and rolled him into the water among
the mud and slime. Kanarik disappeared.

Thereupon Mottke washed himself and ordered Mary to
do the same. Then he took off his torn jacket and boots,
made them into a bundle, weighted them with stones, too,
and flung them into the stream. In Kanarik's bundle he
found his own top-boots that he had been robbed of, and
Kanarik's new suit. He put on the boots. Then he put on the
suit, with red velvet waistcoat, stuck Kanarik's watch in the
pocket and fastened the heavy silver chain. When he was
finished he flung a few more stones into the water at the
point where Kanarik had sunk. Then he took Kanarik's
bundle on his shoulder, and the girl's arm, and set out.

"Don't forget—I'm Aaron-Meier Kanarik now. You
mustn't call me anything but that after this. Remember
that! Do you hear?" he asked the girl in a harsh voice.

"And I'm Chane-Dwoire Silberstein."

"What's that? Since when?"

"Kanarik bought me a pass from one of the tumblers and
gave it to me tonight before we started."

"Good! Now we're new-born. Do you hear? New-born. Both of us. Do you hear?"

"Yes." The girl was trembling from head to foot.

The night was cold and Mary was wearing only a thin coat over her silk blouse. She shivered and gazed up at the young man walking beside her as if he were a god. She clung to him, pressed her quivering body to his, and looked up into his eyes in adoration.

"Mottke, my darling!"

"What's my name?" He struck her in the face with his fist. "What's my name? Have you forgotten already?"

"Kanarik, dearest Kanarik!"

In the stream near by something moved; the water was troubled and beat loudly against the reeds and the thorns, as if at the sound of the word "Kanarik" some one had leapt up and peered out of the water.

But Mottke and Mary never noticed. Holding hands they made quickly for the nearest railway station, to take the train to Warsaw and the dealer whose address Mary carried in her bosom.

BOOK III

CHAPTER XXXI

*

The Old Town

IN ONE corner of the great city of Warsaw some remnants of the ancient medieval town still linger on. The Old Town consists mainly of high narrow houses that look as if they would all crumble to pieces if one of them were taken away. They have no back courts, no windows, no light of any kind, and every one of them is a veritable maze of corridors. Long dark passages wind in baffling labyrinths to the various flats. Only old residents who were born and brought up among them know these passages. Whenever an outsider strays into one of these houses he fancies he has wandered into some ancient monastery, whose walls still hold memories of the Inquisition; he gazes fearfully at the lofty vaulted roof over his head and the severe and gloomy walls on either side of him, and he stops, terrified by the darkness and the gloom.

And it is not only these old houses: the whole quarter gives the same impression. In the middle of the market square there rises on the site of a long dried-up fountain, at one time the pride of Warsaw, the figure of a nymph, half woman, half fish, the emblem of the city. And all round the houses, closely huddled together, stand like hoary grand-fathers, tall and thin and consumptive. Every one of them is painted a different color and bears the arms of some craft.

The square is crammed with booths and stands, and there also is to be found the jumble sale market, where one can buy anything from battered spoons to outworn boots.

In one of these houses, which bore the proud title of "The Ship's Anchor," and accordingly displayed as its coat of arms a green ship on a red field, there was a certain tea-room called "The Warsaw Café." The entrance to the Warsaw Café was illuminated at night by two red lights, which burned just beneath the green ship. Before the place several girls, some young, some not so young, were usually to be seen sitting about in rather startling negligée, neither dressed nor undressed, for they wore thin white silk blouses and white petticoats, generally very short so as to show their legs cased in blue, red or black stockings and high-heeled shoes. Most of these girls wore their hair about their shoulders, or bound with a red ribbon. The older and more sumptuous ones usually forgot to button their blouses—purely by chance, of course—so that their well-developed breasts were casually displayed. These older girls sat stolidly and immovably in front of the café; but the younger and prettier ones kept hopping up and down the steps before the door, showing off their loosened hair, their naked arms and shoulders and finely shaped legs. They chaffed all the men that passed by and even tugged them sometimes by the sleeve.

At night the street was very lively. Red lights burned in front of a great many of these austere old houses, illuminating the ancient coats of arms. Yet, before many a coffee-house door these girls were to be seen sitting about in their curious attire, more suitable for a bedroom. And young lads and old gentlemen, in civilian clothes and uniforms of all kinds, crowded the pavements of the Old Town every night. Sometimes a barrel-organ would play before one of the houses, and the children would dance to its music. Here and there too you might hear the wheezing of a mouth harmonica, on which simple instrument a householder was playing with great expression some melancholy Polish mazurka, as he sat in the bosom of his family and "guarded the house," so that no thief or unlawful intruder might enter. But you may be sure that he paid no attention whatever to the girls passing by with their clients, and watched them vanishing into the dark mazes of the house without giving them a second thought.

That was what the square was like in the evening. But now it is mid-day. The square is crammed with buyers and sellers. Here anything can be exchanged, anything bought and sold. A soldier is hawking army bread, and another, army linen. A Jew is selling old umbrellas and frayed collars; a Jewess, old dresses. The customers put on straight away the articles of clothing they have bought. Others are barter- ing: they hand over some old rag or other for a roll of bread or a packet of cigarettes, and many a man leaves the market without his coat but the richer for a bottle of brandy. For trade here is pushed to the very frontier of decency; you can barter anything, that is to say, but your trousers (for according to the law you aren't allowed to appear in the market without your trousers).

And if the water nymph standing on the sealed fountain hadn't been made of brass, she would often have blushed at the scenes she was forced to witness there.

In the Warsaw Café everything is quiet at this hour. The great samovar simmers in solitude in its corner, and the flies batten undisturbed on the cheese, the cakes and other pastries displayed in the window. The tea-room is empty. But in the little adjoining room, which is windowless and receives what light it gets through a small opening into

another room, a girl is standing at a long table kneading
dough. Some other girls and young women are sitting there,
too, drinking tea. Most of them are still in their dressing-
gowns, although it is already late in the afternoon. Some
are actually in their shifts, others are wearing wraps. A
few of them are drying their hair. The whole room reeks of
powder and cheap scent.

Presently the Lowitch girl entered. She had come from
her little room over the café and she was carrying a half-
dozen silk chemises and some table-cloths and handkerchiefs
of Schyrardower linen, which she kept in a trunk against
her marriage. Full of pride she showed the initials beauti-
fully stitched on the linen. The girls criticized the design,
tried to guess how much she had paid for the table-cloths
and handkerchiefs, and passed the chemises from hand to
hand.

The news that the Lowitch girl had been adding to her
trousseau again drew the landlady from the kitchen, where
she was preparing tea for the children, who would soon be
home from school. Her face was red with bending over the
fire. She was a plump, coarse Warsaw Jewess with a thick
neck and pudgy fingers, and she gazed with rapture at the
fine new table-cloths and handkerchiefs. The cloths were
spread out on the table, the benches and the bed and
thoroughly examined. Everybody tried again to guess the
price.

"What are you going to do with all this finery, Dobsche?"
the landlady asked the girl from Lowitch; a faint smile
passed over her fat face and she winked at the other girls.
"The things only get moldy in that trunk of yours; you'll
never use them."

"Don't you worry. Let them get moldy. A day'll come yet
when I'll find a use for them."

"God grant it! I'll be glad to see that day . . ." said the landlady with the same smile, turning to go back to her kitchen. But Genendel, the girl from Schochlin, struck in:

"Look how sore she gets when any of us girls buy underwear. I suppose it's only her like that can buy decent clothes. Don't you mind her, Dobsche! Health and happiness!"

The landlady of the Warsaw Café wasn't the proprietress of the establishments that the girls belonged to. They had other masters and the café was only their rendezvous. They spent the day there till it was time to dress up for "night duty." The fat landlady was afraid of Genendel; for in the first place the Schochlin girl had a sharp tongue, and in the second a rival café had just opened next door, and girls from other establishments had begun to frequent it.

"Why, I said nothing! It's no affair of mine. She can buy a whole shopful of underwear for all I care!" said the landlady, vanishing into her kitchen.

"What are you going to do with all these table-cloths and serviettes, anyway? Will you ever use them? I would buy a stylish hat and a good coat with the money, if I were you; that would be worth while. But embroidered table-cloths! That's all very well for women who have a comfortable home, but not for us," said Jentel.

The girls smiled at one another. They knew the Lowitch girl's weakness. She always bought expensive underwear with the money she contrived to save, never a new hat or a new dress; she laid out every penny she could squeeze from her clients on her trousseau, and it was moldering in her trunk. Perhaps she still believed that she would find a use for all her linen some day, when she married and began to lead a respectable life; actually that was the secret hope of most of these girls. But it may be that she had given up this hope already and the collection of fine underwear had become a sort of mania with her; for when nobody was there she would take her treasures out of the trunk and do up her little room to make it look like a respectable parlor, with a husband somewhere in the background. She would cover her table with a clean cloth, set her new copper samovar on it, hang her pictures on the walls, and fling an embroidered coverlet over the bed. But in the evening, when the time came to prepare for receiving her clients, she took everything down again and laid it in her trunk.

The girls stopped their talk. A young girl of about eight entered the café, wrapped in a great shawl: one end trailed on the ground after her, and a baby's face peeped out of the folds like a small animal. The girl held the baby in one arm; in her other hand she carried a tin can and said in a muffled voice, for she suffered from adenoids:

"Hot water, please."

"Chanele, Chanele, here's a customer!" shouted one of the half-naked girls.

A girl of about eighteen or nineteen, dressed like any respectable girl of her age, appeared in the kitchen door. She was wearing a cotton print dress, her hair was combed straight back and fell in two plaits down her back, and her face was unpowdered; but among the girls in their shifts and dressing-gowns she had an almost unnatural look, like a man in his clothes among a crowd of naked people. Chanele stepped into the café, took the can from the girl's hand, and filled it with hot water from the bubbling samovar.

"How's your mother today?" Genendel asked the little girl.

"I don't know. She's in bed and father is out," replied the girl in her muffled, singsong voice.

"Give her a bit of cheese cake, Chanele. Here's four

kopeks," said the Schochlin girl, pulling a little purse from her stocking and laying down the money.

Chanele went over to the window. The flies flew up with a loud buzz; she waved them away with her hand. Then she cut a slice of cheese cake and handed it to the little girl, who took it in silence.

"Give her a slice from me, too."

"And from me, too," cried the other girls. Chanele stuffed the little girl's shawl with cheese cakes.

"Take care you don't fall, carrying the baby!" cried the Schochlin girl.

"Go slowly, mind!" the other girls warned her.

"I'm sorry for the cigarette-maker: his wife ill these seven months and all that swarm of children. That's what you get with marrying," said the Schochlin girl, wiping last night's powder from her face with her handkerchief.

"Every man isn't such a helpless ninny as the cigarette-maker," replied the Lowitch girl, folding up her linen in a corner.

The door of the café opened noisily. Two boys who looked like twins rushed into the room swinging their caps and their school-books.

"We're hungry, mother!" they shouted as soon as they were in the doorway.

"Schloime, come over here," the Lowitch girl cried to one of them.

"No, Schloime, you come to me. I'll give you a two kopek piece if you do," said the Schochlin girl, pulling a coin from her stocking.

"Schloime, I'll buy you a pen-knife if you come to me," said a third girl.

The boy stood undecidedly in the middle of the room, his eyes sparkling and his cheeks flushed with running, fiddling awkwardly with the book he was carrying; he couldn't make up his mind between the pen-knife and the two kopek piece.

"Come to your tea, Schloime," said Chanele, taking the boy's hand and leading him firmly into the kitchen.

"She's mighty particular about that boy! You would think I was going to eat him!" said the Schochlin girl in a pique.

The boy flung one more look at the two kopek piece that the girl was holding out to him and reluctantly followed his sister.

Then the empty café woke to life again. Two strangers entered, very unusual visitors they were too, to judge by their appearance and their clothes. The girls retired into a corner and hastily put their hair and their clothes to rights. The landlady settled her hair as she stepped out of the kitchen and went up to her customers. She was pale with fright. But to her relief she recognized a third man she knew along with the two strangers. For red-haired Welwel shouted in his hoarse voice into the dark room:

"Is Kanarik here?"

The landlady and the girls heaved a great sigh when they heard Welwel's voice—for he was the owner of the establishment on the top floor—and shouted in chorus:

"Kanarik, Kanarik, you're wanted!"

A tall young man rose heavily from a sofa in a corner and walked over into the light. Even in the semi-darkness of the café the legs of his top-boots shone; his black hair was ruffled. There was a crafty look in his well-fed but discontented face with its little black mustache. He rubbed his eyes lazily, gazed round him as if he had only caught sight of the place that moment, and asked in a clear young voice:

"Who called me?"

It was Mottke.

CHAPTER XXXII

*

The Herr Director

MOTTKE-KANARIK stared at the two strangers that Welwel
had brought with him. The older one was a slight little man
with black glittering eyes that stared at everything contemptuously and distrustfully: clearly a man who felt firm
on his feet and didn't give a damn for the whole world. A
thick cigar was clamped between his teeth, which were
blackened with tobacco; he coughed huskily every now and
then and kept on spitting. But he simply glittered and blazed
with diamonds. A harp set with diamonds stuck in his tie
showed that he was an art-lover. Great rings set with
diamonds sparkled on his short fingers. On his little finger
he wore a platinum ring with a huge stone. With a movement
that had evidently become habitual he kept rubbing it
against his bright red velvet waistcoat and holding it up to
peer at its bluish fires through his half-shut eyes.

The other gentleman was a good deal younger; he was
handsome, well set up and dressed in the latest fashion. He
wore diamond rings, too, but the stones were much smaller.
He kept fiddling with his mustache, which was trimmed in
the English style.

The young man treated the older one with great deference
and addressed him as "Herr Director."

Mottke examined the two strangers in silence and un-
easily asked himself what could have brought these big pots

to him. But he didn't show his surprise; he simply shot an irritated glance at Welwel and asked:

"What's up?"

"Listen, Kanarik. These gentlemen have come to put you in the way of a piece of business. If you're smart you can pocket a tidy bit, but you must be reasonable and see where your advantage lies."

"What business? Let's hear it," said Kanarik quite calmly, or so he thought· but his nervous movements gave him away.

The older man, the one who was called the Herr Director, cast such a piercing glance at Mottke through his half-closed eyes, that you would have thought he was trying to read the whole life history of that young man. Then he coughed and spat vigorously, as if to show that he had learned everything he wanted. Thereupon he glanced round the café contemptuously and asked:

"You can't even sit in comfort here. What can they give us to drink?"

"Chanele, Chanele come here!" Welwel shouted into the next room.

"Chanele, Chanele!" a voice echoed in the kitchen.

Chanele appeared with a napkin thrown over her shoulder, and gaped with fearful surprise at the great people. Her surprise made a flush rise on her face and gave her eyes a soft glow.

"Tidy this place up, will you, so that we can have somewhere to sit. You see we've got visitors, don't you?" Welwel complacently rubbed his flat nose and glanced at the two strangers.

Chanele hastily wiped a table with the napkin and pulled a few chairs up to it. The men sat down. The Director bored the girl with the same glance that he had tried on Mottke.

Then he pushed his chair a little back from the table and said with a friendly smile:

"Well, now, you bring us a bottle of champagne, but let it be the genuine stuff."

"Chanele, have you got any champagne in the place?" asked Welwel, obsequiously taking up the Herr Director's joke.

Chanele stood where she was; she couldn't make out what they wanted of her.

"What shall I bring?" she asked, flushing a little with annoyance.

"Bring us some of your everlasting tea and cheese cake. It's all you've got," replied the younger man in a crushing voice.

"Who is she?" asked the Director, gazing at the great stone on his little finger, as if he were talking about it and not about Chanele.

"The daughter of the house. Her mother owns the place."

"And she wastes her chances here? A great pity!" said the Director, as if to himself.

"Yes, she's a decent girl. Her mother guards her like the apple of her eye," Welwel went on.

"Oh well, let her go on guarding her! But what are we sitting here for?" asked the Director impatiently.

"Kanarik, do you know who this gentleman is?" asked Welwel, pointing at the Herr Director.

"No, I don't," replied Mottke in mingled awkwardness and irritation. Such unusual company made him feel nervous.

"This is the Director of the Aquarium. You know the place, of course?"

"No, I don't," replied Mottke in a surly voice.

"All the great people go to this gentleman's cabaret, the

Chief of Police does for one thing. You'll find all the highest officials there. Doesn't that convey anything to you?"

"The Chief of Police! And what about the Governor? The higher officers, the colonels, the whole staff, they all come to the Aquarium to drink their champagne and admire the ladies!" said the good-looking young man proudly.

While all this was being said about him, the Herr Director stared indifferently at the stone on his little finger.

"The most famous actresses and dancers in the whole world work for the Herr Director, why, didn't you know that? If a dancer appears in his cabaret she's soon known, and after that she can earn her thousands. All the best cabaret dancers come to Warsaw and beg the Herr Director on their knees to be allowed to appear in the Aquarium, so as to make a name for themselves."

Chanele brought a tray with tea and cheese cakes and put it down before the customers.

"Well, what about the champagne?" asked the Herr Director, staring at Chanele again through his half-shut eyes. The girl flushed and her hands trembled so much that the tea spilt out of the glasses.

"There's a girl that doesn't know her chances. A great pity!" the Director repeated with a sigh. Then he pulled out a gold cigarette case set with diamonds, and handed it round.

"Listen, Kanarik. The Herr Director has heard that your girl the Spaniard can walk the tightrope and do lots of other stunts. He would like to see her."

"This girl here, the landlady's daughter, I like the looks of her too," the Director interposed abruptly.

"But the Herr Director hasn't seen the other one yet, the Spaniard! She's first class, I can tell you. A fiery brunette, pure Spanish type, still fresh and young," said the younger gentleman, who was plainly an expert.

"I'm an honest chap," interposed Welwel, turning to Mottke. "Look here. When this gentleman"—pointing at the young man—"came to me and began to talk about the Spanish girl, I told him right off: 'The Spaniard is Kanarik's girl. He brought her here. She belongs to him. What's mine is mine and what's his is his.' Now I want no rows or unpleasantness. She's your girl; so what you say goes. The Herr Director can make her into something first rate and you can coin a tidy bit of money at the same time. Will you hand her over to the Herr Director?"

Mottke had sat there all the time without opening his mouth; he seemed to be thinking hard about something and kept chewing his mustache. From the very first he had taken a dislike to the Director and felt strongly tempted to give him a black eye. What made him so angry with the Director he couldn't have rightly said. But he didn't like the way the man stared at Chanele. Although he kept women himself and looked upon them merely as his property, he knew the difference between a whore and Chanele, for she was an innocent girl. That was why the behavior of the Director had displeased him. So he held his tongue and made no answer.

"Take your time! No hurry! First we'll have a look at her. I must know what I'm buying," said the Director in an indifferent voice.

"The Herr Director can see her straight off. Where is she, Kanarik?"

"Up in her room," replied Mottke in a surly voice.

"Then why all this endless talk? Come, let's have a look at this Spanish girl from Berditchew!" said the Director impatiently.

"Chanele, Chanele!" shouted Welwel.

The girl entered.

The Director pulled out a great fat purse, looked in it for a long time, and asked casually whether Chanele could give him change for a hundred roubles.

Everybody laughed. Then he asked:

"What about a twenty-five rouble note, then?"

At last he found a rouble note and pushed it into Chanele's hand with a long glance from his half-shut eyes. He refused to take the change she gave him.

"There's a girl that doesn't know her chances!" he murmured yet once more. He was clearly pleased with his aphorism, for like all vain men he liked to give public expression to his worldly wisdom.

They all rose to go. Mottke remained sitting.

"What are you sitting there for, Kanarik? Aren't you coming, too?"

"Come over here, Welwel." Mottke drew him into a corner.

"Who is he?" Mottke asked, jerking his thumb at the Director.

"Why, I've told you. He's the Director of the Aquarium."

"Well, Director or no Director, I don't know much about that—but I don't like the man. If he wants to see the Spaniard he can go up if he likes. It's a public place and anybody can go up there that wants to. But if he ever takes it into his head to play about with Chanele—he'll never leave this place alive, do you hear me?"

"What's biting you? Have you gone off your nut?"

"I've seen what I've seen and that's enough for me! He can go upstairs. I'll wait here."

"Has he any objection to my going up to see the Spanish girl? In that case it's off, here and now. Come, Krumashattko," said the Director, turning to the tall young man.

The Director, Krumashattko and Welwel went up to the Spanish girl's room. They climbed a dark stair, the Director lighting the way with his pocket torch. Children were sitting on the steps, playing in the darkness. A door opened, a woman's head peeped out, they heard a baby wailing.

At last they reached the Spanish girl's door. Welwel went in first. Then he stuck out his head and made a sign to the other two.

They found themselves in a tiny room; the door and window were hung with dusty old red velvet curtains. On a sofa a girl was sitting in a thin silk nightdress; she was smoking a cigarette and humming a song to herself while she manicured her finger-nails. She stared at the strangers with some surprise.

The Director narrowed his eyes and seemed resolved absolutely to transpierce the pretty dark girl with his stare. Then he contemptuously glanced at the stone on his little finger. The Spanish girl seemed to have taken his fancy, for he passed the tip of his tongue over his lips, as he always did when he was pleased. Then he pulled out his gold cigarette case and handed it round.

"Well, Herr Director, this is our dark Spanish girl," said Welwel, introducing her with pride.

The Spanish girl looked up. As she met the Director's contemptuous glance a vague feeling of shame rose in her. She flushed, hastily snatched at the black curls falling over her shoulders and fastened them into a knot with hairpins.

"I can see her, I can see her," replied the Director, as he handed round his cigarettes.

"Can you walk the tightrope, Nina?" asked Welwel.

"Yes, I worked in a circus in the provinces at one time."

"And can you dance Spanish dances?"

"I don't know. I learned to once . . ." said the girl, smiling awkwardly.

"She'll soon manage that. We'll teach her. Ask her to stand up and walk about the room."

Mary, who was used to another tone and other demands from her visitors, was almost frightened by the polite behavior of her visitors and their strange questions, and blushed like an innocent girl. But as she was accustomed to obey men without asking questions, she rose and walked about the room.

The Director and Krumashattko posted themselves in a corner and observed the Spanish girl's walk, her figure and the rhythm of her movements. Then they quietly consulted together, like horse-dealers examining a beast they are thinking of buying. They talked together in what sounded like a Latin language; at least Welwel and the girl could make nothing of it. Thereupon they ordered the girl to stop where she was, lift her arms, bend sideways and so on. She obeyed them, for that had become a habit with her.

"Well, what did I say, Herr Director?" Krumashattko asked.

"She'll do. They'll put her through her paces and then she'll do," replied the Director in a satisfied voice, and he handed round his cigarette case again.

"Who brought her here?" he asked in a low voice, turning to Welwel.

"The chap down below, the chap that calls himself Kanarik. He came with her here from the provinces. He picked her up somewhere in a circus. He had to stand a good few blows here before the profession took him up. They tried to pinch the girl from him at first. But he knows how to look after himself. He's a tough lad, that. He's always got his knife ready. The others are scared stiff of him now.

The Spaniard is his girl. He'll get the money for her; you'll have to deal with him. No use talking to her, he's got the last word."

"So that's it! Then come along, let's settle with the fellow. Nothing more to be done here." And the Director made for the door.

CHAPTER XXXIII

*

Nobody Has a Soft Time

MOTTKE sat on in the café. He felt queerly agitated. The way the Director had stared at Chanele and spoken of her made him see red. Up to now he had never given Chanele a thought. For the year and a half since he had come to Warsaw and installed Mary in the establishment upstairs, he had thought of Chanele merely as the landlady's daughter, the girl that served the customers.

At first he had been surprised that people treated her quite differently from the other girls, and that everybody, down to the lads who lived on the street-walkers and the clients who came in the evenings, drew a line between her and the prostitutes. Nobody ever dared to accost her or say a word to her except when they were ordering or paying for their coffee, tea, or cakes. Even when she was helping in the café late at night, when wild scenes often took place between the men and the prostitutes, she was treated with the strictest respect.

Later Mottke accepted this as a matter of course and tumbled to the fact that Chanele was a respectable girl, while the others were whores. And like the other young men of his trade he felt in a sense bound to shield Chanele; and God help the man who tried to touch her. But that wasn't all. The street-walkers themselves, who usually talked with the greatest freedom, put a guard on their tongues when Chanele was there. It was as if they had an agreement among themselves to save Chanele from the lot they had to suffer.

Mottke followed their example. And when the Director had the impertinence to look at Chanele as if she were a common prostitute, it not only angered Mottke but threw him off his balance; for his thoughts began to occupy themselves with Chanele, and then he began to wonder at himself for never having thought of her before.

While he was sitting thinking of this, Welwel clapped him on the shoulder and piloted him to a table where the Director and Krumashattko were waiting for him.

"Listen, Kanarik. You can get your hands on a tidy bit of cash at one go—more money than you've ever seen in your life before," began Welwel. "And if you know your book you'll make more still later on."

"How much and what for?" asked Mottke sharply.

"The Herr Director wants to buy the Spanish girl off you. But for good, so that you have no claim on her afterwards," said the young man.

Mottke turned pale and said nothing. For a minute he had a strong temptation to jump up and knock out the teeth of the three of them and give them a good hammering. He clenched his hands, but the Director interposed:

"And with me it's cash on the nail. There's no nonsense about me. I have no fear of your running away with the money. Nobody has ever got money for nothing out of me!"

With that the Director pulled out his fat pocketbook, took out a twenty-five rouble note and laid it on the table before Mottke.

"Here's twenty-five roubles as earnest money, and if you bring me the girl—where you're to bring her you'll be told later—I'll let you have another hundred and fifty roubles."

The blood rose into Mottke's face at the sight of the

money. A sudden thought, a hope, made his eyes sparkle. This thought, this hope was connected in some way with Chanele. How and why he couldn't have said. He grew more thoughtful: he did not touch the money, but he replied in a trembling voice:

"I'll think it over."

"What do you want to think it over for? Take the money, you fool!" whispered Welwel. "Haven't you enough women as it is? You can win over the Lowitch girl and the Schochlin girl whenever you like. Or are you scared of Schloime the burglar? How did he come to his women? You know the way to do that as well as he does."

"I'm afraid of nobody," replied Mottke calmly. "But I want to think it over."

"Good!" said the Director. "Think it over. But you can take the money to go on with. I've no fear of your running away with it. And if you decide to bring her along, Welwel will give you the address. And I won't haggle. If you bring her you'll have two hundred roubles. But I must have her by Sunday at four in the afternoon; later than that I have no use for her. Come, Krumashattko, we'll have to go." The Director got up, leaving the money lying.

Mottke sat and stared at the money. He felt alarmed: his face grew red, but he said nothing.

In the doorway the Director and Krumashattko said a few words to Welwel. Then Welwel shouted into the next room:

"Chanele!"

At that word Mottke jumped up like an angry dog. But the landlady's voice answered from the kitchen, and she appeared in person, saying that Chanele wasn't in.

At this news the Director hastily left the café along with his body-guard.

Welwel went across to Mottke to talk over the matter
with him again.

In the next house to the brothel, in a tiny flat on the same
floor as the one the girls occupied, there lived a Jewish
cigarette-maker, a poor, withered-up little man, with a whole
swarm of children. His wife always bore twins. She was
always in bed with her countless confinements. Her husband
went round the smaller pubs every day to sell his cigarettes.
The wife lay in bed and the children were left to their own
devices. Yet the chief income of the family didn't come from
the cigarettes but from the sick woman; for she had once
been a dressmaker and still ran a sort of workshop. She took
in young girls—they were scarcely more than children—and
set them to sew baby's clothes. The woman cut out the
clothes and the little girls finished them off. And the stuff
that was left over or was still unused served as coverlets for
the beds, table-cloths and when necessary blankets.

The girls from the brothel were constant visitors at this
woman's house. During the day, when they had nothing to
do, they looked in on the invalid; they helped to wash the
children and comb their hair, they tidied up the room generally, and even took a hand at the sewing. The girls were
very strongly drawn to their neighbor. And she for her part
had no particular objection to them or their profession. She
had a maxim: Everybody must earn his living as best he can,
and nobody has a soft time. So she was sorry for the
girls, and didn't look down on them. And even her pity for
them had pretty well died out, for she had got used to
them; and she treated them now like her other acquaintances
and had intimate friendships with some of them.

Mary, Mottke's girl, became friendly with her like the
other girls, often visited her, and helped her with the children

and the dressmaking. She liked to gossip with her as she sat at the window trying to get a breath of fresh air. The life in the place where Mottke had installed her didn't appeal to Mary in the least. It wasn't so much that her profession was immoral, as that it was boring. In the first few weeks after her arrival the strange town had thrilled her. But by now she more or less knew it, for she had already seen the Marszalkowskastrasse, the Saxon Garden and the Jewish theater, and she began to long again for the caravan where she had traveled with the tumblers from town to town. She would have run away long ago if her fear of Mottke hadn't held her back. He hadn't merely become her master, but her guardian as well. She worshiped him with an almost slavish love. In the great city of Warsaw he had become both father and elder brother to her, the only human being that she could turn to in the whole world. Everything that he did was right; and she blindly obeyed him, whatever he asked her to do. And his deed in the wood had raised him to a god in her eyes and changed her fear of him into real love. She couldn't imagine how she could live for a day without his guidance. And when he was angry with her, took away the money that she got from her clients and swore at her afterwards, she felt that she belonged to him, that she was his and that she had a home and a father.

So the visit of the two strangers and their curious behavior had alarmed her. She wasn't accustomed to answer any one but Mottke and she felt frightened out of her wits.

Whenever the girls had anything on their minds they went over to the cigarette-maker's wife to tell it to her. Mary did that now.

"Oh, Leah, there's just been two toffs seeing me. They looked at me so queerly, and they didn't ask me for anything, just looked at me, as if they wanted to buy me! I wonder where Kanarik can be. I'm scared. . . . Welwel brought them," said Mary.

"Oh you fool, of course Kanarik knows all about it! Welwel would never dare to take anybody to see you without asking Kanarik. And as long as you have Kanarik you don't need to be afraid of anybody," said the woman.

"They're all frightened of Kanarik. He's stronger than any of them, isn't he?" asked the girl.

"Isn't he, though! As long as you have Kanarik, you stupid . . ."

Mary cheered up and became calmer.

Then Mottke appeared at the door and shouted:

"Nina!"

She jumped up at once.

"Coming, Kanarik!" And she hurried out into the passage.

"Go and dress, I'm going to take you somewhere."

"Kanarik!"

"What are you dawdling there for? Speed it up! I have no time to waste."

When they got to Mary's room the girl took him by the hand:

"Kanarik, where are you going to take me?"

"You'll soon see."

She clung to him and looked into his eyes:

"Who were these strange men?"

"What's that to you?"

She seized both his hands, pressed close to him and looked deep in his eyes:

"Mottke, what are you going to do with me?"

Mottke bit his lip, looked round in terror to see if any one had heard his real name, and clenched his fists:

"What have you done? Anybody might have heard. I'll bash your jaw for you!"

"Strike me, strike me as much as you like, do what you like with me, but don't send me away among strangers! Don't sell me, don't sell me, Mottke, dear, darling Mottke!"

The girl fell at his feet and clung to him. After that she said nothing, but simply looked up at him with the gaze of a dog begging not to be driven away.

"Put on your clothes, I'm only going to take you to a hotel where there's a man that's been asking for you," said Mottke to calm her.

"I'll be ready in a minute!"

She jumped up, threw Mottke a grateful look and hastily dressed.

CHAPTER XXXIV

*

The Tiger Is Tamed

THE street lamps of the Old Town began to flare out in preparation for the night. And soon the yellow gas-lights shone in the shop windows too, and outside the little cinema. They lit up the old walls and threw bluish shadows on the austere house fronts. And in the dark labyrinth of passages girls appeared from the different establishments, dressed in white silk night-dresses trimmed with red ribbons. In the half-light their eyes glittered and their bloodless faces shone with dumb desire, as if they were begging any one at all to lift some of the burden of passion from them. And they found some one to do it.

And soon the more respectable householders appeared in the street as well, along with their families. Women with infants in their arms sat down in the dry gutters to get a little fresh air, and let their infants suck at their bare withered breasts without bothering about anybody. For it was a summer night, and in the little fusty rooms it was stifling. So the quest for fresh air drove people into the street, and their family life, usually hidden behind walls, displayed itself in public, unconcealed.

They had no reason for shame, since they didn't know one another. So they dragged out their mattresses and pillows and made beds for themselves in the open street. And there they gave free rein to their passions under the stars.

227

Friday evening. The Jewish women were already cooking the food for the Sabbath. The smell of stewed fish and roast meat from the houses gratefully assailed the nostrils of the people passing by and the couples lying in the street.

The pavements of the Old Town grew denser and denser with dawdling crowds. They were mainly made up of clients from other quarters come to pay a visit to the girls in the brothels. Young and old men, in civilian clothes and in uniforms, soldiers and officers, officials and private citizens: here they were all on one footing. The thirst for love drove them to the Old Town. And presently the street-walkers mingled with the crowds and with the families camping out in the street. Illegal and sanctioned love went on side by side.

Lost in the stream of pleasure-seekers you might see mothers with infants at their breasts, and loving married couples. Children of every size ran about among the feet of the crowd, and everything was illuminated by the mysterious yellow gas-light that threw blue shadows on the grave house fronts.

And the great civilized city of Warsaw was transformed into a rendezvous for men and women of the jungle, who made love to one another without caring who saw them.

In this love market you might see the guardians of law and order now and then, too; sometimes a policeman would appear and sometimes the police inspector himself would go round and see that everything was done in conformity with the law. But it wasn't an unknown occurrence for some pillar of justice, seduced from duty by his more human passions, to disappear along with a seductive scrap of white into some dark and winding passage.

The Warsaw Café was busy. The counter was piled with cheese-cakes and other pastries that had been kept under

cover all day to save them from the flies, and a huge
samovar sang at the back. The tables were all occupied and
a cloud of cigarette smoke hung over everything. Most of
the people here were pimps or bullies from the brothels of
the neighborhood, but there were ordinary regular customers too, who drank their coffee and played dominoes at
their table every evening. And now and then a stranger or
two would stray into the place; they were generally people
who had come down in the world.

At the back of the room a few girls were sitting, dressed
in bright colors, with their hair done up in a striking style.
The smell of cheap scent and powder told what they were.
They were prostitutes who had stopped at the café for a
rest, or to meet their bullies, or to have a word with the
owner of their establishment.

Chanele and her mother weren't standing behind the
counter tonight. For it was Friday evening and the owner
of the café, who had been out all week on his business, was
sitting in the kitchen with his family holding the Sabbath.

From the kitchen came the smell of fish and the sleepy
drone of Sabbath songs. And behind the counter stood a
Christian woman, the wife of the porter, who had a constant job there on Friday evenings. She raked in the money
from the customers, but a boy was sitting beside her to keep
his eye on her—one of the twins; he was always let out of
school earlier on Fridays to see that the woman didn't
pocket the tips. There was no concealment about it. The
woman knew and so did the customers, and they saw to it
that the four or six kopeks they paid for their coffee reached
the till. And the woman had long since given up trying to
get round these obstacles.

Mottke was sitting at one of the tables with his Spanish
girl. Mary didn't walk the streets like the other girls; he

wouldn't allow her. She was reserved for "better class" clients who could take her to a hotel, or for occasional officers who strayed into the Old Town. So she wasn't wearing the transparent silk blouse that was the badge of the other girls, but was quite respectably dressed. Her white blouse had short sleeves and was open at the neck: a high Spanish comb was stuck in her hair.

Mottke had several other girls who worked for him; he had picked them up at different times. Most of them were old stagers, the cheap kind that had to hawk their wares in the street. He considered it beneath his dignity to sit at the same table with them. Besides, everybody in the café and the brothels round about knew by now that the Director of the Aquarium had been to see the Spanish girl and offered her an engagement in his cabaret. So Mary had become an important personage in their eyes.

Girls from all the different brothels kept hovering round Mottke's table. They all envied Mary and wished that Kanarik were their master. For Kanarik was a strong young fellow feared by all the bullies and roughs, and none of them ever dared to molest his girls. And, besides, he treated his girls well; he often took them for a walk in the park or stood them an evening at the theater, and he saw to it that they were well dressed.

Because of this he was a great favorite with these girls. Tonight it was the Lowitch girl and the Schochlin girl that made for him. As soon as they entered and saw him and Mary, they hurried over with cries of delight.

These two girls belonged to Schloime the burglar, a hardened ruffian at whose name the whole quarter trembled, from Grzybow to the Iron Gate. Fabulous stories were told of his deeds; how he had laid out ten policemen at one go, and how no lock could hold out against him. But that was in the distant past; Schloime was resting on his laurels now instead of winning new ones. In the last few years he had taken to drinking too much beer, and that gave him a big belly and made him slow in his movements. And ever since "that greenhorn, God knows where he jumped from" (so he had called Mottke) had given him a drubbing and he had had to take to his bed for a week after it (it was over Mary, whom he had tried to annex): ever since that day Schloime's prestige was ruined and Kanarik was the rising star. Nevertheless, Schloime's past still kept his rivals in awe, and nobody dared to interfere with him.

All the chief stars in the world of prostitution had their adjutants. These yes-men had somewhat the same powers as a prime minister. Mottke hadn't appointed an official of this kind yet; he was still too young to realize the need for one, and so he kept on rejecting all the offers that were made him. Now Schloime's right-hand man was a little hump-backed fellow with a crooked nose, called Joinele Malpe; he was as faithful as a dog and kept on singing the praises of his master. Every evening Schloime's yes-man strolled about the streets of the Old Town keeping an eye on his master's property, that is, the girls, watching how they comported themselves, and whether they canvassed for clients or idly amused themselves. Whenever the girls caught sight of him they shrank as if they had seen a police spy, and began to accost men as fast as they could to show how enthusiastic they were about their work.

Just after the two girls had walked over to the table where Mottke and Mary were sitting, Joinele Malpe stuck his head in through the door and took a good look round the place. He sneaked off at once when he saw his master's girls sitting with Kanarik. It was an offense against the unwritten laws of the underworld for one bully to sit at the same table as the girls of another. It was accepted as a sign that he wanted to pinch the girls from their lawful owner and establish a claim on them. The two girls had not noticed Joinele Malpe spying on them, and so they contentedly remained sitting at the table. But some other girls presently rushed in to warn them; for the prostitutes stuck together and always tried to help each other.

"Surele, watch your step. Malpe's been here and seen you with Kanarik."

"Oh, God!" cried both girls in terror, flinging their shawls over their heads and rising to go.

But Mottke felt all at once that he wanted to show his power. He made up his mind to let them see he was the stronger.

"Sit where you are!" he shouted. "I tell you, sit where you are!"

The girls did not know what to do. They were quite pale with fright.

Actually they were glad in their hearts that Kanarik was going to take them under his wing and that they would belong to him now; yet they were terrified of Schloime at the same time and of the scene that was bound to follow. But Kanarik ordered them to stay in such a stern voice that they obeyed, pale with terror.

"Some coffee and cheese-cakes here!" cried Mottke.

The other people in the café sat in their places waiting for the row that was bound to come. And a small crowd came in from the street, anxious to see how the fight would go.

"Eat and drink!" Mottke commanded.

The girls sat on in great agitation and started to plead with him.

"Dear kind Kanarik, think what you're doing. Let us go. Schloime will half kill us."

"Don't you worry! I'm here! I'd like to see him touching you! If he does, I'll bash his face in!"

The girls were delighted.

"Eat and drink, I tell you!" said Mottke, his eyes glittering.

Shivering with terror, the girls started on their coffee and cakes without another word. A little time passed, and then Schloime the burglar entered. He was no longer young, by all appearances over forty, broad-shouldered, with a big paunch and a red neck. The gold chain dangling on his belly swung in time to every step he took. In spite of traces of middle age and weariness, his face had still a look of precocious vice. His little mustache, thick eyebrows and the huge ears standing out from his head made him almost uncanny. The room became quiet as soon as he entered, with the quiet that ushers in a storm. The Lowitch girl and her friend made themselves as small as possible, and bent over their glasses so as not to meet Schloime's eyes. With one hand in his trouser pocket and the other behind his back, he strolled over casually to Mottke's table, and looked round him for a few minutes as if he were searching for something. At last his eyes fell on his two girls and he asked in assumed surprise:

"What on earth are you doing here? Why aren't you out on your beat?"

"We're just going, we only wanted to have a cup of coffee," said the Schochlin girl, getting up hastily.

"Sit where you are!"

Mottke banged on the table with his fist, so that the girls and Schloime himself turned pale and started back a step. The girls sat down again.

"What do you mean, you bastard?" said Schloime, pushing his face into Mottke's.

Without looking at him, Mottke turned again to the girls:

"If you rise from this table I'll bash your faces in. You're to sit here with me, at my table. I would like to see the man that has anything to say against that!"

"So that's it?" shouted Schloime, and both rage and fear flashed from his eyes. "Get out into the street this minute! This minute, or I'll break your bones!"

The girls looked about them and did not know what to do. They rose, but Mottke's glance forced them back on to their chairs again.

For a while there was an awkward silence. Schloime grew paler and paler. His nostrils worked out and in, he ground his teeth, and he tried to hold Mottke's eyes with his own, which were flaming with fury.

But Mottke looked through him and pretended he wasn't there.

"Why don't you drink your coffee?" he asked the Lowitch girl, pushing her glass nearer to her.

"You cursed bastard!" yelled Schloime.

Like a snake Mottke reared from his chair and looked deep into Schloime's eyes. They stood like that for almost a minute, ready to spring at each other.

The room became so still that you could have heard the buzzing of the flies as they hovered over the cakes. The members of the confraternity remained sitting at their tables, for they had no wish to mix in the quarrel. Then the Lowitch girl jumped up, rushed to the kitchen, and shouted to the landlady:

"Come here! There's trouble!"

The owner of the café—he was a long, thin Jew—his fat wife, and Chanele came out of the kitchen in their Sabbath

clothes and stopped at the door. They saw two men standing face to face, silently glaring at each other; electric
sparks seemed to flash backwards and forwards between
their eyes. Nobody went near them; in fact, everybody had
drawn back from the approaching storm. Then Chanele
stepped calmly between the two men. She went up close
to Mottke, raised her hands and her eyes to him, and in
her clear voice said:

"Kanarik, what are you doing? They'll shut the place
up if you don't stop. The police inspector will be passing
in a minute. Please, Kanarik!"

He could hear the throbbing of her heart. The people
at the tables looked on in fear. Chanele might get more
than she bargained for if she didn't look out. Her mother
screamed:

"Chanele, come here for God's sake!"

But Chanele stayed where she was and said:

"Kanarik, don't do it!"

And suddenly Mottke took his eyes from Schloime and
turned them on Chanele. He saw the two long black plaits
falling down her back, and the fear in her eyes. But for
a long time he couldn't meet them. He looked at the floor,
a friendly smile flitted across his face. Then he scratched
behind his ear and shouted to the tightrope dancer:

"Come, Nina!"

He took her arm, flung a scornful glance at Schloime,
and growled:

"He can go to the devil."

Everybody wondered why Kanarik had behaved in such
a queer way.

*

The King Is Robed

EVERY Saturday, following a settled habit, Mottke went walking with his girls in the town. He took them to the Saxon Gardens or the Jewish Theater when there was a good play there with lots of singing and children reciting the Kaddish prayer for their dead mother. Mottke's girls always prepared with great thoroughness for their walk. Saturday was their freest and happiest day, for they walked out then not to earn money but for their own pleasure, and dressed themselves up not to get clients but to please themselves and their friends.

So from early morning on Saturday there was a great bustle in Welwel's establishment. The girls prepared for their walk by ironing their blouses, brushing their best dresses and consulting what they should wear. But they were most particular of all about Mottke's suit. They ironed his stiff shirt and his trousers, brushed his velvet waistcoat and his boots. For the more elegant Mottke was on these walks the prouder they were of him.

After dressing up on this particular Saturday they ran across to the cigarette-maker's wife, to show themselves off and get her expert opinion of their clothes. They found her sitting at her window as usual. The children, their mouths and noses smeared with the remains of their Sabbath dinner, sat on the floor in their best clothes, playing with dice. Meilach the cigarette-maker—he came of a pious Chassid family, but had to slave for his living now from early morning till late at night—sat at the table in his drawers gloating over the wisdom of the Patriarchs.

The girls were wearing blue cotton dresses with satin flounces. They displayed their hats, trimmed with all sorts of flowers and feathers, and their new shoes, and asked for the woman's opinion. She gave it with great pleasure. Although she had no good clothes of her own and had never been past her doorstep for years, she loved to talk about the fashions she had known when she was a young girl, and gravely passed judgment on the girls' dresses, deciding whether their hats suited them, or the color of their stockings harmonized with their frocks. And she wasn't ashamed, though her looks were faded, to set the girls' hats on her head to see how they became her. In her heart she envied the girls their finery and told herself that if she had clothes like that she would still be a good-looking woman and make a good show in the park in spite of her state.

"These flounces are a bit too wide, Reisele," she said to one of the girls, an indirect hint to Reisele that she was too skinny.

"That's how they wear them now. All the ladies in the Marszalkowskastrasse wear them wide like that now."

As a pious Jew the cigarette-maker did not by any means approve of such "dirt" (as he called the girls from the brothels) coming to his house and talking to his wife. But he could do nothing. They were neighbors, and the girls liked to come, for then they could talk in a friendly neighborlike way with his wife. After all you couldn't simply shut the door in their faces, especially if you were indebted to them for numberless acts of kindness. Apart from the fact that they often gave the children pennies, bought cakes for them and helped his wife with her work, they sometimes supported himself in his trade in untaxed cigarettes by pressing them on their clients. Such kindnesses could not but lead to friendship, in spite of the girls' profession. Besides his family had actually forgotten by now what sort of girls they were; for they behaved here just like good neighbors and decent women. So gradually the cigarette-maker grew used to his visitors and scarcely thought of them any longer as "dirt." At first, certainly, he had made up his mind to shift from such a disreputable neighborhood, but he never had enough money to do it. And by now the family had got so accustomed to the girls' kindnesses that it couldn't get on without them.

It was only on the Sabbath that he still felt a bit annoyed at the "dirt" blowing into the house on that day when he was buried in the Holy Scriptures. He would turn his back on them, hide behind his book and recite in the prescribed sing-song:

"In the beginning God created the world . . ."

And the girls would listen to the familiar words without showing it, and feel they were at home again.

The Lowitch girl liked best of them all to spend her Sabbath afternoon at the cigarette-maker's. She came of a very religious family. Her father was still a teacher in Lowitch. When she was a young girl she had fallen in love with a barber in that town, but her father had insisted that she should marry a dried-up, almost destitute Talmud student. She was already on her own at that time, for she was an expert stocking-maker. The barber persuaded her to fly with him to Lodz. There he stuck her into a public brothel, from which she graduated to the Warsaw establishment. By now she had come to the stage where she regretted nothing and took pleasure in nothing. Every girl had to bear her misfortunes and nobody had an easy time in this world. She had only one hope left: to escape from the establishment by marrying an honest man. That was why she bought lingerie for her trousseau.

It was a real affection that bound her to the cigarette-maker's family. She liked particularly to go there on Sabbath to hear Meilach reading the sayings of the Patriarchs. That reminded her of her father, her home and perhaps of the future life she dreamt of.

After their visit Mottke's girls assembled in their best dresses in Mary's room and waited for him.

In addition to Mary, Mottke owned three other girls he had "bought" and let out to establishments in the vicinity. They all gathered at Mary's place, for they knew that she was Mottke's favorite and of higher rank; for she never went on the streets but always to some hotel where her services were required. Mottke bought her the best and prettiest dresses too.

It was growing late and Mottke never came. Schloime had already called for his girls; the Schochlin girl, "little Itele," and "red-haired Rosa." (The Lowitch girl had refused to go, and stayed on at the cigarette-maker's, listening to the sayings of the Patriarchs.) Mottke's girls walked impatiently up and down, looked out through the window to see if he was coming, glanced down the stairs, and laid out his suit, shirt, cravat and boots ready for his arrival. But there was no sign of Mottke. At last the Spanish girl flung her hat trimmed with red roses on the bed and swore she would never go walking with him again even if he burst.

"You'll soon change your mind. If he begs you, you'll come," retorted the other girls, who were jealous of Mottke's darling.

While they were sitting in Mary's room Mottke was walking towards the café. It was empty. Saturday was the only day in the week when the great samovar in the corner was silent. Mottke stepped into the dark adjoining room and saw Chanele sitting at the window reading. She asked herself what he was doing there on Sabbath afternoon, when nobody ever came, but pretended that she hadn't seen him and went on reading her book.

Mottke walked about the room and glanced every now and then into the café as if he were expecting some one. The girl still didn't ask what he wanted. He wasn't a stranger and he could come here when he liked, if he wanted to.

Mottke took a look around. The landlady was not to be seen. She and her husband were having their afternoon nap in the next room. There was no sign of the children either. Only Chanele sitting at the window sunk in her book.

At last Mottke plucked up courage, cleared his throat, took a step towards Chanele, but stopped before he reached her and asked awkwardly:

"What's that you're reading, Chanele? A book?"

The girl was not accustomed to have any man speak to her except when he ordered or paid for his food. And she knew quite well that everybody, including the bullies and the prostitutes, had a tacit agreement to behave decently in her presence. They were not afraid to speak with the greatest freedom before the landlady, but as soon as Chanele entered all bawdy talk stopped and the street-walkers would whisper to each other: "Be quiet! Don't you see the girl has come in?" Chanele knew the life of these girls, but she was so used to her surroundings that it never even roused her interest, except that it sometimes excited her imagination and made her think of certain subjects. But the life of these girls couldn't be helped: "Nobody has an easy life in this world." And Chanele simply treated the prostitutes as she treated other people. So she was surprised when Mottke stopped behind her and glanced at the book over her shoulder. Nobody had ever done such a thing before.

She looked up at him and answered his question:

"Yes, a book." Then she went on reading.

"What kind of book is it? A story?"

"Yes, a story. Here, you can have a look at it." And she handed him the book.

Mottke took it and looked at it upside down, blushed like a schoolboy, and said:

"I can't read. Is it an interesting story?"

"Oh, yes, very interesting. It's called 'Jossele.'"

"What is it about?"

"It's the story of an orphan. He was brought up by strangers and they treated him very cruelly and beat him," said the girl, and her face saddened at the thought.

Mottke considered for a while. His face had an innocent look. Then he said with an awkward smile:

"Oh, that must be an interesting story! I would like to hear it. . . ."

"I'll tell it to you sometime."

"You'll tell it to me?"

"Yes," said the girl, nodding.

"That would be fine!"

"Chanele, Chanele! Come here!" cried the mother from the next room, for she was scared of Mottke.

Mottke marched off to his girls. That Saturday he was in a bad temper. He grumbled about the shirt they had ironed for him. Then he suddenly decided not to go walking with them in a row as usual.

"It doesn't look well to have all four of you in a row. Better go two by two."

When he had dressed he examined the girls, and found fault with their finery. He ordered them to take off the big

feathers that they were wearing on their hats. They thought
he had lost his wits, but there was no help for it. Mottke's
word went. Then he led them off, but not in a row as usual
—in couples like geese—and made for the Saxon Gardens.

The great avenue in the park was crowded with people
strolling about. The seats on both sides were filled with
young lads and girls. Mottke marched on with his girls,
and they were proud of him.

He walked on with his hands in his trouser pockets and
his hat over one eye, and glanced neither to the right nor
to the left. His white shirt glittered: the girls had ironed it
as stiff as a board. He was not wearing a collar, but instead
he had round his neck a long red neck-band that one of the
girls had made for him out of a silk ribbon; the polish of
his top-boots could be seen from afar.

The people in the Saxon Gardens knew him. The lads
nudged each other:

"Look, look, there goes Kanarik with his girls!"

The girls knew that people gazed after them, and were
hugely pleased.

On their promenade they met Schloime, who was taking
his girls for an outing too. But Mottke's girls were far better
dressed and showed their awareness of it in their proud
bearing. Schloime's girls envied them, for they knew that
Mottke would take them to the theater afterwards, while
as for their own master, he grudged them every penny, for
he wanted to save up and get married.

The two rivals stared at each other. Mottke raised his
eyes and measured Schloime with a sarcastic smile; Schloime
turned his eyes away.

Mottke did not stay very long in the park. He took the
girls to the Jewish theater in the Kuhstrasse. The young
man who sat at the ticket window knew him, for he was

an esteemed patron of the Jewish theater: he always bought rouble seats for himself and his girls, a thing which rarely happened there. The managing secretary, a fat man with black teeth and a golden harp on the lapel of his frock-coat, rushed up to him, showed him to his place and obsequiously addressed him in Polish, using the expression "Prosze pana" instead of "Please come this way."

In the play that came on there was a great deal of singing, and boys recited the Kaddish prayer for the dead. Mottke's girls cried and wiped their tears from their powdered cheeks with their silk handkerchiefs. In the interval Mottke bought them chocolate and treated the managing secretary and another young man belonging to the theater —he seemed to be both actor and dispenser of tickets—to a glass of brandy. Then he took his seat again and listened gravely to the songs, which he sincerely admired. As a token of appreciation he sent up to the stage a box of chocolates for the comedian and another for the boys who recited the Kaddish prayer.

The girls were in raptures. Everything pleased them and they fell in love with all the actors. For a whole week they sang the songs they had heard in the theater. and told the other girls, the cigarette-maker's wife and Chanele, how the boys on the stage had recited the Kaddish prayer for their dead mother. They waited impatiently for the next Saturday, when Mottke would take them to the theater again.

But since Mottke had talked with Chanele that afternoon he was no longer pleased with himself at all.

CHAPTER XXXVI

*

Mottke Makes Up His Mind to Marry

MOTTKE didn't know what to do with himself. Every day he thought more and more about Chanele. He was in love with her, but did not see how he was to tell her. He, a man who had the lives of four women in his hands, who was accustomed to command and see his orders carried out without question, who recognized no obstacle to his will—neither God, nor the law, nor conscience—he felt completely helpless and behaved like a green boy when he met this girl with the two long black plaits and the eyes that looked you so frankly and fearlessly in the face that everybody in the café kept his distance. He actually became awkward in the girl's presence. Since that afternoon when he found her reading and spoke to her, he had not been able to look her in the face without feeling ashamed. He cursed himself for letting himself be played with by a chit of a girl. He told himself it was ridiculous for him to be led by the nose by a mamma's pet. But it was no use; Chanele occupied all his thoughts. He began seriously to consider how he could win her for his wife.

And to the great surprise of all his friends and acquaintances he began to change his ways of life. He treated his girls exactly like Schloime. He looked upon them merely as chattels and entirely broke off his former friendly relations with them. He had as little to do with them as he could, no longer took them to the theater, and very seldom

even went walking with them in the Saxon Gardens. He
grew mean and actually groused—a thing he had never done
before—over every article of dress, every pair of shoes that
they asked him for. And, just like Schloime, he swore at
them whenever they asked him for money:

"What are you thinking of? Every week you have a new
hat! The old one will have to do."

Nobody could understand what had happened to him.
He sat all evening in the café, or patrolled the street to keep
an eye on his girls. As soon as one of them returned from
being with a client he would search her on the spot for fear
she might have hidden some money away, in her stocking
or elsewhere. He became a hard master. When the other
lads of the confraternity saw that he was doing everything
he could to save money and didn't fling his roubles about
any longer, they laughed at him behind his back, and one of
them, "Slim Chaiml," actually dared to ask him to his face:

"What's gone wrong with you, Kanarik? Have you made
up your mind to marry, seeing you're so careful of your
coppers?"

"Don't worry your head over me! You'll see sometime,
if the lice haven't eaten you up before that," was the retort.

And indeed Mottke's behavior was incomprehensible. He
had a fine suit made, dressed on the Sabbath like a young
man belonging to a good family, and in this outfit promenaded back and forward before the Warsaw Café. Nobody
could make out what was wrong with him; while he himself
thought of nothing but how he could get at Chanele and talk
to her.

For when he took up any idea he was accustomed to carry
it through at once. So he could not bear to wait now, and he
firmly believed that Chanele would agree to become his wife.

For he could not picture to himself that anybody could refuse him anything: "Why should she? I'm certainly just as
good as the next man, and I can make money too. But how
am I to get a talk with her?"

He bought a watch and a gold ring with a diamond inset,
and it cost him forty-five roubles. He carried these presents
under his shirt, tied up in a rag. But how was he to give them
to her so as to show her that his intentions were honorable?

He pictured to himself how he would take her home and
show her off to his mother on one of the great holidays.
For the memory of his mother had risen in him again, along
with a burning wish to give her a happy surprise. But not
his father, only his mother! He made up his mind to buy
fine presents for her; a new wig, a cloak with a wide border,
and a great woolen wrap. And at the New Year festival he
would bring his bride home and walk with her through the
streets of the town. That would create a sensation! All the
windows would be filled with people looking. The women
would whisper to each other:

"Who's that?"

"Why, don't you recognize him? That's Mottke, Red
Slatke's son. He's come to see his mother, bringing his
bride."

"Can it be that little thief Mottke, the brat that was
always pinching rolls and cakes from the other children and
making off with them?"

"Yes, that's him, the thief. You couldn't let your children
out in the street because of him. Yes, Red Slatke's son—just
look what a fine fellow he's turned into. Ah, there you can
see what a big city can do for a man."

"It was nice of him to remember his mother and bring her
such fine presents."

"Why shouldn't a poor woman have a bit of enjoyment

once in a while? She's earned it! The things a woman has
to bear before she can bring up a child to be a grown man!"

So the women would talk on Friday evening, standing before their doors, while Mottke walked past with his bride.

But he would behave as if he had never heard, merely
unbuttoning his jacket to show his gold watch-chain. And
Chanele would be wearing a hat in the latest Warsaw fashion, costing fifteen roubles at least. In the whole town there
wouldn't be a girl as lovely as Chanele, or as well dressed.
And this girl would be the wife of Mottke the Thief! They
would burst with envy.

His thoughts floated in these blissful dreams of the future.

But how was he to get at Chanele? Simply go across to
her and say that he wanted her to be his wife? He was
afraid she might get scared and run away. He wanted to
tell her of his feelings very gently and delicately so as to let
her see that he was in earnest about her and wanted to make
her his lawful wife, not treat her like his girls.

He had no friends, nobody he could trust, and so he had
to bear his secret and think everything out for himself. At
last he decided to go to a match-maker and send him to Reb
Meilach Lichtenstein, Chanele's father, asking for her hand.
The match-maker would smooth the road for him and put
things right.

In the neighborhood there was a Jew, a worker in leather.
But he was much more than that. For he led the singing in
the little synagogue, and also supervised at circumcisions.
When the feast of the Vine Grape came on the leather vanished from his workroom, and he sold instead palm branches
and "ethrogim," a fruit somewhat like a citron that was used
as a fertility symbol during the festival. The leather-worker
was a respected citizen and wore a long well-groomed beard;
all the people in the Old Town saluted him when they passed

his shop. Mottke chose this man as his ambassador. He knew he was a man whose words would be listened to, and he told himself that a serious man was needed for such a serious business. He had heard, too, that the man occasionally acted as match-maker for better-class families, and he was resolved to send nobody less than the best and most respected match-maker to Chanele, no matter what it cost. He wanted to make a good impression upon her from the start by his choice of the man he sent to sue for her hand.

As soon as Mottke entered the leather-worker's shop there was such a to do that you might have thought a fire had broken out. The man grew pale at the very sight of Mottke, and his wife followed by all her children appeared at the inside door, as if they were seriously concerned for their father's life. Mottke could not understand why his coming should cause such a commotion, and looked round him in amazement. But when he announced that he wanted to talk to Reb Berchie privately their agitation grew still worse. And the man's wife said she wouldn't move from the spot, no, not even if it cost her her life. But Mottke soon reassured her, for he gazed at the floor and said quite simply:

"I want to ask you, Reb Berchie, to go to Reb Meilach at the Warsaw Café and ask, for Chanele's hand in my name."

On hearing this the Jew could hardly help bursting out laughing. But as he was afraid a laugh might cost him his life, he remained quite grave and said nothing.

"Why don't you answer? You needn't worry about the money, I'll pay you as much as any of your rich customers." And Mottke put his hand in his pocket.

"Well, you see . . . it's a matter of . . . I mean . . . just to go to Reb Meilach. . . . Have you spoken to the girl about

it yet?" At last he thought he had got a loophole to slip out
of this disagreeable business.

"I haven't spoken to the girl yet, but I think she won't
say no. Besides, that's nothing to you. Speak to Reb Meilach
and tell him that I sent you."

"But surely you see ... a modern young man like you. . . .
As a man of the world . . ." Reb Berchie tried to get out
of it with a small piece of flattery. "A young man nowadays
speaks to the girl first and only sends the match-maker later
on. You must know that yourself."

Mottke had to admit that the man was right. Besides, the
compliment—"a modern young man," "a man of the world"
—caught his fancy, and he rolled it on his tongue. So he had
to admit that he must speak to Chanele first.

"If the girl's agreeable, then that's a different affair. In
that case it's a simple matter to get the father's and mother's
consent."

Mottke couldn't but admit that, too; so he left the shop
with the firm resolve of speaking to Chanele.

He fixed the interview in his mind for Saturday. On Sabbath afternoon, when her parents were having their nap and
she was reading her story book, he would speak to her. With
a beating heart he awaited the Sabbath. When the fateful
day came he shaved carefully, put on his good suit, which
had cost him twenty roubles, donned a collar and tie, and
paraded in front of the café in his shining top-boots. His
girls waited for him in vain; he no longer took them for
walks. He had deposed his favorite too, the Spanish girl,
and now she walked the streets just like the others. The
prostitutes piously accepted their fate. On the Sabbath they
sat like prisoners at their windows or gathered at the cigarette-maker's house, for they knew that Mottke was occupied with other matters.

He waited until the street was empty, and then walked into the café. He found Chanele in the little room. She was sitting by the stove reading her book. The faint light falling through the dirty panes made a halo round her head. Mottke cleared his throat, smiled, and awkwardly rocked on the heels of his new boots. Chanele never lifted her eyes from her book. She knew that Mottke was there, but never troubled to look up.

"How do you like my new suit, Chanele?" he asked with a smile, pointing to his jacket.

Chanele looked up, flung a casual glance at him and his suit, said with a smile, "Very nice," and went on reading.

Her smile gave him courage, and he asked again:

"What are you reading? The story about the orphan again?"

"No, another story."

"Is it interesting, too?"

"Yes."

"And that story about the orphan—you said you would tell it to me. Will you tell it to me now?"

"Oh go along! What do you care about stories like that?"

Her face was lit up with a smile that went to his heart. He smiled back and put his hand in his pocket. Then he drew something out, held it hidden in his huge hand, and began to stutter like a greenhorn:

"Chanele, I . . . I would like . . . to say something to you."

The girl was startled when she saw him becoming serious. She had never seen him so embarrassed before. What was he stuttering like that for? She got up apprehensively.

"I've wanted to say it to you for a long time, but I couldn't. But I must say it now."

Chanele glanced at the door. She did not know what to do and her fear made the blood fly to her face.

Mottke unrolled a watch from the cloth and said in a stifled voice:

"Chanele, I want you to marry me...."

The girl flushed and then turned pale. She opened her mouth to call for her mother, but terror paralyzed her tongue. Her eyes begged him for pity. He felt as if he were strangling some soft helpless thing in his hands. He wanted to say something, but couldn't find the right words and blurted out:

"Chanele, I don't mean it in the same way as with the other girls! God forbid! ... I want you to marry me.... Really and truly.... You would be my wife."

The girl came to herself. Mottke's last words actually brought a smile to her lips.

"What do you want *me* for? Surely you have enough girls already!"

Chanele ran into the next room.

Mottke was left holding the gold watch in his hand.

CHAPTER XXXVII

*

Mottke Writes to His Mother

Soon Welwel's establishment, the Warsaw Café and all the Old Town knew that Mottke had proposed to Chanele and wanted to marry her. And wherever he went he heard sarcastic sniggers behind his back: "Here comes the bridegroom!" He felt that people were sticking out their tongues at him, and he thought he could see an ironical grin on the faces of all his acquaintances. He couldn't make out why they all laughed at him. But it put him on his mettle, and one day he stopped one of the jeerers, struck him in the face with his fist and yelled:

"Devil take the lot of you! I suppose nobody is supposed to get married but you?"

After that they were afraid of him and avoided him. But he became the talk of the whole street, and the people had something they could joke about at least.

Chanele had disappeared. Her mother was terrified of letting her serve in the café while Mottke was about, and so she sent her to live for a while with an aunt in the Pfauenstrasse. That hurt Mottke more than anything else. He felt then how deeply Chanele's father and mother despised him and how greatly they feared him. They had actually sent the girl away in case he did something to her! At first he fancied they had done it because they disbelieved in the honesty of his intentions and were afraid he merely wanted to get hold of her and make her a street-walker like the

252

others. So he feverishly began to think of some means to win the trust of her father and mother. He treated his girls like beasts now, as if he didn't know them, and grew more severe than Schloime himself, just to show the landlady that he had no personal relations with them and that they were merely a source of income. When the landlady was there none of his girls dared show her face; if she did Mottke would shout at her:

"What are you doing here? Why aren't you out on your beat?"

But all his conscientious efforts to reassure the landlady were useless. She stubbornly avoided him, and all her family went about in terror of him.

He was filled with a deep longing for Chanele, a longing so deep that it completely crushed him. He got a little comfort out of talking to her young brothers. He won over the twins, played with them on their way back from school, and gave them money and sweets. When he was with the two children it gave him a feeling that Chanele was not very far off either. But the mother was afraid for her boys, and whenever Mottke appeared in the café she would send them packing to their room at once, as if some monster had entered:

"Moischele, Chaiml! Go to your room. Go along!"

Mottke would have liked to speak to the woman about her behavior and ask her why she wouldn't let the children come near him. But as he wanted to remain on friendly terms with her and did not want to anger her he pretended not to notice anything.

The lights had just been lit in the Warsaw Café and people were beginning to go in. Mottke decided to go in, too. As he approached the door he could hear voices raised in loud talk. As soon as he entered they fell silent. He

knew quite well that the talk had been about him. He felt
everybody looking at him as he passed. But without bothering about that he walked over to the back room and shouted
for Chaiml, who was a great friend of his. The boy rushed
out. Mottke asked him something or other. Then one of
the customers made a sign to the landlady—she was standing
behind the counter in Chanele's usual place—and she called
to Chaiml sharply:

"Chaiml, what are you doing here? Get into your room!"

The boy obeyed. Mottke was furious. He strode over to
the landlady and said quietly, doing his best to control his
anger:

"What are you frightened of? Do you think I want to
eat the boy?"

"Of course not, Kanarik. It isn't that at all! But he's
only a child and he should be in the other room," replied
the woman, pale with terror.

Mottke was silent for a while, then he asked:

"Where is Chanele?"

The woman turned as white as a sheet. She was terrified
of Mottke, yet she could not resist showing him for once
how much she despised him. No matter what happened, he
must be made to put Chanele out of his head.

"What right have you to ask after Chanele?" she asked
sullenly.

Mottke said nothing but merely looked at the woman.

"You have no right to ask about my daughter. Perhaps
you think that because I have to run a place like this, God
help me, anybody can have my daughter. Don't get any
such notion into your head. My daughter isn't for people
like you and the other men that come here. This wretched
place, God help me . . ." She burst into tears and wiped her
eyes in her apron.

Mottke stood gaping at her without knowing what to say. Her words hurt him, but he didn't want to offend her. For he saw Chanele before him with her two black plaits, and his heart longed for her again. Suddenly he felt deeply sorry for himself, and for his mother, too. She had been insulted. He banged his fist on the counter, making everything on it rattle, and shouted:

"You think I'm a bastard, maybe? I have a mother, too!"

The woman grew more terrified than ever and tried to appease him:

"Who said anything against your mother? God forbid! Of course you have a mother. Everybody has a mother. May she live till she's a hundred and twenty!"

"I thought . . . I would be sorry for you if you had said anything against my mother. I would be sorry for you. . . ."

He held his fist under her nose, and she collapsed on her chair with terror.

Then he turned away, thought for a while, and decided to do something that would show everybody in the café that he had a mother. He walked hastily to the door and called in the Lowitch girl:

"Genendel, come here!"

The girl rushed in in her dressing-gown; her cheeks and lips were heavily rouged. She asked fearfully:

"What is it?"

"Sit down there." Mottke pointed to a chair at one of the tables. "Sit down, take pen and paper and write a letter for me to my mother."

The Lowitch girl could write Yiddish and attended to the correspondence of the establishment. All the girls who had anything to get off their minds turned to her, and she wrote their letters for them.

As there was no note-paper in the café, Mottke sent out

one of the customers to the shop opposite for some and an
envelope. Then Chaiml fetched pen and ink from the kitchen.
The Lowitch girl dipped the pen in the ink and asked:

"What shall I write?"

"Write this." Mottke dictated in a loud voice so that
everybody could hear, walking up and down as he did so.
"Write: 'To my dear mother.' Have you got that?"

"Yes. Go on."

" 'I send you twenty-five roubles.' " He drew a twenty-
five rouble note from his pocket and flung it on the table
with a resounding blow of his fist. "Have you got that?
'Twenty-five roubles. Buy a wig with it, a pair of shoes and
a woolen wrap. But don't buy anything for my father, for
he thrashed me when I was a little chap. All the money is
for you. I'm staying in Warsaw now, and I am a cobbler.
I make a lot of money. I'm going to be engaged shortly.
She's a lovely girl and belongs to a fine family. As soon as
we're engaged I am going to bring her home to see you, and
I'll bring you presents at the same time.' ..."

"Oy, oy!" moaned the landlady, clasping her head in her
hands, when she heard what he was saying.

Schloime's faithful henchman Joinele Malpe was sitting
at one of the tables along with some other young men.
They had been watching Mottke ever since he came in,
smiling to themselves. When they heard what he was dictating they pinched one another with joy, stuck their heads
together, and made obscene jests about his mother. He
knew quite well that they were laughing behind his back,
but he controlled himself and went on with his letter.

"Write: 'And when the people see Red Slatke going to
the synagogue along with her son's bride they'll burst with
envy.' ..."

"Red Slatke! Did you hear what he called her? She must

be the right sort!" The men held their hands over their mouths to keep in their laughter.

Mottke looked around for a table that wasn't occupied, and while he went on dictating: " 'You must make the house nice for our visit,' " he seized it by two legs, swept off everything that was on it, and flung the heavy table at the men's heads.

"Who laughed at Red Slatke?"

Next minute he had Joinele Malpe by the scruff of the neck, and in another the man's face was streaming with blood as he struggled to get free.

"You laughed at Red Slatke, did you?" Another blow came down on Malpe's face. "Go down on your knees! Like this," cried Mottke, kicking his legs from behind till they caved in. "Here!" he pointed at the filthy floor. "There's Slatke's footsteps. Kiss them! ... Kiss the feet of Red Slatke!" And he beat Malpe on the head till he touched the filthy boards with his outstretched lips.

"Nobody'll laugh at Red Slatke! And anybody that even sneers at her will have to kiss her feet like you!"

Then he gave Malpe a kick that sent him flying back to his table. Thereupon he went back to his place and continued:

"Write this: 'And I'll bring you a roast goose and fresh fish, so that you can have a real spread ready for me and my bride.' ..."

CHAPTER XXXVIII

*

Mottke Fights Against Himself

MOTTKE was wounded in his most sensitive spot. And he decided to put Chanele out of his head, no matter what it cost him. He was furious that the woman should be ashamed of having anything to do with him, and he wanted to show everybody that he had no need of them.

So he restored his former favorite the Spanish girl, though he had almost completely withdrawn from her in the last few weeks.

In doing this he was moved by jealousy, too, to some extent. For Mary had risen immensely in prestige recently, having acquired a rich admirer: it was no other than the Commissar of the quarter, the sole ruler over the Old Town, the ruthless and much feared Wassili Nikolaiewitch Chwostow

Chwostow had the Old Town so completely under his thumb that it was as good as his private property. The shops virtually belonged to him, the wine cellars, the drapers, the confectioners, the public brothels, the cabarets. As he strolled through his domain of a morning, the shopkeepers and brothel-keepers trembled.

"Who'll he come down on next? Who'll he pitch on this time?"

Chwostow always appeared in uniform and top-boots— their creaking could be heard a mile away—and the buttons on his cloak shone. His neck was thick and red, and he

had a puffy bloodshot face, almost blue. His beard fell
in two points over his breast, on which gleamed a long row
of orders. With measured pace he walked through the streets
of his little kingdom, and his glittering eyes darted about
on every side to see that every policeman saluted him
and all the people bowed and took off their hats. And if
anybody passed without making a deep bow and doffing
his hat, Chwostow would stare at him suspiciously and
make a sign to the two policemen who always followed at
his heels to stop the "revolutionist" and examine his papers.
But very rarely was anybody guilty of omitting to take off
his hat on seeing the "Colonel" (as Chwostow loved to hear
himself called). They were all good subjects, and served
their Emperor faithfully, as well as his Commissar, the
Colonel. If he happened to pass a shop-window where there
was fresh caviare set out, or smoked fish, or choice fruit,
he coveted these delicacies straightway and went in. The
merchant, his wife and his handsome daughter would rush
up at once to serve their distinguished customer. He had
the caviare, the fish and the fruit brought, and ordered a
selection of them to be wrapped up on the spot to take with
him. The shopkeeper, his wife and his handsome daughter
bowed humbly, smiled devotedly, and hastened to comply
with the commands of the all-powerful potentate. And presently one of the policemen would be lugging the package
of caviare, smoked fish and fruit behind his Colonel.

Thus our absolute monarch made his round of his kingdom every forenoon. And when he got back both the policemen escorting him would have their arms full of the best
and tastiest tit-bits that he had "observed" on his way.

He considered it beneath his dignity to show any interest
in the brothels in his district. He left this to the inferior
officials, his subordinates: the local inspector and the police-

men. For himself, he frequented only the Aquarium and similar better-class places of amusement that happened to lie within his jurisdiction. Nevertheless, he looked on it as the duty of the inspector and the policemen to report at once if any particularly striking girl appeared in one of the brothels. In such cases he paid a visit to the establishment in person, so as to see the girl with his own eyes and decide whether it would be worth his while to get into closer touch with her.

In any establishment found worthy of such a distinction, the appearance of the Commissar was an event. The owner straightway bragged about the excellence of his goods, and the girls felt honored and looked upon themselves as belonging to a better class than the girls in the other places.

This good fortune came the way of Mottke's favorite. And at the very first glance the Commissar fell for her and thereafter visited her every night. He saw her exclusively in Welwel's establishment and never appeard until late in the evening, when the other girls were out on their beat. And he ordered his wines, his caviare and his choice fruits to be sent here now instead of to his residence.

When he arrived he shut himself up with the Spanish girl in her room, drank till he was senseless and held wild orgies. He smashed everything that came his way; yet although Welwel got nothing but damage out of these visits, he was intensely proud of the honor shown to his establishment. The citizens of the Old Town were soon courting him and begging him to put in a good word for them with the Colonel. For Welwel had suddenly risen to the distinction of being an "influence."

At first this affair with the Commissar interested Mottke only in so far as it reduced his income from the Spanish

girl. For now she was officially booked by the Commissar
every night and brought him in nothing.

But after he had made up his mind to put his silly fancy
for Chanele out of his head, the question of "prestige" became urgent. He would show them that he was still a power.

So he gave a ball for his girls in Welwel's place. Fruit,
wine and all kinds of delicacies were as plenteous as at a
royal gala. The Colonel could send the best and tastiest
things from the shops every day if he liked: good luck to
him! In fact, he had done it so well that since his affair
with Mary the children of the cigarette-maker had begun
to look distinctly healthier and redder in the cheeks. The
whole neighborhood was living off his bounty, and Mottke
could have given a banquet any day he liked. But this
evening was a special one. For Chanele had returned to her
father and mother, and he made up his mind to show her
and her mother that he didn't give a curse for them, and
that he had been a fool to run after an empty-headed chit
of a girl who looked down her nose at him. He would show
them that he needed nobody and was afraid of nobody, not
even the great Chwostow. For he would drink the wine that
the great man sent. And he would take the Spanish girl
away, too, and install her elsewhere. And she would go with
him! For his sake she would leave even a Colonel and a
Commissar!

Mottke lay like a pasha on Mary's bed; he had taken off
his coat and boots. On the table beside him stood in grand
array several dozen bottles of wine, liqueurs and brandy.
On his right sat the Spanish girl in her best silk dress with
the lace trimmings: her arms and bosom were bare, and
from her ears dangled two great ruby earrings which had
been given her by the Colonel; she looked as stylish as any
cabaret singer. And Mottke carelessly pushed on her finger

the diamond ring he had bought for Chanele. The strong
wines and liqueurs had gone a little to his head, and he sent
the other girls away; actually he had only called them in
to show them that the Spaniard was his queen again (Mary
herself had begged him to do it, for she wanted her rivals
to "burst with envy"). So now he was alone with her. She
danced naked before him, as she had done before the
Colonel. Mottke lay there like a king, sipping every now
and then at his liqueur, and gazing complacently at his
property. He ordered her to call him "Herr Colonel" and
do everything that she had done before the Commissar. And
he pretended that he was actually the Commissar.

"Who am I?" he asked.

"The Herr Colonel, the Commissar of the Old Town,"
said Mary, rolling out the words as if she were addressing
the Colonel.

"And how do you salute the Herr Colonel?" asked Mottke
in the Colonel's voice.

"Like this, sir." Mary, naked as she was, stood to attention and put her right hand to her forehead.

"And how do you address a Colonel and Commissar?"

"Your excellence, Herr Commissar Colonel Wassili Nikolaiewitch Chwostow," replied Mary.

"Mottke Kanarik!" Mottke shouted at her.

"Mottke!" cried the girl in terror, when she heard his
own name coupled with the name of the murdered man. At
once all that had happened that night rose before her, and
she felt as a woman might feel, looking back on her wedding
night.

"And you love a Commissar, a Goy, a Chwostow, a
monster! And you show yourself off before him every night
as you've done to me now. . . . Get out!" shouted Mottke,
pushing her from him in disgust.

"But Mottke, darling, you surely don't think I'm in love with him? I loathe him, but what can I do? He sticks to me like a filthy slug. Take me away from here, take me away where he'll never find me again!"

"I take you away? He won't have that satisfaction! Mottke doesn't run away, it's the others that will have to do that. I'll soon find something that will keep him from coming here again, your fine Colonel and Commissar!"

"How—as you did with Kanarik, eh? Kanarik was a sort of Colonel and Commissar, too!" said Mary, laughing.

Mottke turned pale and put his hand over her mouth.

"Leave Kanarik out of it! Hold your tongue! He got his, he's dead. And you mustn't laugh at the dead, do you hear? And I must stick up for him. I bear his name. . . . Kanarik."

The girl looked at him blankly. He was suddenly very serious.

"What is it, Mottke?" she asked, pressing close to him.

"Listen, Mary. You know that Kanarik is lying there in the water. We flung him in and went away. He wanted to run away with you and I ran away with you. He was called Kanarik and I'm called Kanarik. I've got his pass here under my shirt. I am Kanarik. I have neither father nor mother. I'm nothing more than Kanarik. Kanarik went away with you and Kanarik's living with you now. We must stick together, stick as close together as this," he pressed his palms against each other. "We must stick together, just as if we had got married that night. Whatever comes. . . . Otherwise everything will go wrong. I'm afraid that if I ever stop being Kanarik he'll rise up again and come here and revenge himself on me and take you away, too. So stick to me, Mary! Stick to me, whatever comes between us. I'm Kanarik and you're Mary. And if anybody was to plank down a whole pile of thousand rouble notes before me I wouldn't part with you. They've offered me a lot of money for you already, a great lot of money. . . . But I won't sell you! We're tied to each other. For ever."

They clung together and gazed at each other. In their gaze was the fear of death that they had shared together, the mystery of the sin they had committed, making them one. Without speaking they looked long into each other's eyes and lived again what they had lived through that night in the wood, where Kanarik lay in the water. And it seemed to Mottke he could hear some one calling his name.

"Mottke, darling, take me away from here! I don't want ever to see him again, that man."

"You little fool, I'll soon arrange things so that he'll never come back again. I'll slip into your room masked when he's with you, I'll take away his revolver and drive him out into the street in his drawers. You'll see!"

"Like the Pole, can you remember him still? You were only a little smout then," said Mary, laughing.

He drew her down on his knee and they began to laugh at the Commissar and all the people that feared him. They thought out all sorts of plans for playing tricks on him and then running away.

"Yes, yes, Mottke, let's go away from Warsaw altogether. I wish it was burned down! We'll be artists again, as we were before. I would love to be back on the tightrope again. . . . Do you remember the rich landlords that followed me from fair to fair when I was a tightrope dancer? Oh, what have you made of me, Mottke?" she cried, bursting into tears.

"Shut your mouth, you little fool. I'll get you a place in a cabaret or a great circus or something. You'll work for a rich company and make lots of money. I'll get you fine dresses yet, you'll see, Mary."

"Mottke, my darling, my darling. . . ."

Then a girl's voice could be heard in the passage:

"Chaiml, Moischele, come to your breakfast, it's almost time for school. . . ."

Mottke turned pale. It was Chanele. Since her return he hadn't seen her, and this was the first time he had heard her voice. A sea of memories broke over him. He was dejected all at once. He felt sullied and he was disgusted with the wines, the liqueurs, the naked girl, with himself and his whole life. But he tried to drive away his thoughts, laughed, gulped down a glass of brandy, and kissed the Spaniard on the mouth. But this girl who belonged every night to another man horrified him now. He pictured the fat Commissar lying on the couch with her. . . . His huge belly. . . . And he couldn't stay there any longer. . . . He saw Chanele's black hair.

No, he couldn't bear this room any longer. Putting on his clothes, he went downstairs. He didn't dare to go into the café; he was ashamed to look Chanele in the face. But he cast a hasty glance into the kitchen and saw her there. She was setting her brothers' breakfast on the table and talking to them. He saw her black hair, with the smooth parting in the middle. He saw her hands as they set the plates down. He saw one of her brothers smiling at her and saying something. He saw no more and wanted to see no more. His heart contracted and he went away. For a long time he wandered through the streets. When he came to the Iron Bridge he climbed down to the Vistula, sat down on a stone and stared at the water. He sat quite still. Then a sudden rage came over him. He felt angry at some one—but who was it? And then he knew; he was angry with Kanarik lying there, dead, in the wood under the water. He took up a stone and flung it into the river, as if he were trying to hit Kanarik.

"It was all his fault that I killed him!" he cried. "All his fault, from beginning to end!"

Then he began to smile. He saw Chanele decking the table on Friday evening. And he was her husband. He had just come home. He had driven some people from the station; they had been late. He clumped into the room in his muddy top-boots, though the floor was swept and strewn with sand. Chanele was annoyed at his dirtying the floor again. Then his mother—she was staying with them—brought him a basin of hot water from the next room. He washed himself. A smell of stewed fish came from the kitchen. The room was filled with the fragrance of the new bread set out on the table.

He saw himself as the master of the house. He walked to the synagogue, a prayer-book in his hand.

And he smiled to himself. . . .

Rage seized him again. Who was it that was standing in his way? Who was hindering him? Why had they made him into what he was? And who had done it? Everybody, everybody! They had all wanted him to be a thief and to murder Kanarik; they had all brought him to the point where he must live with prostitutes for the rest of his life and never have a wife of his own or a mother; they had beaten him down till he had a brothel for a home and a whore who slept every night with the Commissar for a bride. And he felt the full injustice that the whole world, everything, the sun, the sky, the earth, mankind, had committed against him in forcing him to become what he was. . . . He blamed everything, everything but himself. He looked upon himself as clean and free of all guilt. And that roused his spirit. Simply because they all wanted him to remain what he was now, to spend his life in a brothel and never have a wife like Chanele to light the candles on the Sabbath

Eve—simply for that reason he would show them that they could go to the devil and that he was capable of bringing about whatever he set his mind on. . . . Oh, he didn't want to be a respectable human being for *their* sakes! They were all robbers. But he would fight on till he got a wife and a mother and a home of his own, and for his *own* sake, not theirs. Even if they all burst with envy. . . . Kanarik could lie in the water and rot if he liked. . . .

And now he had the feeling that Kanarik was a living creature struggling with him. He picked up a big stone and flung it into the river. And he kept on flinging stones into it, as if he wanted to hit Kanarik's body, which lay somewhere else, weighed down with such stones as these. He decided to part with the Spaniard that very day, and to sell the other girls cheap to Schloime: "I'll take whatever he offers." With the few hundred roubles he got in exchange he would look round for some business, and either buy a cart or else set up as a cobbler. "I'll find something or other to do." Oh, he would risk everything, everything, to get himself a wife, a home and a mother of his own, if only because the others were so set against his doing it.

And with his usual energy he started upon the execution of his resolve: to become a decent human being in spite of all the world,

CHAPTER XXXIX

*

Mottke Sells Out

NEAR Welwel's establishment the barber Jankele had his
shop. There the men of the confraternity foregathered, the
procurers, bullies, pimps, and owners of the Old Town
brothels. But while you went to the Warsaw Café for
amusement or to kill time, you went to Jankele's for business reasons. Here deals were closed, here the brothel-
keepers and bullies sold, exchanged, or bequeathed their
living wares. And sometimes a procurer would lead the pro-
spective buyer through a separate door and up a stair to a
little room where he could display his goods—generally a
naked girl—in safety. In this way you could decide whether
she was worth the price or not.

But this day a regular market was being held in Jankele's.
For dealers had arrived, big dealers covered with diamonds,
who were laying in goods intended for export to distant
lands, and they paid for them to the tune of hundreds of
roubles. Everybody waited for this market day with great
impatience, the bullies as well as the girls belonging to the
brothels; for on it many of them were delivered from the
Old Town and sent out into the great world beyond the
sea, to acquire riches.

The Old Town was quiet this day. Not a girl was to be
seen in the streets. A few young men promenaded the
pavements. All were worried over the dealers. If they took
fright the whole business was as good as lost.

But there was no real cause for such fears. The police themselves would see to that. The Commissar, Colonel Chwostow, who knew quite well when the "Turks," as they were called, were to be expected, had sent two of his most reliable men to patrol the street. The policemen walked the pavement before Jankele's shop and saw to it that there was no hitch in the smooth running of the business.

In Jankele's shop there was a great bustle. His wife had been early to the market and bought the best fish and the fattest geese. In the kitchen, feverish activity. The smell of roast goose filled the whole length of the street, for a real banquet was being prepared for the dealers.

Up in the little room next door to the barber's shop, which was reached by a back-stair, and whose window looked out on a high gray wall, the dealers were sitting on two beds piled high with cushions: a fat woman in the fifties dressed in rich silks, with diamond rings on her short, stubby fingers, and a long chain of pearls round her bloated neck and falling on her immense bosom; opposite her a young man, her son. He was equally well dressed and equipped with diamonds. His whole appearance, and particularly the red spots on his cheeks and his thin pointed fingers, showed that he was consumptive. He kept glancing about nervously, smoking one cigar after another, and tugging restlessly at his little mustache. So as not to be understood by the others, mother and son talked in a sort of Spanish-Jewish dialect, mixed with Turkish phrases and expressions drawn from every conceivable European language. They spoke Yiddish to the sellers, although neither looked Jewish and were of a pure oriental type, with their brown complexions and brownish-black eyes. But they rarely addressed a word to the procurers and the brothel-owners. When a girl was offered to them their first question was always: "Is she

fair?" in which case they didn't even bargain, but paid at
once the sum that was asked. On the table before them lay
a whole pile of photographs showing girls in the most various
poses; some of them looked like respectable girls of good
Jewish family, while others were quite naked and taken in
daring postures. Mother and son examined these pictures
with indifference, listened to the sellers lauding the points of
their girls, and nodded now and then. Then they would
glance at each other, exchange a few incomprehensible
Spanish or Turkish words, and the deal was closed.

The chief middle-man in this business was Jankele the
barber, a broad-shouldered Jew with a lock on his forehead,
a fat belly and a dimple on each cheek. He called the
woman "aunt" and her son "cousin." They consulted with
him, for they trusted him and relied on his word, since he
was a relation. Every now and then Jankele's wife appeared
bearing a tray with stewed fruits, brandy and oranges, which
she offered to her guests with a hospitable smile:

"Now, you must eat something, Auntie. And you must
take something to strengthen you too, Cousin."

And when Jankele made a sign to her to leave the room
she would retort:

"What are you thinking of? They've been at it talking
and bargaining since early morning. They must be feeling
quite faint!"

The woman dealer smiled condescendingly at her niece,
tasted a little of the stewed fruit, and with a few words in
Spanish pushed it across to her son.

But usually these two strangers had no time for such
trifles. Business demanded their full attention. Such girls
as they couldn't come to terms about because of the highness
of the price, they made a point of inspecting personally.
Then everybody left the room, for nobody must know what

happened now. The fat woman and her son were left alone.
After a while the door would open, and a girl stood there.

"Does Gedalje the glazier live here?" she had to ask.

"Yes. Just come in, child," replied the fat woman.

Mother and son scrutinized the girl and winked at each other, because of Gedalje the glazier.

Although the visitors knew what was what, and would have liked to say so openly, the conversation was always confined to Gedalje the glazier.

For greater safety a pack of cards lay on the table. For if the police chanced to come in you could say you were playing cards.

Yet Gedalje the glazier was very seldom called in, for generally the deal was closed straight off by word of mouth. No business is more dependent on mutual trust than the business in living flesh. One's word is one's bond, and everybody watches jealously over the honor of the trade. That applies not only to the actual dealers but to the objects they sell. For nobody is so delighted by a deal as the girls themselves.

They become so weary at last of their monotonous life in these places that they acquire an almost pathological longing for change, for some event that will free them from their narrow rooms and launch them into the "great world." And the words "Buenos Aires" and "The Argentine" are for these girls surrounded with the gloriole of legend. There, in Buenos Aires, girls were free, made lots of money from the "Blacks," and then acquired a husband and themselves became proprietresses of establishments; all the rich women dealers who came from Buenos Aires had been in establishments themselves once upon a time; lots of girls who had gone there wrote to their friends, saying that they were growing richer and richer every day, and sent money to their old folks to get their sisters married; over in the Argentine all the girls wore gold fillings in their teeth and cleaned them with gold tooth-brushes.

And the legends that went round the brothels told of girls who had won the love of black princes and black sultans and lived now like queens.

So all the girls in these places had a burning desire to be bought for export to the Argentine. And when the dealers came from Buenos Aires to replenish their stock the Old Town held high holiday. All the girls bleached their hair or tinted it yellow and put on their gayest dresses. For the dealers always gave blondes the preference, because the "Blacks" in Buenos Aires would have nothing but blondes.

But Mottke's girls were most elated of all.

"Kanarik's selling off all his girls," the word flew round.

And in fact all Mottke's girls had become blondes at one stroke. He sold them with relief. True, he wasn't allowed to enter Jankele's Holy of Holies, where the market was held. He wasn't a tried and trusted dealer yet, to be admitted to the presence of the Argentinians or, as they were called in jest, "Gedalje the glazier." More, he didn't even know where the market was being held. Welwel put through the deal for him. All the same Mottke came out of it with "a pocketful of hundred rouble notes," at least so it was said in the town. "That fellow has the devil's luck. As soon as he wants to get rid of his girls these dealers arrive; it must be Gedalje the glazier himself that brings him his luck." The Old Town enviously told how Kanarik had made his pile and was a rich man now.

"But what will he do without his girls?"

"Don't you worry! He'll soon find other ones."

"Rubbish. He's giving up the business. He wants to marry Chanele."

"But she won't have him."

"She'll have him now, all right. The lad has money, and she'll have him."

"And what has he done with the Spaniard?"

"He wanted to sell her too, but Welwel wouldn't let him for fear of the Commissar."

"No, he didn't want to sell her. He was offered a pile of money for her some time ago, but he wouldn't give her up."

This is what was said in the Warsaw Café and the Old Town about Mottke. His girls floated in a dream of bliss and good fortune. For Gedalje the glazier had helped them all. Mottke had made a pile of money, and Welwel hadn't come off badly either. But the happiest of all were the girls themselves, for they had escaped from their slavery. They were all blonde and wearing their brightest dresses. They did not go on the streets to earn money any longer, but made preparations for the long journey to the land where black princes awaited them, black princes who absolutely raved about blonde Jewish girls. And all of them dreamed of a black prince who would fall in love with them and raise them to be princess of his black kingdom.

CHAPTER XL

*

Mottke Becomes an Honest Man

THE time came for the girls to be shipped across the sea. They wept bitter tears, and a great paying of farewell visits began in all the neighborhood. In the cigarette-maker's house there was deep mourning. The girls came to say good-by to the sick woman. They all cried and wished one another good luck.

"Don't forget me when you're across the sea! When you're happily settled remember me and the children."

"Do you think we could ever forget you, Leah? You've been more than a mother to us, more than a sister," cried the girls, bursting into fresh tears. "We'll never, never forget you."

"Dear Leah, take these things for the children." The girls brought her their spare underclothes and dresses and everything that they didn't want to take with them.

Only one of them gave her nothing, the Lowitch girl. She kept the trousseau she had gathered together safely under lock and key.

"How'll you be able to get a great big trunk like that over the frontier? What will you do with all that stuff on the other side? Lingerie is dirt cheap there," the other girls told her.

But the Lowitch girl wouldn't listen to them. "You can find a use for lingerie anywhere." She would sell nothing and give nothing away. She would have renounced all hope of another life if she had parted with her things: the hope of

marrying and becoming respectable. The trunk with her bed
and table linen was to her a symbol of purity and hope.
And she guarded it carefully and took her spotless linen
with her into the "black kingdom," where she hoped to become a queen, the wife of a black prince.

"As soon as you're safely over the frontier, do write to me
and the children, even if it's only a few lines," the cigarette-
maker's wife said to them as they were going.

The children flung their arms about their necks, clung to
them and wept bitterly because their "aunts" were going
away.

The whole street gazed after them with pity when they
left. The people knew where they were going and felt sorry
for them, not because such a dreadful destiny waited them,
but because they had to face such a long journey across the
great ocean, and they were terrified of the sea. There were
others who envied them and wished they were in the shoes
of these girls going off to a country where you could pick
up money in the streets. They would have been glad to go
too, if they only had the money for the journey. But everybody hoped that the girls would safely reach the land of the
"Blacks."

Meanwhile Mottke had given up his old profession and
become an "honest man." He no longer dressed like a bully,
but went about in "civvies," as they said in the Old Town.
He wore a decent new suit, a collar and tie, and a gold watch
and chain. Dressed up like this, he sauntered through the
streets of the Old Town. And strange to say, since people
had learned that he had made "a little pile" by selling his
girls, that he had money to spend and had become a man just
like them, they didn't fear him any longer. Certainly they
still fought shy of him and no respectable citizen would have
stopped him in the street and spoken to him. But the veil of

mystery that had enveloped him when he was the king of the prostitutes was gone, and nobody trembled now at the sight of Kanarik, or crossed to the other side of the street on seeing him. And when he went into a shop to buy something the other customers didn't leave at once. He was just an ordinary citizen of the Old Town and people looked on him as one of themselves.

Since his metamorphosis into a respectable man, Mottke no longer showed his face in the Warsaw Café. Yet he didn't leave Chanele entirely out of his sight. Every evening he stole to the kitchen window that looked out on the back yard, and watched Chanele giving her little brothers their supper. And when he saw her black plaits hanging over her shoulders, a sense of ineffable purity filled him. This feeling was a reward for all that he had suffered for her. Looking at that head with the black hair he saw his whole future life as he dreamed of it. And that head was bound up in his mind, too, with something in his past that was dear to him, for it reminded him of his mother. He couldn't think of Chanele without thinking of his mother. These two women, Chanele and his mother, melted into one woman in his mind. And he loved them both in one.

And strange to say, he felt pained now by the thought that Chanele should live in the Warsaw Café and have to serve the people that went there. He felt a deep disgust for the Café and the whole quarter, and wished that Chanele, his Chanele, were well out of it and that her mother would send her to her aunt's house again, as she had done before. Nobody must be able to touch Chanele, nobody must know where she lived. He himself mustn't know.

But he couldn't send the match-maker to Chanele's father for a while yet. Mary still stood in the way. She was still in Welwel's establishment, and the Commissar visited her

every evening. Mottke's heart was divided between Chanele
and Mary. He couldn't bring himself to sell Mary like the
other girls. They had been mere chattels to him. But Mary
was very near to him, a living being that belonged to him.
He knew this was so after carefully examining his feelings.
Yet he saw that he could never win Chanele if he didn't get
rid of Mary, if he didn't put her out of his life. And Chanele
was dearer to him than his life. His one ambition now was
to have a wife and a mother of his own, like any other man.
And he would see that he had them, if only because everybody was against it. But he wanted to come to Chanele with
pure hands and a pure heart.

For a long time he fought with himself Then he went to
Mary one day and opened his heart to her. He spoke to her
as a brother might talk to a sister, as a human being to another human being:

"Mary, we must part. I'm leaving this place."

"Whatever are you saying, Mottke?" she said, looking up
in alarm. Then she asked: "You want to get married, don't
you?"

"Yes," replied Mottke.

"Why?"

"I don't know.... I must.... I want to.... I can't help
it."

Mary looked at him sharply and saw his great longing for
Chanele in his eyes. She saw his eyes shining, his lips trembling, his face growing pale. She loved him and she couldn't
bear it. She flung her arms round his neck and kissed him
passionately.

"Mottke, my darling, whatever you do I'll always love
you."

"Whether you love me or not, I know my life is in your
hands. You can give me up to the Commissar for having

murdered Kanarik, and tell him that I have a false pass and a false name. Give me up if you like, but I'd marry Chanele all the same, even if I knew it meant death or disgrace. I'm going to marry her; you can have me sent to Siberia afterwards if you like. But I'm going to marry Chanele."

Mary grew jealous when she realized how deeply he loved Chanele. She bit her lips till they bled, clenched her fists and leant against Mottke so that she mightn't fall.

"Why can't you have me and Chanele too? Take her if you like. Steal her away some night and put her in one of the houses. We could be all together then, and she'd earn you lots of money. We'd both love you, both of us, and work for you. . . ."

Mottke turned pale. His heart beat like a hammer. More than once he had thought of the same thing, but he had never dared to follow his thoughts to the end. It was only deep down in his mind that he had ever dared to think of such a thing, and now Mary spoke his thoughts straight out. He said nothing. Good and evil fought within him.

"I'll manage to persuade her, you'll see. I know about such things. I'll bring her to agree to it," Mary went on hurriedly.

Then Mottke saw his mother before him. She was sitting at the table sewing his trousers. He was lying in the corner of the cellar, black and blue with his beating. He was crying and gazing at his mother as she sewed his trousers.

Yes, that was her! Her face looked just like that— wrinkled, tanned as hard as a piece of leather, tears running down her yellow cheeks, her lips dry and cracked, the veins on her shriveled neck sticking out like those on a plucked hen's; her eyes glazed like a hen's when the slaughterer held it between his knees to cut its throat.

And Mottke couldn't tell how it happened—Chanele suddenly turned into his mother, and his mother into Chanele. They were one person, one being, and if he hurt Chanele it was the same as if he were to hurt his mother. The thought agitated him so deeply that he forgot everything else. He knew that his life was in Mary's hands, but that didn't matter to him now, and he stamped his foot and shouted:

"Hold your tongue! Do you think that Chanele would ever do what you do? Come along! Come along with me at once! Come along!"

"Where?" asked the girl in terror.

"What's that to you? What right have you to ask? Do you think I'm going to leave you here with your Colonel, so that you earn nothing? Come on, come along, I tell you! I'm going to take you to the Aquarium. They want you there for some turn. You'll be able to dance on your tightrope at last. And you won't be working for me. I don't need your money. You can work for yourself and make something out of yourself, so that you needn't stay in these houses."

He began to bundle up her things, stuffing her silk underwear, washed and unwashed, her silk blouses, stockings, shoes, hats, into a trunk; and that very evening he appeared with her at the Aquarium. There he sold her, as he might have sold a prize dog or a favorite horse, for two hundred and eighty roubles, after prolonged haggling.

Before he left he took Mary's hand, looked deep into her eyes and gave her the money he had got for her:

"Here. Take this, I don't want it. It belongs to you. Buy yourself some hats."

Mary felt as deeply insulted as if he had struck her. She flung the money in his face and shouted:

"I'm your whore! You've sold me! It's your money! Why do you offer it to me?"

Mottke stuck the notes in his pocket and said in a low voice:

"My life's in your hands. You can give me up to the police if you like. What does it matter to me? I'll only be sent to Siberia."

The girl was silent. But her sharp teeth, white as ivory, bit deep into her red lips.

CHAPTER XLI

*

Mottke Becomes Engaged

A LITTLE while after that Mottke disappeared from the Old Town and took up his domicile in Grzybow near the Iron Gate, where the fish-dealers lived who handled the frozen fish that came from inner Russia. In Grzybow Mottke went into partnership with another young man and bought a horse and cart and started carting fish from the railway station to the town. His reputation in the Old Town was well known to the carters and feared by them. So they made no objection to his entering the union, and gave him his permit to carry out his trade. Soon they forgot his former profession, accepted him as one of themselves, and never brought up his "brilliant past" except when they quarreled with him. But lots of the men in the fish trade had equally "brilliant pasts," and Mottke was soon as highly respected in Grzybow as he had been in the Old Town. His few hundred roubles he lent to one or two fish-dealers, and, according to the common talk, he was going to be taken in as a partner by one of them presently.

The reason for Mottke's doing all this was a wink he had got from Reb Meilach, Chanele's father. For the old man had kept his eye on him ever since he had made his little pile off the girls. And when he saw that Mottke was leading a steady life he decided, after careful consultation with his wife, that this fellow Kanarik mightn't be at all a bad husband for Chanele.

"A young chap with a few hundred roubles—what does his past matter? It isn't as if he was a girl who had to be careful of her name. There's lots of things a girl daren't do, but a young fellow can do pretty much what he likes."

"That's true. He hasn't scattered bastards round him, anyway," agreed his wife. "And if a fellow turns respectable, it shows he must have something good in him deep down. He may turn into a respectable father of a family yet. And he's head over heels in love with Chanele, he would let his eyes be put out for her."

"The main thing, don't forget it, is that he has a few hundred roubles tucked away, and when a fellow like that starts on the right road he works like a horse. Who's to know how he got the money? There's no record of it on his pass, and money isn't to be sneezed at, let me tell you!"

But Reb Meilach didn't speak to Mottke himself. He took care not to meet him; for God forbid that anybody should sniff out his ideas about Mottke. But he had his middlemen, friends and acquaintances, and they advised Mottke and pointed out what he should do. One of them, in fact, was the same Reb Berchie, leather-worker and precentor at the synagogue, that Mottke had asked before to arrange a marriage with Chanele.

"A young fellow like you with a few hundred roubles in his pocket shouldn't be idling about the streets. You'll soon have eaten it all up or squandered it on your friends, for there's never any lack of that kind of friend," Reb Berchie lectured him, after he had sold the Spanish girl and appeared in the shop to beg him again to arrange a marriage with Chanele.

"Don't you fear; I won't fling it away. I swear by Chanele herself that I won't spend it on drink or enjoyment; I'll stick to my little nest-egg."

"If you want to marry you must start on something.
For instance, you might go to Grzybow, look for a partner,
and buy a horse and cart. What are you doing here? You
must get out of the Old Town. People must forget who you
were and what you were—don't you see?"

That was Reb Berchie's advice: he had got a wink from
Reb Meilach.

Mottke did as he was advised.

But not till after he had been away from the Old Town
for a fairly long time, so that everybody had almost forgotten him, did they arrange a meeting between him and
Chanele, so that the two young people might get to know
each other. Reb Berchie took over the match-making after
all. He described Mottke as a "fish-dealer from Grzybow,
a healthy young fellow, exempt from military service, with
a few hundred roubles of his own, and a cart and a pair of
horses." Reb Meilach and his wife quietly let the broker
say his say to the end, and then enquired more particularly
into the qualities of the suitor, as if they had never seen
him in their lives. The meeting between the lovers was
arranged for next Saturday. And at the agreed hour on
Sabbath afternoon Mottke and Chanele met each other at
the house of the girl's aunt in the Pfauenstrasse.

Mottke sat in his chair, pale and perturbed; he was wearing a new suit, and didn't dare to move for fear he might
break something. Opposite him, at the other side of the
table, sat Chanele, equally pale, in a new dress, her hair
braided in two plaits. Her whole appearance awoke his pity
and yet attracted him. He looked across at her and his heart
almost burst with pity. She was like a little bird that hadn't
got its feathers yet, like a little bird he had seen in its
nest when he was a boy. It had trembled with cold in his
hand. . . . fluttered its little wings . . . and he had put it inside

his shirt to warm it. . . . He would have liked to take Chanele to his breast like that now.

The conversation turned on family affairs. They got to know the young suitor. Chanele's mother wanted to know all about her future son-in-law, and asked if his father and mother were still alive.

"I've a mother. She's a good mother, a very good mother. . . . When I was quite small—a little smout I was too—they wanted to beat me. But my mother wouldn't let them . . . and she . . ."

"Is your father living too?" Reb Meilach broke in, for he thought Mottke's remarks were out of place.

"Yes, he's alive too, but I don't like him. . . ."

"Where do they live?"

"In a little town, Schochlin."

"And what is your full Jewish name? I mean your first name," asked the marriage-broker.

"Mottke."

"Mottke? This is the first I've heard of it!"

"Oh . . . they only called me that when I was a little chap . . . they called me Mottke then," the suitor went on hastily. "My real name is Aaron-Meier Kanarik. I have it on my pass. Here it is."

Mottke pulled out his pass.

"Aaron-Meier is a good Jewish name," said Reb Berchie, turning to Chanele's father.

But Mottke felt as if something had snapped in him.

He realized, as if for the first time, that he bore the name of a stranger and had lost his own. And he had a passionate longing for his own name; never had he felt such a longing for his own name as now, just before his betrothal.

The thought made him sad, and he fell silent.

"Let's leave the young folk to themselves for a little," said Reb Berchie, making a sign to the others.

"Perhaps they've something to say to each other that they wouldn't like us to hear," added Chanele's aunt, leading the others into the next room; she had read Mottke's silence as meaning that he wanted to be alone with his betrothed.

Mottke became paler than ever when he found himself alone with the girl, more perturbed and silent than ever. Though he had destroyed a man's life with his hands, he felt quite helpless before this girl, and couldn't think of a single word to say. Chanele, too, felt constrained. Mottke could hear the beating of her heart. And yet she found her tongue first:

"It seems settled that I'm to be your wife. It must be the will of God. . . ."

"And you yourself? Do you want to be my wife?" asked Mottke.

"I want to do whatever father and mother wish. They know better than I do what's good for me," replied Chanele, looking at the floor.

"But you yourself, do you want to be my wife?" Mottke asked again.

"I'll tell you the truth. I'm terribly afraid, I'm trembling with fear. . . ."

"What are you afraid of?" asked Mottke in deep alarm.

"You know yourself. I'm afraid you might return to your old ways some day. Do you expect me to lead a life of that kind with you? It would be far better if we parted now before we're united in the eyes of God and man."

Chanele's mother had coached her to say this to Mottke, so as to work on his feelings. But Chanele was really afraid of him, and her eyes filled with tears.

Mottke couldn't bring out a single word. He wanted to fall at her feet and tell her everything about himself as he might tell it to God or a great Rabbi; all about his childhood and everything else that he kept buried in his heart: that he wasn't Kanarik at all but Mottke, and that he had murdered the man whose name he bore. He felt he must tell her all this, but then he thought of the people in the next room. He bit his lips and stammered in a voice that could hardly be heard:

"Chanele . . . I would rather die . . . kill myself . . . fling myself in the river, than hurt you. . . . Not even *that* much. . . . I'll be a faithful husband to you, Chanele! . . . You'll see. . . ." And he burst into tears.

Chanele took pity on him.

"Don't cry. I believe what you say. If I didn't believe you, do you think I would agree to be your wife?"

Mottke hastily wiped his eyes with his handkerchief and fought back his tears, for he could hear steps in the next room. The door opened:

"Well, are you agreed?"

Mottke and Chanele remained silent.

That evening the official betrothal took place, quietly, and without fuss. That the ceremony might be valid ten men were present. Chanele's father didn't want it to be known in the Old Town yet that she was betrothed to Kanarik. At first he had intended to postpone the ceremony till later, but Mottke had begged that it might be got over as soon as possible. When they were signing the agreement Reb Berchie signed for Mottke, since he couldn't write:

"Aaron-Meier Kanarik."

"*Maseltow*, Aaron-Meier, here's good luck!" all the men cried.

But that name seemed quite strange to him now, and he had a feeling that it wasn't he but Kanarik who had been betrothed to Chanele. For the name under the agreement wasn't his, but Kanarik's.

CHAPTER XLII

*

Mottke Confesses

ALL the week Mottke and Chanele did not see each other. But to make up for that they spent Saturday together. Mottke always went to the aunt's house then and found Chanele there. After dinner they went for a walk, not in the Saxon Gardens, where he was too well known, but to the Citadel behind the Jewish Hospital; there was an alley of tall poplars there where the young couples of Warsaw went when they wanted to be undisturbed. Chanele herself had no wish to go to the Saxon Gardens or the Jewish theater. She was afraid of Mottke's being recognized there.

In the few weeks of their engagement they had come to know each other. She taught him how to behave and treated him like a younger brother. And Mottke did all she told him, for he was resolved to become a thoroughly respectable man. Already she had got him to the point of attending the synagogue every Sabbath with her uncle. He dressed now, too, as every decent young engaged Jew in Poland did: that is, he wore a frock-coat not much shorter than a caftan. In his button-hole he pinned a sort of medallion with a photograph of Chanele, and another portrait of her, in another medallion, hung from the gold watch-chain that she had given him as a wedding-present along with a watch. He had no traffic now with the other carters in Grzybow, and no longer drank with them in the taverns. He made friends instead with the fish-dealers who had businesses of their own, for that was more respectable and high-class. It was Chanele's idea and he did whatever she asked him. She showed the greatest skill in getting her way, and when she wanted him to do something or other she would begin:

"You see, Aaron-Meier, you're engaged now, and when a man's engaged he really doesn't. . . ."

Naturally, she always called him Aaron-Meier Kanarik, not Mottke. As they walked together through the lonely poplar avenue towards the Vistula, she would sometimes call him "Aaron-Meier, my darling." That sent a pain to his heart. For it was as if she didn't mean him, and he was only Kanarik's substitute. And in a minute Kanarik would rise from the dark water, walk up to Chanele, take her by the hand and claim her. And when they sat on the hill behind the Citadel, and Chanele pulled his head down on her lap with her cool hands and pressed her cool lips to it and whispered: "Dearest Aaron-Meier, my own Aaron-Meier," he would shut his eyes and whisper to himself softly, so that she couldn't hear: "Mottke . . . Mottke . . . Mottke."

Once—it was on the eve of the Feast of Tabernacles—they were out walking together. Chanele was wearing a new frock with a blouse that looked almost like a man's and had a soft collar; it was the latest fashion. Mottke was struck dumb with admiration when he looked at her. How stylish she looked, how high-class! He was wearing a new suit, for the wedding was coming near now and they were buying new clothes almost every day in preparation for it. They went out to the Citadel as usual. It was a real June day. Everything was in blossom, and the scents were intoxicating. As they neared the poplar avenue a great green plain opened before them under the wide sky. One half of it was in the sun, the other was bathed in dark bluish shadow. And down below them the opposite bank of the Vistula was a whirling shower of fiery red points, like a little inferno. They felt as light as if they had wings instead of feet. They felt they couldn't walk any longer; they must run. So they raced each other to their favorite spot, a little patch of sward on the hill behind the poplars, sat down on the grass and looked at their reflections in a dark brown pool close by the trees. They spoke of their wedding, made plans for the future, and were as happy as the day. Suddenly Chanele asked:

"Aaron-Meier, why don't you get your mother to come? I want to meet my future mother-in-law."

Mottke replied, his heart beating faster:

"Will you like my mother, Chanele?"

"Of course I'll like her! How can you ask such a question? Who else should I like? She's your mother and so she's my mother too."

Mottke's lips twisted; he managed to say:

"I'll write home tomorrow and send her some money and tell her to come."

"I want both your mother and my mother to be at the wedding, else I wouldn't like it in the least."

Mottke felt by now that they both belonged to the same family; as if Chanele had been born along with him and was of the same blood, not his bride only but something more, as his mother was.

And when Chanele snuggled against him and said: "Aaron-Meier, I've got a nice present for your mother: a wig and a black lace shawl," he caught her hand in his and whispered very low:

"Chanele, my name isn't Aaron-Meier. It's Mottke. Call me Mottke. Please!"

"Mottke!" the girl laughed heartily. "Go along! You're trying to have me on. Mottke! What sort of a name is

Mottke? It's the kind of name you would give to a thief."

"I'm not trying to have you on, Chanele. The name I use isn't my own."

"What do you mean? Do you go under a strange name? But nobody goes under a strange name! You're joking."

"I'm not joking. Listen to me, Chanele. I've wanted to tell you for a long time, for I must tell you everything. . . . Before we get married you must know everything about me, just like my mother. You'll be like a mother to me from now on. I must tell you everything. . . . Everything!"

Chanele held her tongue. She felt that he was going to tell her something very important, but she was afraid to hear it. Yet she felt curious at the same time.

"You see, Chanele, when you spoke of my mother just now I saw all at once that you and I—how can I put it?— are one and that I can tell you everything. Listen, Chanele, I bear a stranger's name, the name of a man who isn't living now, who isn't living. That man wronged me deeply, very, very deeply. . . . And he had a name and I had none. . . . I ran away from home when I was a little chap, I hadn't a name or a pass. People struck me and I struck back. They searched for me and wanted to lock me up, but I ran away. . . . I hadn't a pass, and if you haven't a pass you haven't a name. Nobody can go about without a name. . . . The other man had a pass and a name. . . . I envied him for that and kept thinking and thinking how I could take his pass and his name from him. . . . And I thought and thought—and at last I managed it. . . ."

Chanele sat without moving. Her heart was beating fast. She didn't feel the dew piercing through her dress, she only saw Mottke's wide-open eyes, which held hers like a magnet; she could feel the warmth of his hand and his breath.

". . . And one time, after that man had done something

very, very cruel to me—he and his friends beat me up so
that I lay on my back for a long time—I found out that he
was going to run away . . . with some one else . . . so I consulted with . . . with the one he was going to run away with.
Then I watched for him one night on the road he was taking,
and . . . did something that made him disappear, disappear
from the face of the earth. And now I have his pass and
call myself by his name. Don't be afraid; he'll never come
back again. He's lying at the bottom of some water with
stones on the top of him to keep him down. . . . That was
the way I saw it. He struck me, and I struck him back.
Now I'm sorry I did it, very, very sorry. I've been sorry
ever since I knew you. I can't sleep at nights. But it can't
be helped now. I must put it out of my head. He's dead,
and whatever I do it won't help him. It's all one to him now.
But I'm alive: I *must* go on living! But I can't live as I'm
living now. God knows, I can't, I can't! Since I've known
you. . . ." Mottke broke off and looked questioningly at
Chanele:

"What do you say to it?"

Chanele was struck dumb with terror. She looked at
Mottke.

"So now you know everything. You can give me up if
you like. I won't do anything to you if you do—as God's my
witness, I won't do anything to you! But I'll do something
to myself. I can't live any longer with a rope round my
neck! I can't. . . . I can't. . . . Don't you see that? . . ."

Chanele mechanically nodded her head.

"I know it was God's punishment on me that I became
a thief and murdered a man. But I don't want to be a thief
any longer! I won't be a murderer any longer! I won't! . . .
I won't! . . . Why should I be different from other people?
I'll be a poor cobbler or a porter. . . . Believe me, do believe

me.... I want to earn my livelihood like other people; I don't care how small it is. And I'll show them yet—you'll see, I'll show them.... Just because they're so set on my being a thief. And you, will you help me? You'll help me, Chanele, won't you? If you don't, I don't want to live any longer. Better die now than lead such a life!"

Mottke stopped and looked imploringly at the girl.

Chanele was trembling. Her mouth was open and her teeth were chattering.

"I'll go home to my mother's town. I'll bribe the police there and make them give me a pass in my own name. I'll be Mottke again, and I'll shake Kanarik and everything connected with him from my back forever. I'll shake it all off my back as if it had never happened. Ever since I've known you I've been Mottke again—the Mottke that my mother knew."

He gazed imploringly at Chanele again.

"So you know everything now. Tell me: do you still want to be my wife? Don't be afraid to answer—I won't do anything to you. As God is my witness I won't do anything to you, I'll disappear, you'll never see me again; I swear it by the life of my mother! Tell me: do you want to be Mottke's wife? Not Kanarik's wife—Kanarik is dead and buried. Mottke's wife—my wife...." He began softly to stroke the girl's hair.

Chanele started up as if she had wakened from a dream. She realized everything. And in a breaking voice she shrieked:

"Mother! ... Mother! ... Mother!"

Her voice terrified Mottke. He came to himself and realized what he had done, saw that he had betrayed himself. But he didn't repent of it; he was glad that he had eased his conscience and said:

"Don't scream! The people will come. Come, I'll take you back. Don't be afraid, I won't do anything to you."

"Why should I be afraid?" said the girl. She had her wits back now and told herself that it would be best to go on playing her rôle. "We're engaged, aren't we? So why should I feel afraid of you? I was only startled. . . ."

"Chanele, Chanele, is it true?" he cried, falling on his knees before her and burying his face in the folds of her skirt.

"Come, çome," said Chanele. "It's late. Mother will be anxious if we stay longer."

The spring night arched dark and glowing over the earth, drenched in the scents of blossoms opening in the darkness and breathing out their fragrance. Through the perfumed night the betrothed pair walked towards the town without saying a word.

CHAPTER XLIII

*

The Engagement Is Broken

CHANELE arrived home half dead with fright. She called her father and mother into the parlor, and trembling violently and with many stops told them what Mottke had told her. When Reb Meilach heard the dreadful tale and realized the kind of man he had betrothed his daughter to, he was almost frozen with horror and couldn't utter a word. His wife wrung her hands and burst into tears.

"Stop that noise, for God's sake, they might hear us!" whispered Reb Meilach.

After their first agitation they began to consider what was to be done.

For a long time the father and mother gazed at each other in silence. Then Chanele began to sob.

"What are you crying for, child? You should thank God he's told you now. What would you have done if he'd waited till after you were married, which God forbid?"

They tried to soothe Chanele and led her to her room.

"The first thing is to hide Chanele away from him," said the mother, when she was alone with her husband again.

"No, the first thing is to go to the Commissar and tell him everything we know," retorted the father.

"Meilach, you would never do that!"

"I'll do what I've said. Or do you want the Commissar to hear of it from somebody else and arrest you and Chanele

along with her fine bridegroom? God knows what trouble
this may get us into yet!"

"That's all stuff. Have we done anything? We never knew
anything about this!"

"That's just why we must go straight to the Commissar
and tell him everything. 'Panie,' we must say, 'that's how
the matter stands. We knew nothing about it. Our daughter
was betrothed to him. We've just found out what he did
and we've come straight to you to tell you all about it.
We're innocent.' Is that understood?"

"I'll have nothing to do with it! It isn't for us to give
him away!" cried the woman.

"Do you think the Commissar won't hear of it if you
don't tell him? He'll find it out all right. There will be other
people ready enough to tell him. If Chanele knows about it
there must be others that know too. Murder will out, don't
forget it, and if it doesn't come out now it will in a year or
two. By that time he'll be your son-in-law and you'll be
drawn into the business, too. Chanele certainly will, for
she'll be his wife by then and she knows about it and hasn't
given him in charge. I won't let my girl ruin herself! I don't
care about anything else; I'm going to the Commissar now,
this minute, and I'm going to tell him everything. I refuse
to be mixed up in this business; the police are going to have
no handle against my girl."

The last words convinced the woman that if her daughter
was to be saved they must charge Mottke. She fell silent
and began to cry quietly.

Chanele was called back into the room. She was pale and
trembling and hardly knew what was happening.

"Don't cry, child! Thank God everything has turned out
as it has. You aren't his wife yet nor he your husband. Being

betrothed isn't the same as being married. He's still a stranger as far as you're concerned."

Chanele knew all this, but it brought her closer to Mottke. He was the first man who had ever kissed her.

"We must shake off this burden, child, or we'll be ruined, too. We must rid ourselves of the whole business. After all, we had nothing to do with it."

When Chanele realized that her father was asking her to go with him to the Commissar to tell everything she broke out into such a sobbing that her father and mother grew alarmed. Could she have been more to that man than she should have been?

Chanele flung herself on the bed, covered her face with her hands, and buried her head in the pillow. She wanted to see nobody and hear nobody.

"Hindel, I'm afraid, I'm afraid, he has made us unhappy. The fellow has made donkeys of us!"

"What an idea! How dare you talk like that of the girl! She's as innocent as a babe unborn, and the poor fellow treats her like a lady, he does."

"But I'm afraid, all the same, we must hold our tongues after all, the business has gone too far. Look how the girl is crying."

"Meilach, get out of this. I never thought you would say such a thing. Leave me with the girl."

"Make sure you get the truth out of her, Hindel. We must know where we stand. If it's too late, then we must just hold our tongues, and that means ruin. See that you get at the truth."

Meilach left the room.

"Chanele, tell me, my child. . . . Don't be ashamed to say it, I'm your mother. . . ."

The mother gently drew Chanele's head on to her shoulder.

"Why, what do you want me to tell you, mother? I've told you everything already. . . ."

"Has he ever done anything to you?"

"Who, mother?"

"Mottke."

"No, no, he's treated me like a lady, he's been so nice to me. He's only stroked my hair and told me that he loved me, loved me dearly. He's done everything I've asked him. He's gone to the synagogue every Sabbath with uncle. He's given up all his old friends. He's done it all for my sake, for he wanted to be respectable and he wanted me to love him. And that's why he told me that story. He wanted me to know everything about his life, he didn't want to have any secrets from me. That was the only reason why he told me. . . ."

"And he never went any farther with you than that? Listen, child. Has he gone so far that our hands are tied? In that case we must just bear it and hold our tongues. We must just swallow our shame and the wedding must go on. . . ."

"No, mother, I've told you already that he's treated me as nicely as any high-class gentleman could have done. He told me that if God was good to him and he had the joy of standing before the altar with me he would be the happiest man in the world."

"He'll get his happiness all right, we'll see to that. . . . It's lucky for you, my girl, that you didn't let yourself be led astray by him. Meilach," she cried, "I knew you were talking nonsense! What an idea to have about the girl! He's treated her like a fine lady all the time. He couldn't have treated her better."

"If that's how it stands, then all the blame for this business falls on him. We're out of it. Come, my child, come with me."

"Where, father?"

"To the Commissar. You must tell everything to him just as you told it to me, everything. . . ."

"Father!"

"I'll drag you there by force, if you don't come. You must save yourself, girl! What is he to you? You aren't married to him. The engagement is broken off. . . . He's a stranger, as far as I'm concerned. What does he matter to us? Come."

CHAPTER XLIV

*

Mottke Finds a Guardian Angel

THAT very night Reb Meilach dragged his daughter to the Commissar.

"I can't afford to keep this secret another night!" he cried.

Chanele's tears were useless; he took her by the hand and she had to follow.

But they did not find the Commissar either at his office or at his house. He was spending the evening at the Aquarium, where the Spanish dancer Isabella was appearing, of whom the papers and all the young bloods of Warsaw swore that she had the loveliest legs in the world. Colonel Chwostow was her closest friend, and many an officer envied him his success with the beautiful dancer. And they whispered to each other where Chwostow had made her acquaintance. These rumors about the place where the loveliest legs in the world had come from gave the dancer an additional glamor. Everybody envied the Commissar and congratulated him on having such a charmer. And he was proud of his "discovery."

As he couldn't get hold of the Commissar either at his office or his house, Reb Meilach dragged Chanele to the Aquarium. His wife tried to prevent him and said he should put off his visit until next morning. But Reb Meilach stood firm:

"The sooner the better. Don't you see that, you fool?

300

Who can tell what may have happened by tomorrow? He's likely to be sorry by now he ever told about it, and preparing to skip. Or he may do some harm to us; he may still bring us into it if we don't take care. We must strike while the iron's hot. They must come down on him when he isn't expecting it."

And when Chanele began to cry again he whispered in his wife's ear:

"And we'll rake something off it too! The police always give a tidy reward in cases like this; a hundred roubles at least, sometimes more. It'll help to provide a dowry for Chanele."

His wife could bring up no objection after that. And she turned to her daughter reproachfully:

"Chanele, do you want to bring us all to ruin? Us and yourself? We must get this secret off our chests as soon as we can."

But at the Aquarium they were refused admittance to the Commissar. Herr Chwostow was engaged, for Isabella was doing her turn at that moment. She wore short black silk tights with glittering jet spangles. Barefoot, her hair hanging down her back, she danced on the tightrope stretched across the stage. The music broke off. The lights in the hall were turned down. The audience rose to their feet, even the officers and their ladies in the boxes. All eyes were fixed on the stage, which was bathed in a blood-red light. With a little parasol in one hand the dancer glided over the tightrope, swaying her sinuous body and showing the loveliest legs in the world. The blood-red background and the black dress made her legs show up a dazzling white. The rope was high enough for everybody to see these legs. And all, even the officers' wives, were enchanted by the soft, velvety, harmonious lines of that body and those lovely legs. Blue veins

gleamed through the white skin, the red light giving them a
warm glow The women were even more ravished than the
men, and everybody gave a cry of delight when the dancer
suddenly turned a somersault, her legs describing a graceful
curve through the air. A second later she was standing
once more on the rope. The audience raised their glasses to
her and bawled their applause. She thanked them with a
gracious movement of her legs.

At that moment an attendant announced to the Commissar, who was standing near the stage devouring the
dancer with his eyes, that a Jew, along with his wife and
his daughter, wanted to speak to him. He replied that they
could go to the devil and turned his eyes on the dancer
again.

But Reb Meilach refused to budge.

"I'll wait here, even if I have to wait all night!" he stubbornly declared. For he was afraid that if he were to go
home now and put off his business till next morning, the
rascal might escape and lie in wait for him. Filled with a
hardly understandable feeling of revengefulness, he told
himself that Mottke must be arrested that very night while
he was asleep and unconscious of danger. Reb Meilach set
his whole mind on this purpose.

Soon afterwards the Commissar and his party—a staff
officer and a judge—made their way to a private room that
had been reserved for them. There, well provided with
flowers and champagne, they waited for the dancer. The
door opened and Krumashattko, handsome and young, entered bearing the lady in his arms. He was followed by the
Director, breathing hard. The gentlemen greeted the dancer
with loud applause and hand-clapping. The Commissar knelt
down before her; she lightly stepped on his bald poll with
one naked foot and from there leapt on to the sofa.

"Now, Krumashattko, let's see what you have to offer us," said the Colonel: Krumashattko sold jewelry to the patrons of the cabaret to give to the artistes.

"Two precious rings with large rubies, from a pawnshop in Petersburg. The Pearl Queen herself pawned them there."

"Let's see them."

The Colonel gave the handsome young staff officer the honor of presenting them. He knelt down and slipped them over Mary's toes.

Then the attendant announced again that the Jew was waiting:

"Herr Colonel, the Jew simply won't go away. He's standing out there with his wife and daughter. They say they've something of urgent importance to tell you."

"What do these Jews want? I've told them already they can come tomorrow to my office."

"They say it's something that can't be put off," replied the attendant; Reb Meilach had tipped him.

"Maybe he wants to sell his daughter. The people in this district know that you're a lady fancier and have an eye for pretty girls, and pretty Jewesses, too."

Flattered by this tribute to his good taste, the Colonel turned with a complacent smile to the attendant and asked:

"Is the daughter pretty?"

"A fine looking wench, a dainty little Jewess."

"Then bring her in."

"No, no, not here! Better go and see her in another room. There's a lady present," said the judge with a bow to Mary. "I fear the gracious lady might find it embarrassing."

"I don't like the idea of leaving you two alone with my charmer," replied the Commissar. "You might say nasty things about me behind my back. I have no fear of you,

you old dog," he went on, turning to the judge, "but that young greenhorn ... he's different," and he pointed waggishly at the young officer. "These young lads, they snap all your conquests from us, these greenhorns."

"Herr Colonel could perhaps receive these people in here," said the Director, pointing to a glass door leading into an adjoining room. "Then Herr Colonel will be in touch with his lady and be able to interrogate the Jews at the same time."

"Take them in there," the Colonel ordered.

He went into the next room. The others began to drink champagne. The Director left the room to fetch a different brand of champagne, and Krumashattko continued on his round. The dancer held court, coquetted with her admirers and led them on, not because she liked them particularly but out of habit and to annoy the Colonel. She laughed, showing her white sharp teeth, which threw the judge into a perfect ecstasy.

Suddenly she heard a sound of weeping in the next room, a young girl's weeping. She became rigid with fear. Then she got up, glided in a dance step to the door, opened it softly and peeped into the room. Chanele was standing before the Commissar sobbing. She put her handkerchief to her eyes now and then with a despairing gesture. Meilach stood beside her shouting at her:

"Tell the Herr Colonel everything! Tell him everything as you told it to me! Tell him about your fiancé in the same words that you told it to me!"

Mary understood at once. She became pale as death. With assumed composure she shut the door and returned to her admirers.

"How inquisitive you women are! As soon as you hear another woman's voice, there's no holding you."

"The gracious lady is jealous of the Colonel; she's afraid he might be faithless to her, what?" asked the judge, taking Mary's hand.

"Do you think I would be jealous of you, old bald top?" asked Mary, laughing and giving the judge a slap on his bald head.

She knew that Mottke's fate was being decided in the next room. And she saw at once that she must save him. She decided that she must keep the Commissar here until morning. That was the only way to give Mottke time to disappear and find a safe hiding place.

She lifted the champagne bottle from the ice-holder, filled the glasses and cried: "Come, let's drink!" To make the Colonel jealous she laid her naked legs on the officer's knees, stroked his hair and let him kiss her feet.

Chwostow entered, purple in the face with excitement. He twirled his mustache and muttered to himself:

"An important case! An interesting case! Very interesting! Something must be done about it at once. . . ."

Mary pretended not to hear. She clasped the officer with her legs.

"What must be done at once? Don't you see the danger that's threatening you here?" said the judge, pointing at Mary's legs.

"Duty calls, brother. Duty first, pleasure afterwards. A very interesting case. Huh, a fine fiance!" grunted the Commissar to himself, ringing for the attendant.

"Have you gone off your head? Where are you off to? Are you going to leave her here alone with him? I'm superfluous here, brother. When they're together they quite forget that I'm here, these two!" said the judge.

"Oh, you let him go. We don't mind. And I'll show you the snake-dance that the manager and I have been rehears-

ing, after he's gone. Just wait till he's gone!" said Mary,
taking the young officer's glass, sipping from it and then
putting it to his lips.

"Well, this is fine news for you, Chwostow! We're old
wrecks, both of us, and should be in the lumber room, it
seems," said the judge, laughing. He was drunk.

"Oh, I won't go now till you've danced that snake-dance.
You've never shown it to me, and you're going to dance it
before them!"

"And I won't dance it till you've gone! So go."

"Heigho, Chwostow! Now you've fairly put your foot
in it!" said the judge, roaring with laughter.

"And I won't go until you've danced!" retorted Chwostow
obstinately. "Get to the devil!" he shouted at the attendant,
who had appeared in answer to his ring.

"And I won't dance while you're here!" retorted Mary
teasingly. "Chwostow, give me a cushion," she commanded.

Chwostow obeyed.

"And now go, go to your duty!"

"I've no intention of doing anything of the kind. I stay
here."

"Then send your Jew to the devil and sit down. The man
invites people here and then leaves me alone with them.
A nice host, a gallant host!" cried Mary, putting her handkerchief to her eyes.

"Quite right! She's quite right, Chwostow," said the judge
and the officer. "You'll have to beg her pardon."

"I don't want him to, I don't want him to!" cried Mary.

"Now you see what you've done with all this fuss about
your Jews, Chwostow. You've insulted her and spoiled the
evening for us."

"Peccavi!" said Chwostow, striking himself on the chest.
"I acknowledge I'm to blame, but—the law demands it

and duty calls. If she promises to dance the snake-dance to me, then I'll send the Jews to the devil and stay here."

And a few minutes later Chwostow passed behind the glass door again and spoke to Reb Meilach, intentionally loud so that the judge and the officer might hear how important his business was:

"You! Go home now. And don't say a word to anybody about this. We'll settle up everything tomorrow. When does he come to you, to your daughter?"

"Every evening after his work, about six."

"Good. I'll be waiting for him with my men at your house. That will be the easiest way and it won't cause any scandal either. You hear?"

"Yes, Herr Colonel."

"Go home and speak to nobody. You'll get a reward."

Mary listened attentively so as not to lose a single word of what was said.

"An important case! An interesting case!" the Commissar cried to his guests as he entered. "I should go, really, my duty demands it, but my heart keeps me here." He bowed to Mary. "So I've arranged things so that the demands of the heart and the law are both satisfied. Oh, you only need a good head in these matters. And now, darling, the snake-dance. I think I've deserved it."

"Yes, that's right, he's deserved it," the gentlemen agreed.

"There's lots of time. He must drink something first. We were all drinking when he was busy with his old case."

"That's right. Chwostow, you're a lucky dog! Just see how she looks after you."

"It's my heart that's my worst enemy, my good heart!" said the Commissar.

An hour later they were all drunk. Law and justice, represented by Chwostow and the judge, knelt before the dancer. She poured wine over their bald heads, and law and justice gratefully kissed her hands.

Then she danced her snake-dance for them. She stood on her head and stretched her naked legs in the air; the legs caressed each other, clasped, kissed, loved each other.

In this way she kept them all till morning and then dismissed them drunk with wine and love.

At last Chwostow escaped her embraces, where she had kept him until late next day. Mary hurried down at once into the street, jumped into a droshky and drove to Mottke's lodgings.

But she didn't find him there.

CHAPTER XLV

*

Why, Chanele?

THAT morning Mottke awoke feeling happier than he had ever done before. He had opened his heart to Chanele, and she knew now that he wasn't Kanarik but Mottke: the thought made him feel as if he had been new-born. Even if he were to lose everything; even if Chanele didn't want to marry him now and broke off the engagement: he felt unspeakably happy that she knew everything. It was as if he had become really betrothed to her only after his confession to her yesterday. Before that it was Kanarik that had been engaged to her, Kanarik that had gone walking with her. But yesterday he had flung Kanarik in the brook for a second time. There he lay, and Mottke was Chanele's betrothed. And now it was Mottke that Chanele loved.

He got up earlier than usual, with the bounding energy of a man who is set on building his future. He yoked his horse in the cart and drove to the railway station to fetch a load of frozen fish that had arrived from inner Russia. He sang as he drove along and thought of his meeting with Chanele that evening; he would ask her to write a letter to his mother inviting her to Warsaw.

"But no, perhaps it would be better for me to go home first and bribe the police to give me a pass," he thought, and decided finally to talk it all over with Chanele. He would do whatever she advised him.

But when he drove into the market place with his first

load the other carriers shouted to him that a woman had been asking for him and looking for him everywhere in a droshky: "A fine bit of stuff—you know the kind!" Mottke was greatly surprised, for since he had taken Mary to the Aquarium he had never seen her again. And it must have been Mary. He spat, muttered a curse and set about unloading the fish.

Then a droshky drove up alongside his cart. He saw Mary bending out of the carriage and waving to him.

"Devil take her!" he growled. "What does she want?" And he stepped across to the droshky.

"Save yourself as quick as you can. They're after you. The police are looking for you. Chwostow knows everything."

Mottke turned pale. He bit his lip and asked quietly:

"Did you give me in charge?"

"No, I didn't. Your girl was with Chwostow last night, and her father too, and they told him everything."

"Don't tell me any such fairy-stories! Hell freeze you! . . . Chanele blab? No, if you didn't blab, nobody else did!"

"Listen, for God's sake! The police are looking for you. Get into a droshky and follow me. . . . I have money. . . . We must leave Warsaw at once"

"Oho! So that's how the wind blows! I see your game now. You want to get me away from Chanele. I'm to fly with you, am I? You needn't say another word. Have you got tired of your Chwostow? You've got fine rings on your fingers—and under your eyes, too!"

"Mottke, listen, for God's sake. This isn't the time for talking. I don't want to steal you from Chanele, I want you to save yourself and me, too. Chwostow knows everything . . . Chanele told him everything."

"Hold your tongue, I tell you. Or else I'll bash your face

in. I'm going to Chanele now. I'll ask her, ask her, mark this, whether she told on me or not."

"What are you thinking about? The police are at Chanele's waiting for you!"

"I don't care. If Chanele wants me to give myself up, then I'll give myself up. I'm not afraid. If you haven't given me away then nobody else can have done it. And leave Chanele's name out of it, please, or else you'll get hurt! Here, driver!" he shouted for a droshky.

"Where are you going?"

"That's nothing to you. You drive to Chwostow . . . give me in charge, if you want to! A nice trap! Very nicely arranged. Tried to scare me away from Chanele, did you? Driver, take me to the Pfauenstrasse."

Mary drove after him, tried to stop him, flung herself at his feet when they got to the Pfauenstrasse, and begged him to save himself and her and fly with her at once. But it was no use.

For where could he fly without Chanele? What was the world to him, or life, without Chanele? He pushed Mary away, then knocked her down and shouted:

"I'm going to her! I'm not afraid! If she wants to give me up to the police, she can!"

Mottke wasn't expected so soon. Chanele's uncle, who already knew everything, had made arrangements with the father for Mottke's arrest. But they hadn't expected Mottke to appear before the evening. Chanele would have left the house before that—so it was agreed—and instead of her Mottke would find the police waiting for him. So when Mottke entered the uncle was quite taken aback at first, but soon pulled himself together, and being both cowardly and sly, did his best to seem friendly:

"What's gone wrong that you've come so early to-day?"

"I must speak to Chanele for a little. Is she here?"

"Why, where did you expect her to be?" replied the uncle with a smile, and he shouted into the next room: "Chanele, Chanele, here's an unexpected visitor for you!"

Chanele hurriedly dressed. When she heard that it was Mottke she did not want to come out.

"She's just dressing, she'll be here in a minute. Wait just a minute, I'll be back in a jiffy," said the uncle, slipping out through the door. "Leah, Leah, bring a drop of tea, here's an unexpected visitor," he cried, and he left the room.

Mottke was left alone. An inexplicable fear and uneasiness took hold of him. He stepped to the door of the next room and cried:

"Chanele, Chanele, will you be long?"

"Coming in a minute," Chanele replied, and then asked, to gain time: "Why have you come so early? Has something happened?"

"No, nothing has happened. I only want to speak to you."

No further delay was possible. Chanele entered at last. She went over to Mottke. Her face was white and her hands trembled:

"Good heavens, how you frightened me! To come so unexpectedly! What has happened?"

"Nothing, Chanele." A happy smile lit up Mottke's face as soon as he saw her. "Why are you so frightened?"

When Chanele saw that he knew nothing she got back her composure and replied:

"Oh, it's nothing. But when you come here so unexpectedly . . . What has happened? Something simply must have happened. . . ."

Mottke thought her uneasiness was due to his confession the day before, and blamed himself for having frightened her. He took her hand. She was too frightened to withdraw it. Then he stroked her hair and asked:

"Chanele, are you still afraid because of yesterday? Chanele, tell me. . . . I must know! Don't you want me as your husband any longer? Tell me, I won't do anything to you. I'll wait as long as you like, until you don't fear me any longer."

"But I'm not afraid of you. Why should I be afraid of you?" said the girl. Then she suddenly buried her face in her hands and burst into sobs:

"Oh, my God, can all this be true?"

A pain shot to Mottke's heart. He felt he must die. He didn't know what to say. Then he became angry and shouted:

"Chanele, I'll tell the police everything! If you ask me to, I'll give myself up. Shall I, Chanele?"

For a moment Chanele lost her composure, but then got it back again:

"No, don't do that! Why should you?"

"Oh, Chanele!"

Tears burst from his eyes. He flung himself on his knees and began to kiss her feet.

Chanele was in despair. She stroked his hair. Mottke snatched her hand and covered it with kisses. Then he looked up at her and asked:

"Chanele, will you marry me?"

Chanele did not reply. She was crying.

"Why are you crying, Chanele? It breaks my heart. Don't cry, please don't cry!"

"All right, I won't cry any more," said the girl, wiping her eyes.

"Tell me, Chanele, do you still want to marry me? Don't

MOTTKE THE THIEF

be afraid, I won't hurt you. I'll go away and never say a word."

"Maybe it would be best . . ." the girl murmured as if to herself. "Go, go now!"

Mottke shrank and looked at her, his eyes wide open with amazement and despair. His look frightened her. And with her eyes fixed on the floor, her cheeks red with the lies she had told, she stammered:

"Where are you going now? As it is, there's no . . ." She did not end the sentence and turned red with shame and fear.

"Chanele! Mother!" cried Mottke, burying his face in her skirt and sobbing like a child.

When the police entered (they had been secretly summoned by Chanele's uncle) they found Mottke cowering at the girl's feet.

Slowly he raised his face from her dress and looked round in wondering amazement. He looked at the policemen and then at Chanele, who was standing with her hands covering her tear-stained face, her father and mother on either side of her. Mottke's great, clear, child-like eyes had the same expression that they had had when he lay in the cellar in Feigele's fruit-basket and they put a piece of wet rag between his lips for the first time: an expression of astonishment at being torn away from his mother's breast.

THE END